A CANDLELIGHT REGENCY

CANDLELIGHT ROMANCES

182 Dangerous Assignment, JENNIFER BLAIR
183 Walk a Dark Road, LYNN WILLIAMS
184 Counterfeit Love, JACQUELYN AEBY
185 The Gentleman Pirate, JANETTE RADCLIFFE
186 The Golden Falcon, BETTY HALE HYATT
187 Tower in the Forest, ETHEL HAMILL
188 Master of Roxton, ELISABETH BARR
189 The Steady Flame, BETH MYERS
190 White Jasmine, JANETTE RADCLIFFE
191 Cottage on Catherina Cay, JACQUELYN AEBY
192 Quest for Alexis, NANCY BUCKINGHAM
193 Falconer's Hall, JACQUELYN AEBY
194 Shadows of Amanda, HELEN S. NUELLE
195 The Long Shadow, JENNIFER BLAIR
196 Portrait of Errin, BETTY HALE HYATT
197 A Dream of Her Own, MARYANN YOUNG
198 Lord Stephen's Lady, JANETTE RADCLIFFE
199 The Storm, JACQUELYN AEBY
200 Dr. Myra Comes Home, ARLENE HALE
201 Winter in a Dark Land, MIRIAM LYNCH
202 The Sign of the Blue Dragon, JACQUELYN AEBY
203 A Happy Ending, ARLENE HALE
204 The Azure Castle, JANETTE RADCLIFFE
205 Never Look Back, JACQUELYN AEBY
206 The Topaz Charm, JANETTE RADCLIFFE
207 Teach Me to Love, GAIL EVERETT
208 The Brigand's Bride, BETTY HALE HYATT
209 Share Your Heart, ARLENE HALE
210 The Gallant Spy, BETTY HALE HYATT
211 Love Is the Winner, GAIL EVERETT
212 Scarlet Secrets, JANETTE RADCLIFFE
213 Revelry Manor, ELISABETH BARR
214 Pandora's Box, BETTY HALE HYATT
215 Safe Harbor, JENNIFER BLAIR
216 A Gift of Violets, JANETTE RADCLIFFE
217 Stranger on the Beach, ARLENE HALE
218 To Last a Lifetime, JENNIFER BLAIR
219 The Way to the Heart, GAIL EVERETT
220 Nurse in Residence, ARLENE HALE
221 The Raven Sisters, DOROTHY MACK
222 When Dreams Come True, ARLENE HALE
223 When Summer Ends, GAIL EVERETT
224 Love's Surprise, GAIL EVERETT

LOVE'S UNTOLD SECRET

BETTY HALE HYATT

A CANDLELIGHT REGENCY

For Mister B. Always. . . .

Published by
Dell Publishing Co., Inc.
1 Dag Hammarskjold Plaza
New York, New York 10017

ISBN: 0-440-14986-X

Printed in the United States of America
First printing—February 1978

CHAPTER ONE

The room was full of moonlight when I awakened. I was aware of a draft of night air, and my eyes focused on what seemed an apparition hovering between the bed and the moonlit window. Fear prickled the back of my neck, bringing instant cold moisture to my palms.

For one dreadful moment, I believed the ghost of Mullins existed! My heart beat erratically as the apparition wavered; then all at once, to my utter relief, I saw that it was only the white gauzy curtains being lifted in the slight breeze.

For a while, I lay very still, listening to the unfamiliar sounds around me, of the countryside in the night and the sudden rustle of leaves, the chilling call of some bird from the estuary. Then I heard the clock in the stable tower strike two.

I rose from the great deep bed with its dark blue silk curtains tied back to the thick posts and went to the window, leaning out from the wide casement. The moon traced a thin gossamer web of light down across the wide sweep of lawn beyond the small courtyard below the window, and touched the tops of the tall copper beeches that crowded along the estuary.

The branches stirred against the sky, and again the strange churring of that bird came, unlike any other sound I'd ever heard—low, primitive, insistent and oddly compelling, and I shivered involuntarily. I remembered what Trevor had told me of Mullins long before Lucretia and I had arrived yesterday.

"There is a wide path from the gardens of the house down along the estuary, passing the old stone quay, to Poppy Meadows which juts out nearest the sea, and it is quite beautiful in any season, but especially so with the deep foliage of trees," he'd explained. "This estuary, unfortunately, was always a favorite haunt of pirates and smugglers, and Mullins was always involved at some time or another in those dark deeds, for my ancestors were never above such acts themselves." His laugh had been a dry one,

I'd thought at the time, as though he'd resented the memory.

"We still have smugglers, Roma," he'd continued, "and although I haven't been there much in the past seven years, I'm told it is still a haven for these rogues. There are many little creeks off the main estuary deep enough when the tide is high for a ship to hide in, and no one at the house would ever guess they are there, as the trees provide a natural cover."

Trevor had been contemptuous of these smugglers, but he felt with the garrison of Revenue Men posted in St. Austell he would have no trouble harassing them himself, and he talked as though he even hoped he would have this chance.

"My father, Edward St. Coryn," he'd gone on to explain, "was notorious for being a smuggler, a fair-trader, as they're called in Cornwall. He had his own ship, *The Petroc*, a fast lugger built in Polporro, and until he was caught, which he well deserved to be, and made to pay a steep fine, he did his share in these illegal runs, as everyone at Mullins knows."

All this he had told me during those long evenings we had walked beside the Thames on the Chelsea Embankment, more than a year ago. Even then it had sent little chills of excitement and something close to fear tingling down my spine.

But now, as I stood at the window, the night seemed expectant, I thought uneasily, and I felt some unreasonable fear touch me like an icy hand. Then, as I watched, a figure of a man stole out from the belt of trees into a patch of bright moonlight, and looked up towards the house, his white shirt gleaming like alabaster.

At once, I drew back into the shadow of the room, screened by the curtain, my heart pounding so heavily that my body trembled. The man cupped his hand to his mouth and gave a low whistle.

Almost directly beneath me, I heard what sounded like the cry of a sea gull, and suddenly, from the same belt of trees from where the man had come, other shadows crept out, bent under the weight of wooden casks carried on their shoulders, and made their way single file towards the house.

I stood frozen at the window, still hidden by the curtain, my whole being locked in a peculiar paralysis of panic as I watched what was like some nightmarish dream, and I guessed I was indeed witnessing what Trevor had described as a "run of contraband" being smuggled into this old manor house.

My first thought was to wake the household, but with this thought came a far more logical one: someone within this house had given the signal to enter, someone who knew the master was away.

The long file of figures hurried from the bank of trees without so much as a break, and I dared hardly to breathe lest I be heard or seen by the man who kept vigil standing just within that patch of moonlight, bold as day. I had always believed this had to be carried out on the blackest of nights. What utter gall that man had to stand there in the bright nocturnal light, defying all the rules of the daring game he played with the law, just as if it were he who made the rules to suit himself.

I cringed inside, knowing Trevor was not back from Falmouth, where he had gone a few days before. He hadn't been able to meet us at Bodmin, but had sent his coachman, Hamilton, to bring Lucretia and me down to Mullins, with a message that he had urgent business that would keep him away for several days. Now I knew that someone in this household—was it one of the servants Lucretia and I had met lined up in the hall yesterday?—was betraying Trevor in his absence.

Some minutes passed and the men returned from the house empty-handed and, like phantoms, moved into the crowd of trees and disappeared along with the man who kept the watch. I waited, listening, while my pulse raced madly, but no sound save that of the wind stirring the trees came, and no one returned.

The breeze was cool on my thin chemise, and I shivered, aware now that I must have been standing there for some time. I turned back to the room and pulled the pale pink silk peignoir over my nightgown, my fingers trembling as I tied the satin ribbon under my full breasts.

I was not easily frightened, nor was I frightened now, but something like a wild flame was burning through me. I knew I should warn the household, but because Trevor was gone, I could think of no one to warn. I did not know the servants well enough yet, and certainly I had no way of knowing just who was loyal and who was not. It seemed that this would have to wait until I could tell Trevor.

I decided to look in on my cousin to see if she'd been disturbed in any way. I went through the arched door which led from the bedroom into the small boudoir, my feet tucked in soft leather slippers making no sound over the carpet, the moonlight drifting into the room so that I didn't need a candle.

I had been given this suite of rooms as a second thought, because they were the oldest rooms of the house and supposedly haunted, and Lucretia had been too frightened to accept them once she'd learned that. And because she was the bride-to-be, she was naturally given her choice of rooms.

With vivid clarity, I again recalled the warm summer evening more than a year ago, when Trevor and I had talked of Mullins.

"The house," he'd said with a curious light in his eyes, "is one that has grown over the centuries with the increased wealth and importance of its ancient family. Its origin goes back to Queen Edith, the wife of Edward the Confessor. Additions were made throughout the centuries, of course, giving the house its own peculiar style." In the distance, Westminster Abbey's bells had begun to ring, and I had looked up at his profile in the dusk, knowing he was telling me all this for a reason.

"The first one was the Norman wing, built onto the southwest corner of the Great Hall. You will see," he said, turning suddenly and looking down into my face. "I want to show you Mullins one day."

And I wanted to see it with him.

He went on describing the house. "That particular wing was called the Ladies' Bower, because they withdrew there after the dinners in the Hall. The Solar above it, quite the fad in those days because it was the latest French trend, you see, was reached by a marvel of a spiral stone staircase which we still use.

"This old Solar was made into bedrooms later, and the Bower is now the library. It has always been referred to as the Bower though, just as the Solar is called the Blue Boudoir. It's supposed to be haunted by a woman in a blue gown who used the rooms, which are done all in shades of blue." He laughed, as if he thought it a joke.

I knew he was telling me all this because he was going to ask me to go with him as his wife to Mullins. "Then Mullins does have a ghost, like all the old manor houses in

Cornwall are supposed to?" I laughed, delighted. How I wanted to be the mistress of such a house, and I recalled the romance I had attached to his description of it.

"By all means, Mullins does have its ghosts. But my favorite one is the mistress who was carried off by the Spaniards. After being rescued by her husband, she was caught one night running away to the man who had abducted her, and was shot by her husband in the courtyard beneath the window of the old Blue Boudoir! They, and by that I mean the servants, say her ghost appears every midsummer's night, for that was when she was seen climbing down from the window to meet her waiting lover."

He'd stopped talking, and turned to take my hand in his. "We are not a pious family, my dear Roma, with no aristocratic bearing. I'm afraid we made our history by living it, and siding with the luckless Charles was the downfall of the St. Coryns. No saints seem ever to dwell among us, I fear, and the wealth of the family often veers into poverty."

That was a very long time ago, I thought now with a touch of impatience and with wounded pride. I was here at Mullins, but it was my cousin Lucretia, not I, who was the chosen bride-to-be.

Now I stood in front of the portrait of a young woman, the woman I knew to be the latest ghost of Mullins, and I thought guiltily of poor Lucretia. She had clung to me like the child she was when she'd been told about the ghosts, desperately frightened. I bit my lower lip, remembering with a pang how pale she'd been when she looked up at me for protection.

She had gratefully accepted the mild sedative Cook, as Mrs. Combes was called, had given her with the hot milk, and I had remained with her until she'd fallen asleep. What on earth would she have done had she witnessed what I had just seen from my bedroom window? I grimaced and thought that Lucretia would never rise from her bed anyway, not for any reason at all during the night.

With a touch of exasperation, I wondered how she had been brave enough to consent to marry Trevor St. Coryn, a man who could be ruthless, especially knowing she would have to come down to "the ends of the earth" in Cornwall, as she so often referred to it, to live at Mullins. It was so far away from the elegant and safe Chelsea town house she'd known all her life.

"But you will be with me, Roma," she'd said over and

over again. "I shan't need anyone with me as long as I know you are there too." I knew she was frightened of Trevor although she had not admitted it, and I knew, too, that she would never be able to know him as I knew him. I had to choke down my hurt pride whenever I thought of their coming marriage.

However, my conscience always reared up to mock me in moments like this. She depended on me, guileless child that she was, and she couldn't know my true reasons for accepting her pleas to come with her to Mullins. Even as I had done in the past, I knew I would protect her; I had to, for she was such an innocent.

My glance moved swiftly over the young lady in the portrait and then I went to the door. I moved along the corridor and made my way quietly to Lu's rooms, just to look in and make sure she was asleep. Past experience proved that sometimes she cowered under the covers, terrified at the slightest noise.

Cautiously, I opened the door and peeked out into the darkened corridor. Someone had extinguished the light in the wall lantern. I could almost hear Mrs. Pascal's warning as she had brought me up the spiral staircase last evening to the Blue Boudoir:

"We don't have gaslight here as yet, Miss, so we must use candles and oil lamps, and it do get dark in this part of the house, oh it do," she'd explained. "Mind the step here. It's uneven and you must take care not to trip. We do keep a small candle burning in this lantern here all night." And she'd pointed to the wall where a red glass globe covered the lighted candle.

But now I stood there staring into the inky darkness, wondering about that candle and deciding that it had been put out for fear of fires. I remembered the tricky step and hesitated for a fraction of a moment, and in that moment I was certain that I must go look in on Lucretia.

I stepped out into the corridor, still hunting for the tricky step, and suddenly I sensed another presence in the hall. A dark figure stepped out in the corridor and before I could cry out, a coat was flung over my head, blinding me, and hands pinioned my arms to my sides so that I could not move.

I was helpless and I knew it, and for the first time in my life, I was gripped in a spasm of real fear. Strong, rough hands lifted me and I was flung over a man's broad shoulder with my head downward in a most degrading manner, but even my indignation at this manhandling could not spare me the horror which washed over me in great suffocating waves.

I must have blacked out, for without a doubt I felt all the breath in my body leave me, and I succumbed to that merciful oblivion. The next thing I knew, a cold breeze hit my face and I gulped it in, fighting for it, and opened my eyes.

A face stared down into mine, and in the glow of a lantern swinging above me I saw it was an evil face, the mouth cruel and almost leering under the black mustache. I must be dreaming, I thought, for the man was the one I had seen at the edge of the trees, standing in the moonlight!

I was lying on the deck of a ship. I felt the sway of it beneath me and heard a dry, creaking sound as the ship pulled on its moorings, but I was barely conscious of any of it. My attention was riveted on the man who stood above me, and for one long moment he stared at me in silence.

Then he stood back. "Bring her to the cabin, Robin," he said in a low, harsh voice, and in perfect English, not in the strange foreign tongue I thought all pirates were supposed to have. And surely, this man must be a pirate. Had he not abducted me in the dead of night and brought me to his ship?

The man behind me laughed as if I amused him, then he lifted me to my feet and gave me a little shove, as the man who had given the order turned his back upon me and strode through a swinging door and down the steps. I stumbled after him, prodded by the swarthy man behind me, as if I were indeed living a nightmare.

All sense of logic had fled. I was kidnapped by these pirates, as bold as any I had ever heard about, and I believed I was being taken down to some dark and filthy hole to rot away as the ship sailed out to a foreign port, where I should be sold at some slave market. In London, there had been rumors of white girls kidnapped and sold into slavery, into the harems of rich, powerful sultans and sheiks of the Arab world. So was this to be my fate? My heart thudded against my ribs as I dumbly followed the tall man in front of me.

He opened a door at the end of the galley and went inside, and in another moment I stood on the threshold of a cabin, stunned, blinking at the steady glow from a lantern which hung from a low, polished beam, and which cast soft patterns on the rich dark paneling. I saw that the cabin before me was not the dark hole I'd envisioned, but a comfortable room with a handsome table of dark mahogany, and a wall cabinet with books and silver goblets behind glass doors. A rich Indian carpet covered the floor, and a large globe stood on a heavy oak stand in a corner near the porthole.

I barely took notice of the bunk bed under the high poop-deck window, curtained with fine red damask. It was the cabin of a gentleman, worthy of the finest of ship's captains, but certainly not fit for this pirate!

The man behind me pushed me inside with a rough gesture, then closed the door at the other man's silent signal, and I stood face to face with this tall, angry man.

At once, I was aware that he was dressed in the clothes of a gentleman, if one could call the casualness with which he wore the fine white shirt open at the collar and tucked into dark breeches which ended in black Hessian boots the manner of a gentleman. But the look on his face was not a kind one, and somehow with this thought I overcame my great fear, and I was angry as well as indignant. That he was English and not some Spaniard or Arab or Frenchman, made it at least plausible to speak to him, in spite of the fierce look on his face. The close-clipped beard made him seem even more sinister, I thought.

He was staring at me with what could only be described as the most arrogant scowl I had ever seen on a man's face, and I resented it deeply.

After what seemed an eternity of silence, in which he seemed to be forming some plan, it was I who spoke first, and with indignation, intending to cut this man down verbally as he deserved to be.

"What right have you to abduct me in this manner, pray tell, sir, and in the dead of night?" I demanded, lifting my chin defiantly, trying hard to control my quivering body.

For a longer moment, he did not answer but stared at me with those cold, calculating eyes, and I thought perhaps he hadn't heard me.

"You are Miss Kendal, are you not?" He ignored my question, his manner impersonal as well as insulting, as his insolent eyes raked over my body, then up over my face and throat.

Suddenly, I was conscious of how my long hair trailed

over my breasts, which were barely concealed under the thin night clothes. I had every reason to fear this man and I knew it, but even in this moment of fear, I felt a strange, attraction to him. I did not want him to know my fear *or* this other feeling, which somehow flustered me and brought the blood to my cheeks in a revealing rush.

I wondered how he could know my name, then defiantly, I lifted my eyes and met his with a coldness to match his own.

"Yes. I am Miss Kendal. It does seem strange indeed that you should know my name, sir, when I've not been aware of meeting you before."

I wanted nothing more than to cut him down to size, but I saw that he too could scarcely conceal the contempt he felt for me.

"You are the intended bride of Trevor St. Coryn, Miss Kendal. I am making it my personal right to abduct you, and, yes, in the dead of night." I could hardly believe the derision I heard in his voice.

Stunned, I opened my mouth to protest that I was not *that* Miss Kendal, but he came and stood over me, so threateningly tall and close that I felt a greater sense of horror move deep inside me, weakening me, and took an involuntary step backwards.

He moved that step closer, his face poised just above mine. My throat constricted and my heart hammered so loudly that I believed it must betray the fear his presence aroused in me.

I tried to keep my voice level and cool. "Pray tell, sir, do! Can you possibly know Trevor St. Coryn?" I arched my brows, implying my doubt.

A mockery of a smile curled the sensuous lips in that dark, bronzed face.

"Trevor St. Coryn is the man who cheated me of my inheritance, Miss Kendal," he whipped out. "He didn't tell you of my existence?" He threw back his head and laughed; it sounded cold and mirthless in the cabin. "I am Roc St. Coryn. I simply intend to take back what is mine, and make him suffer in the process."

I must have shown my great surprise for he seemed satisfied as he stared at me so intently. "It's just as I thought, Miss Kendal," he said, and I saw the flash of his white teeth. "Trevor would never reveal his black secrets to the woman he intends to marry for her wealth. No. He would have you ignorant until he had you in complete possession, wealth and all, and there would be nothing then that you could do about it."

He was much too close to me. I could feel the hot breath coming from that proud, cruel mouth. It was all too much like a nightmare, and I was alarmed now more than ever.

"You are Trevor's brother, then?" I hoped he did not see my fear, or the shaking of my knees that was making it difficult for me to stand in front of him.

He lifted those magnificent brows, his smile contemptuous. "Half-brother, Miss Kendal. Yes, we have been classed as such." His eyes narrowed and the brutal lines about his mouth now caused me to shudder. There would be no mercy given if this man were ever crossed, I thought.

That Trevor had never mentioned a half-brother, which this man claimed to be, did astonish me. And the fact that this man harbored such deep resentment that it had festered like a sore for years seemed all too unreal. The man was evil; he was eaten to the core of his being by this hate. The thought sobered me, and for a fraction of a second I somehow understood how he felt.

He stood back and walked over to the cabinet, where he took down two silver goblets and a silver flask, and placed them on the table. I was aware of his height, of the strength in that lean and muscular body. When he spoke, his softened voice gave a new sense of deception.

"First we shall have a drink, Miss Kendal. I see you are trembling. Perhaps you are cold? There's no need to be frightened of me. Come." He pulled out a chair, and gestured to it. I moved toward it with as much disdain as I could manage, but took the seat gratefully, for I was indeed trembling and could not seem to control it.

He had poured what looked like wine into the goblets, and handed me one. "This will warm you. Drink up." It was an order, but as he lifted his own goblet to his lips, I did the same.

He saw the look on my face, and seemed amused by it, "This is sweet wine from Burgundy, Miss Kendal, smuggled into Mullins for the great wine cellar old Combes keeps vigil over, under lock and key. Those are his orders from Mister Trevor St. Coryn."

"And you smuggle it in, as you did tonight," I said bravely, with as much acid in my voice as I could muster, to express my contempt for him. I sipped it and found it sweet, and liked it in spite of myself.

His laugh was dry and mirthless. "So you watched my men perform tonight? It is well you did. Mullins is a lair for smugglers, Miss Kendal, and those who don't participate are most often caught and hung by the neck for being obstinate. This is a warning."

I took another sip, eyeing him over the brim of the goblet. That he thought me to be Lucretia was clear enough. But in the seemingly long interval in which we eyed each other, sipping on the wine which indeed began to warm me, it occurred to me that he'd abducted me to hold me for ransom, thinking me to be the heiress. I wanted to laugh, but of course I knew now I would play the game with him. If he knew his mistake, would he not abduct poor Lucretia as he'd done me?

He seemed to be waiting while I finished the wine, and I felt a warm glow spread through my body. I asked archly, "Then sir, what can you want of me, unless, of course, you mean to hold me for ransom?"

He threw back his head and laughed, and I suddenly thought of a Roman god defying the earth with a laugh such as that. His eyes were tilted slightly and his eyebrows followed this upward slant and gave him a satanic expression. One could almost have believed fire and smoke to come from those arrogant nostrils!

"I have no plans to hold you for ransom, my dear Miss Kendal. No." He stood up and placed the flask we'd used back into the cabinet, then turned back to me. "My plan is to break the back of Trevor St. Coryn, to rob him of what he thinks will be his. And you," he said, pulling me to my feet, "are in those plans."

A sudden flame touched those dark eyes and I stepped back, but he caught my arms and pulled me close to him.

"You must be mad, sir," I said, not quite convincingly enough. It seemed all wrong as his arms went around me, and yet I was aware of a strange pulsating feeling within me as he caught my head and pulled it back. His mouth was upon mine, forcing it open, hot, demanding, revolting. I tried to fight, while a stronger sensation, totally unknown to me, scorched through my whole being.

I was swept away, thinking only that no man had ever kissed me in this manner, not even Trevor. It seemed indecent. It was! But for some reason, I didn't want it to stop. I seemed to melt in the man's arms, and was on fire at his touch.

He lifted his head and his face was close to mine. Then he took me in his arms, and carried me to the bed. He kissed my eyes, my lips, my throat, and again my mouth, and I was in a world I had not entered before, nor was I able to resist it. He was possessive and in this all-consuming desire, I didn't want him to stop kissing me.

I felt his hands upon my breasts. There was a thin ripping sound, and my body was bare to his touch as my nightgown and peignoir fell from me.

Somewhere in that moment of uncontrollable desire, a warning sounded in my head and I tried to heed it. I said, "No. Oh, no, please don't!"

"You cannot mean that; not now, my dear Miss Kendal. You are already mine. Don't you know this?" His voice was tender. He bent his head over mine, and his kisses were demanding once more.

I forgot that he was my enemy; I forgot that he had abducted me, that I was just a means by which he was to get revenge on the man he most hated. My body yielded, his warm, strong hands expertly stroking my softness. I felt his hardness. Then he stood back from me.

In a daze, I saw him as he began to remove his shirt, the thick dark hair curled on his broad chest beneath it. I tried again. "You are . . . mistaken, sir," I began. "I am not the heiress Trevor St. Coryn is to marry."

He laughed, no trace of belief in his expression. "You do me an injustice, to suppose I would fall for your bluff. I have seen you with him in London. You are the kind of woman Trevor St. Coryn would want for his own. But I will make you my woman." His strong, white teeth dazzled as he laughed again and descended on me, touching me with his magic fingers, and I had no power whatsoever to free myself from him.

His lips were on my throat and my mouth, my eyes and my long hair, and desire flooded through me. He meant to take me then and there, and as if in a dream—for this could not truly be happening—I waited for it, even desired it, and closed my eyes as his warm mouth covered mine once more. I seemed to be floating and time passed, or so I thought, and I opened my eyes to find him staring down at me; I was sure I was mistaken about what I saw, for there was unspeakable tenderness in the mold of his mouth, and the dark eyes saddened. It left me bewildered.

All of a sudden, he moved off and left my side, throwing a robe down over my nakedness. I heard him moving about the cabin, and I was aware of the gentle sway of the ship on the water, but unable to understand why I could so succumb to this man's advances, and what I had done to make him change his mind. Hadn't he meant to . . . ravish me completely? I closed my eyes again.

It was some minutes before he spoke, startling me. "Here. Drink this." My eyes flew open to see him standing beside the bunk, holding a goblet. "It's brandy. It will help." I blinked up at him, disbelieving. He thrust the goblet toward me, but I pushed it away. His hand caught my wrist in a grip that made me wince. "Drink up and now!" he ordered, and I dared not refuse. "All of it!" he demanded.

As I drank, the fiery liquid burned along my throat and brought tears to my eyes. I wanted to hate him, but I was powerless to do so. He took the goblet from me, his face a mask of inscrutable darkness, but his voice, rough before, was now suddenly gentle.

"I gave you an aphrodisiac powder in your wine, Miss Kendal. A *cantharidin,* which made you quite willing. It will wear off after a time." He touched the dark velvet robe he'd flung over me and said, "There's water to wash in, and then you may wrap yourself in this. I will be back soon." With that, he turned and strode from the cabin, leaving me alone.

Stunned by what he'd said, I fought down a new kind of panic. He'd admitted to giving me a drug, to render me helpless, and I had just melted in his arms without a struggle! As reason came back to me, I knew a sense of anger and despair, and something else I did not care to admit even to myself; I had enjoyed it, much to my sudden shame, and my face stung with hot color as I recalled how his fingers had caused my body to tingle.

Even as I blushed in remembrance, I knew I would not be the same woman again. But, I thought with mounting panic, what did he intend to do with me now? Supposing he meant to keep me drugged? My cheeks blazed, and I glanced around me, at my torn garments thrown on the floor, and the nakedness of my person. Hot with shame, I clutched at my clothes and, to my despair, I saw they were indeed torn beyond repair.

But I was stimulated too by the brandy he'd forced me to drink, and I quickly calculated the freedom of this moment, and hurriedly rose from the bed and began to wash at the ewer.

My eyes smarted with tears of anger as I bathed my body with trembling fingers, wanting to wash away the memory of this past hour, of his touch on me. But I knew I could never do so, and lest he return to find me in this state, I grabbed the robe and wrapped it around me, tying the sash tight around my waist. Then I stared at my reflection in the mirror, the glow of the lantern behind me swinging gently to the sway of the ship creaking on her mooring.

Shocked, I saw a face glowing with defiance rather than white with fear and shame; my dark eyes were too bright, I thought, my lips too red. My hair was a dark cloud of tangles, and I had no brush to smooth out the curls nor a ribbon to tie them back.

From the bow of the ship, the smell of hot bread and bitter black coffee came to me, a tantalizing aroma. I turned and picked up my torn clothes with unsteady hands, bundling them up just as the door opened and my seducer entered, a tray in his hands. He placed it immediately on the table, and turned to me.

How tall he was, I thought, and I steeled myself, for I believed he was going to touch me again, but he did not.

He had the audacity to smile, and he gestured towards the table. "I will pour us some coffee. Please sit down." His eyes moved boldly over my face, and he seemed satisfied, I thought contemptuously. He pulled out the chair, and because I could not think of a hasty retort, I sat down with as much dignity and defiance as I could muster.

There was a crusty loaf of bread, freshly baked, with butter, and a dish of peeled oranges and some cheese. He poured out the steaming brew from a jug and placed one cup in front of me, then sat down and, without formality, cut the bread into thick slices and buttered them. He gave me one and then began to eat and drink his coffee.

Reluctantly, I accepted the fare, for my appetite was ravenous. I drank the coffee, grateful for its strong warmth, all the while watching him over the brim of the cup as he was regarding me. For a while we did not speak, and I could not help but wonder what his plans were now. Was this the way he treated all women he took by force? Did he render them helpless, then afterwards feed them, trying to make them feel that the worst was over and they should be grateful to him for what he had done?

I was uncomfortable under his thoughtful gaze.

"Yes, Miss Kendal. The worst is over. Believe me." It was as if he'd read my thoughts, the *odious* man! "And I'll wager that you'll thank me one day for this 'awakening,' shall we call it? It happens to every woman," he said as he began to eat a section of orange, "and it is best if you can accept it." He was serious, although his smile seemed mocking and it amused him to see me so discomfited. I wanted nothing more than to reach out and slap him.

"You mistake me entirely, if you think I shall ever thank you for what you have done!" I retorted, angrier than I'd ever been in my life.

But I knew I would have the last laugh. I would see him when he learned the truth, and I also knew that I would do anything now to prevent him from learning that truth until the moment when he could not take his revenge out on poor frightened Lucretia.

His eyes continued to appraise me, as if I were his possession. My heart raced erratically, however, for I knew I had been but putty in his arms. I hated myself for that, yet I could not banish from my mind the sensuous warmth with which his mouth had touched mine. I loathed him, but I could not deny what he'd aroused in me.

He laughed. "You will," he said, "but I do not expect Trevor will thank me." He was mocking me, and I felt my whole being tingle with a new kind of shame. I would never be able to explain this to Trevor, and he surely would have the right to know, wouldn't he?

All at once, and with a bitter taste in my mouth, I realized what I had sacrificed. Lucretia would be "safe" for Trevor, but I had been ravished by this man's evil desire for revenge. There could be no one for me to confide in, for it was all some horrible mistake, a comedy of errors that I should have to bear alone. I bit my lower lip to keep it from trembling, and I took a sip of the hot brew.

A cruel light touched his eyes as he watched me. "Trevor did not tell you of me, or of Edward St. Coryn's death?" I was surprised, and shook my head.

He scowled darkly. "It's ironic that he would not tell you

everything of our illustrious past. He himself is not above the dark deeds our family is known to participate in. Has he not told you of his business abroad? Of his slave trade?"

A shiver ran down my spine at his sinister accusation. I had certainly known of his business abroad, but I had assumed it was above reproach, and not what this blackguard was implying it to be. When I did not answer him, he went on.

"My father was a smuggler, Miss Kendal, a true buccaneer. This ship was his, and it is mine now. I trained under my father before I went to school, and two nights after his death, I took *The Petroc* to the Spanish Main, and there learned the trade of my father firsthand and quite well." I heard the sarcasm in his words. He had been hurt, and deeply so.

"My father married a woman for her wealth, and because it had been arranged for him by his own father. But he loved another woman, who was his life, and whom he could not marry because she had no dowry. He was a scoundrel, but he loved this woman with all his heart. She was my mother, and when she died, he brought Kate and me to live at Mullins. We were illegitimate, Miss Kendal, our father's bastards. But we were *his* children of his own blood. True St. Coryns!"

I had no words for him. I met his eyes, willing him to go on, for I was certain he was telling me all this for a purpose.

"Trevor St. Coryn! His name sticks in my throat! He had the audacity to override my father's will, to use his 'legal birth' to gain my inheritance. I didn't know all the circumstances, even when my father died, but I have since learned the whole truth, and I have returned to see justice done. Trevor's not my father's son. His mother had been set upon by a notorious sea captain, a rival of my father's, before my father ever touched her, and she was pregnant when he took her to the altar. My father didn't know this until after the child was born. She forced him to accept her son and give him the St. Coryn name so that Trevor would inherit Mullins."

For a long moment, I could think of nothing to say, for I was stunned by the similarity of this man's situation and my own. It seemed that we both had been robbed of our rightful inheritances. And I knew that in his anger he wanted me to be impure, as his mother was when she married Edward St. Coryn. Why, then, had he not taken me completely? I would not have thought he'd have spared me—and in truth he had shamed me enough—but he had not forced upon me the fate Trevor's mother had suffered. How would this threatening man react when he learned of his mistake, and knew that I was to be Trevor's mistress but not his bride? And that Lucretia, the heiress, and wife of Trevor in a short month's time, would be unmolested? It was ironic, and I wanted to laugh.

"I see this amuses you, Miss Kendal," he said, his voice booming.

"You are telling me that you are setting up the same situation that existed in your father's time, and should I not find that amusing?"

"So you do follow my plans, Miss Kendal." I did not like his smugness. "I do intend to carry them out and to break this man, for what he did to my sister, to my father and to me." He did not go on with this, but stood up and walked over to the porthole and looked out.

"The night my father was killed, he and I had quarreled over the inheritance. I, in my youth, did not know that he had always intended Mullins should go to me, for I believed that Trevor was his legal son by that loveless marriage. I wanted my portion, however, and that was his ship, for he could no longer sail her, afflicted as he was by drink. He was having troubles, too, from another quarter—Trevor was making his life miserable, demanding money. He never had the slightest interest in Mullins, not even as a young boy, and my father knew this. And it came as a shock to me when I learned that all my father had left to me, including the estates of Mullins, was craftily stolen by Trevor, thinking himself legally justified. Oh, yes, I intend to make him pay dearly. He will suffer. I shall see to that."

He turned and faced me, a brutal look on his face. A hot flush stained my cheeks as I tried to meet those evil eyes.

"Then you are no better than the man you intend to crush under this revenge, if all you say of him is true!"

He took three long steps over to me, then reached down and grabbed my wrists in a strong grip, pulling me to my feet. "It is true. All of it. You have been used for Trevor's purposes and for my own. But make no mistake about how he will use you once you are his wife. I know him. He will take a mistress once he is tired of you, but he will continue to use your wealth, just as my father did his wife's fortune.

But I intend to make him know how much he has to lose."

Stung deeply, tears stood at my eyes. How despicable he was!

"I see," I cried, unable to control my anger at the injustice of it all. "You intend to ruin me, just to satisfy your own immoral lust for revenge! You must be mad to think I shall be persuaded to believe you, after what you have done to me! Indeed, you must know I intend to reveal what you have done—" My heart faltered, for I saw that his defiance matched mine. And he could do exactly as he pleased with me, for I was his prisoner.

Then he laughed, a most wicked laugh, I thought, as if I were the source of his amusement. "I have no doubt as to what you will do in the near future, my dear Miss Kendal. You will be angry. You see yourself now as an injured young woman, but you will see that you aren't injured at all, for you have spirit.

"And then," he continued, "you will fume, be indignant, but you will see the sense in being discreet, and you will never mention this to Trevor. A woman like you does not scream for help, but rather keeps silent. You see, I know your kind. And Trevor would never believe you, not being the hot-blooded woman you are. He is a jealous man, and a possessive one."

He stood over me, his face inscrutable now. I hated him more than ever.

I could not trust myself to speak. Then he said, "If you are ready, I shall see that you are taken safely back to Mullins. It will soon be daylight, and we mustn't run the risk of the servants seeing your return." His words mocked me, and he saw the intake of my breath. He was saying that he was setting me free!

"Yes. I am letting you go, Miss Kendal. I know I shall be able to rely upon your discretion. You will think over what I've said, and see the sense in it. Mark my words."

He turned around and brought a long scarlet cape from the hook in the corner. Roughly removing the robe he'd not long ago thrown over me, and without so much as a glance at my nakedness underneath, he flung it around my shoulders, fastening it at the throat, then quickly took the bundle of torn clothes still in my grasp.

"You will not need these, I am sure," he laughed, and I bristled, full of anger, my cheeks staining crimson. He threw my clothes down inside the chest, closing the lid.

"This cape will hide you from my men and their prying eyes." And before I could protest, he took my arm in a firm grip and opened the door, pulling me through it.

We came out onto the deck just as the first pale streaks of daylight crept into the sky. There was no sound save that of the water lapping against the ship, rocking it with a gentle moaning sound as it pulled at the anchor. I noticed some men working to mend the sails on the far side of the deck, and they looked up as we came out. I fancied that they laughed to themselves. They were all deeply tanned, men of the sea, and most of them were foreign, I guessed by their looks. We went to the bulwark.

The ship was anchored in a deep pool and I noticed that on either side the mud banks rose steeply as the tide ran out, and that the creek itself wound around a bend and turned toward the estuary, which I knew ran in front of the manor house.

A few yards from where we stood on deck there was a small boat tied to the quay, and a man stood there, pulling in a line with a catch of fish.

Roc turned to me with a serious look in his eyes.

"Miss Kendal, before you go, let me ask you this one question. Do you know what he intends to use your money for? And how he intends to use Mullins?" He placed both hands on my shoulders.

I said nothing, for naturally I did not know, and I waited for him to go on.

"He is in slave trade, Miss Kendal," he said, his voice low and cautious. "He intends to use your fortune to back it up, and to bring the slavers into the estuary. I am here to stop him."

Horror rushed over me in great waves. My heart sunk. Surely the man would blacken Trevor's name and reputation only to vent his own anger. So why was I afraid? I trembled, and turned away, my hand clutching the bulwark.

"The payment will be just, Miss Kendal. You aren't ruined, and perhaps I've even done you a service if, perchance, your husband discovers our little tryst and refuses to have anything to do with you!"

"Oh!" I put my hand up to my flaming cheek. What an insolent creature, to remind me of what he had the gall to do to me, and to boast so! Before I could retort, he pointed to the river where the small boat was now being rowed towards the ship by the man who had so roughly pushed

me down the galley-way. His little monkey face was smiling as he came alongside the ship.

"Here's Robin. He will take you back to the house." His
words were full of confidence as he looked down at the
man in the boat.

Up until that very moment, I'd feared the worst: that
Roc St. Coryn would not set me free, but keep me a prisoner. It was only when he began to help me over the bulwark that I realized he meant to send me back to Mullins,
and it came as a genuine shock. I swung myself gingerly
over the side and clung to the ladder, the cape swirling out
around me as I let myself down into the rowboat, refusing
Robin's offered hands. I glanced up once, and to my dismay Roc St. Coryn leaned against the side, holding Robin's
catch of fish in one hand, watching me with knowing eyes
and that secretive smile I'd already come to loathe. The
men who had been mending the sails now stood alongside
him, grinning as if they enjoyed the scene of my departure
immensely.

Insufferable rogue! Enraged but powerless, I sat down
and Robin began to row. As we moved slowly away from
the ship, I saw the name beneath the windows inscribed in
gold lettering: *The Petroc.*

When we reached the far bank and quay, a shaft of red
sunlight struck the ship and its masts. It stood out in its
bold coloring—remote, unreal, a thing of beauty touched
by the new light of day—and I could hardly believe that I
had been so unwilling a captive in the cabin where those
windows were flung open to the morning glow.

As I stepped from the boat onto the quay, I looked back
and saw the herons still standing in the shallows, but now
their heads were sunk in their pearly, hooded shoulders.
Farther down the creek a solitary curlew paddled in the
mud, but the oyster-catcher was gone.

CHAPTER TWO

We walked through the trees, and as I followed Robin over
a worn path I had the thought that this must be the very
path the smugglers had used earlier for their "run of contraband." That seemed far away, as if it had been a dream,

for now day had come and there was a reassuring bright-
ness in the air. The scent of moss and wet pine permeated
the woods and the bracken was thick and already a rust
color on the forest floor, wet with the heavy autumnal dew.

For some time we walked through this deep forest, and I
knew we must be quite a distance from the house. I kept
the cape pulled tightly about me, but the hem of it was
soon soaked by the damp grasses it brushed as I went by. I
believed we were not far from the Channel but I had no
way of knowing, except for what Trevor had once said of it
to me.

"Mullins," he'd said, "is built on a rise of land along a
narrow tree-lined estuary, which forms an irregular peninsula, and the Barton Farms take most of it. Poppy Meadows is at the far end, facing the Channel, and it's the high-
est point of land."

The house itself, I knew, was built well above the flood
level and behind it was a copse of copper beeches through
which an avenue ran to the Bodmin Road.

Now, I could almost see the land as he'd described it, as
I followed Robin through the deep forest. Trevor had been
sensitive about Mullins. I knew he had not lived here for
very long in the past but he'd explained it in such detail
that I felt I already knew it, and I was greatly disturbed at
what I'd been told by Roc St. Coryn. I was determined,
too, to prove him wrong.

At last we came to the gardens of the house, still in the
shadows of early morning. I noticed that smoke curled
from the chimney pots and knew the servants were already
up.

Robin bade me enter through what I saw must be the
entrance to the Little Hall. Again, I had the strange sensation of having been there before, for with vivid clarity, I
recalled what Trevor had said of this portion of the house.
He'd told me that when the second story was added over
what had always been the Little Hall, where the steward
presided over the food stores and wine cellar, a stone pas-
sage built over a trickling stream of water separated it from
the kitchens.

"It's their wing of the house now, and the stream is
blocked off to preserve the house from dampness. Done in
my father's time, I suspect," he'd said. "There's a marvel-
ous old stairwell which can be approached from inside or
out, stairs that were made crooked by design," he'd ex-

plained. "Pirates and smugglers often raided houses along this coast, and if they didn't know these stairs, they would stumble and fall, which kept them from being too successful.

"But, of course, the irony of it all lies in the fact that the St. Coryns were the pirates and smugglers themselves, even then." He had laughed and because I thought it amusing myself, I told this to Lucretia yesterday, as we took a tour of the house. But she hadn't been amused at all and had almost fainted from sheer fright.

Now, Robin proved that he too knew this stairwell, and very well indeed, for he said in his guttural English, "Be 'ee careful like, Miss, for them stairs be crooked, and 'eel throw 'ee one, 'tis for sure. But 'eel take 'ee back up to the old Solar, it 'eel, and to the Blue Boudoir."

I turned to stare at him, stunned that he even knew the name of the room I'd been in. But why not? I thought at once, since I knew he must be receiving information from one of Trevor's servants. I tried to imagine which one it could be, remembering the line-up of the household staff that greeted Lucretia and me yesterday. One of the sly maids? Maybe my own maid, I thought ruefully, as I glared at Robin. But even as I thought it, I believed Pansy would not give this little monkey of a man a second look. Or would she?

I turned around to face him. "I know my way from here," I snapped. "You may return to your master." I wanted to slap the smirk from his funny face, but even more I wanted to slap his despicable master. I was furious that he could have crept up these very stairs and waited for me, abducting me at the instructions of Roc St. Coryn, and that he had carried me down these stairs without a misstep because he knew them so well.

He just stared at me with that foolish grin, not perturbed in the least, which increased my ire all the more. I turned around and started up the steps, realizing as I did so that they were indeed tricky, and I stumbled rather clumsily. I wanted to lash out at the gaping little man at the foot of the stairs, but I did not, and instead hurried as best I could out of sight. I soon found myself in the corridor which I recognized would lead me to the Blue Boudoir.

It was just as I was passing the landing at the top of the spiral staircase and was almost at my own door, that a servant reached the top of those stairs and saw me. My heart fluttered in fear.

It was Combes, the old steward whose wife was the kindly Cook. He had a strange look on his face, as if he knew he'd caught me up to something. I could not imagine what duties he could be about at that time and it occurred to me he too was waiting for an explanation. My face reddened with guilt and embarrassment, and I was glad of the dimness that kept him from seeing me very well.

"Good day, Miss. 'Hap 'ee gave me quite a turn there, 'ee did. 'Ee do be up so early?" His dialect was as thick and quaint as the speech of all the Cornish folk I'd met, and I noticed that his lower lip seemed to pout rather stubbornly as if he were displeased at my being up already.

"Good morning, Combes," I answered as calmly as I could. "I wanted to go look in on my cousin, Miss Lucretia. I do so worry over her," I lied, and I was aware this seemed to surprise him. How much did this old man know, or even guess? Was he one of the servants loyal to Roc St. Coryn, or to Trevor?

Suddenly, I wanted to escape him, for I could envision him giving the warning signal to the crew of *The Petroc*. It seemed in keeping with his character, I thought, and I turned my back and hurried toward the door of the Blue Boudoir.

I rushed into the bedroom, kicked off my wet, grass-stained slippers and flung off the red cape, then rolled them together and hid them under the huge wardrobe.

I pulled out a fresh white chemise and slipped it over my shivering body, then hurried to the bed and under the covers, waiting for the day to begin.

It was only then that I realized I had done exactly what Roc St. Coryn had predicted I would do. I had not screamed for help or aroused the household in hopes of having the man hung for abducting and ravishing me, and I realized that I would go to any lengths to keep my secret, even from Trevor.

To my dismay, I knew he was right. Trevor would never accept the truth of it. But what Roc St. Coryn didn't know was the reason I could never speak of this interlude to Trevor. How, indeed, could I tell the man whose mistress I was prepared to become that I had been seduced in such a wicked—but almost delightful—manner?

I could not. Trevor St. Coryn was a man who would

believe the worst, and I was not going to be humiliated by telling anyone of this incredible encounter with Roc St. Coryn.

No matter how I tried, I could not put from my mind the man who had seduced me. I wanted to forget, but my thoughts went over it all in detail, and I found I was not injured in the least, not as I knew Lucretia would have been had Roc St. Coryn's diabolical plan of revenge been correctly carried through.

That she had been spared this fate was not much consolation to me in this moment. It seemed ironic that it was always I who had to protect my frail little cousin from the outside world.

Lucretia had always evoked a strong protective sense in everyone, including me. But it seemed unfair, I thought now, as I too longed to have that comforting sense of being protected by someone stronger than myself. I knew I would never be able to tell anyone what had happened to me this day, but all I desired now was to get even with Roc St. Coryn, who had so cunningly drugged that wine and seduced me.

I was strong-willed, giving everyone who knew me the impression that I could look after myself in any situation. It took a man with diabolical cunning to shake this strong will, and I couldn't protect myself from him.

I blushed as I remembered how his hands had moved over me, his strong fingers exploring with the greatest skill, and arousing within me an emotion so wanton that I had abandoned all sense of discretion under his influence. In spite of my anger at Roc St. Coryn, I could not forget that feeling, so alien to me, so unlike anything I'd experienced before.

So I couldn't protect myself from a man like him. But I had come through it all, hadn't I? I was stronger than my cousin Lucretia and totally unlike her. She was timid, while I was resolute in everything I did.

This came from having parents who were so engrossed in themselves that they had no room for a third party when I barged into their world so unexpectedly. I learned to be independent at an early age, while they played in London society circles.

When I was ten years old, my parents were drowned on holiday at the Isle of Wight, in a sailing mishap on the Solent in a sudden summer storm. Orphaned, I arrived at

the Chelsea town house of my uncle, Doyle Kendal, my
father's older brother and Lucretia's father, ready to protect her from the cruel world and the pains it could inflict
upon the young. She had looked up to me from the beginning, for she too was motherless.

My life in Chelsea was not unhappy, but rather what one
would expect it would be. My father had been a very
wealthy merchant, owning a shipping company in India,
and my mother had been an Earl's daughter. It was expected that when I reached the age of twenty-five, I would
come into that more than considerable wealth.

I had believed that my care and my keep, as well as my
expensive education in Miss Spring's School for rich young
ladies and my coming-out season, had come from my
inheritance. I believed myself the heiress I should have
been. What I hadn't known was that my Uncle Doyle had,
by some crafty means, used my fortune, investing it in his
own interests and cheating me out of my own father's
money. My mother's wealth had reverted to a distant male
relation, and I was left penniless, as I learned when Uncle
Doyle died quite suddenly last autumn. Sir George Thorpe,
Uncle's solicitor, had stood in the drawing room of the
Chelsea town house and read Uncle's will.

I was stunned at the distorted words spoken by the solicitor. According to him, Uncle Doyle had taken me, penniless daughter of a wayward brother, into his house and
bosom, out of the goodness of his heart, and had treated
me as he would his own daughter, paid for my expensive
education, given me his home, launched me into society.
Upon my twenty-fifth birthday, if I had not married, I
would have to seek employment suitable to my education,
but I would receive a (very small) lifetime allowance, half
of which would cease upon marriage.

Nothing had prepared me for this. Angrily, I had gone
to Sir George and protested, but he only said, "You are
indeed fortunate you had a generous uncle, Miss Kendal.
Your own father, I might say, was thoughtless and made
no will. Under the circumstances, Mister Doyle deserved
the wealth left by such a negligent brother. Consider yourself fortunate."

I hardly paid attention when Lucretia was mentioned in
the will as Uncle's heiress; indeed, it seemed the whole
household staff, and Lucretia, expected this, and that I was
the only one who had been duped. I was devastated.

So I found myself at the age of twenty-four a penniless relative. I could not, and *would* not, forgive Uncle Doyle for this piracy of my rightful inheritance. I had only one friend who had been totally shocked at this turn of events. She was my godmother, a close friend of both my parents who often included me in her dinner parties and lavish balls. Lady Cecilia Lebrun had taken a fancy to me, and had done her best to see that I was introduced to the most eligible bachelors. She had believed I was to inherit a vast fortune, and it was she to whom I went, to relate all.

Ironically, I had met Trevor St. Coryn two months before Uncle's death. Uncle Doyle had taken Lucretia down to Bath for those two months, and I had stayed in Chelsea. Lady Cecilia gave one of her many balls during that time, and there I met Trevor. She herself had introduced us.

Lady Cecilia informed me that Trevor, with his many business ventures abroad, was most useful in helping locate the families of the poor, unfortunate victims of the guillotine, and in helping them establish a new life in England. She herself was deeply involved, and though we were just beginning a new war with France after the awful Terror, she did her best for these destitute refugees. Her own husband had lost his head to the guillotine, and thus her sympathies had been unflagging during the intervening years.

Trevor had courted me with all the ardor of a man in love. I found him to be the most exciting man I'd yet known, and when he spoke so passionately of returning one day to Mullins in Cornwall, with a lovely wife, I felt my prayers were answered. That he expected to marry a woman who was an heiress meant little to me in those days; I *was* that heiress, and I knew what I wanted.

Shortly before Lucretia and Uncle Doyle returned from Bath, Trevor had to go abroad again, this time to the Ivory Coast of Africa. He gave me every reason to expect a proposal of marriage when he returned.

The night my uncle and cousin came back to Chelsea, Uncle Doyle's heart gave out and he died totally unexpectedly, sending Lucretia into the most pitiful of shocks. It was all I could do to ler her cling to me during the weeks that followed. I had written to Trevor the news of my uncle's untimely death, and when I wrote him of my penniless state, I was dismayed that he kept silent until he returned to London.

He called at the house, and I introduced him to Lucre-

tia, who was distraught with the grief of losing her dear
Papa. She turned to Trevor for the strong protection a man
could always give to such a pathetic child as my cousin.
Had she not been so guileless, I would have been envious,
but I could not find just cause to vent my anger upon the
helpless Lucretia.

That she had my fortune, given to her by a devious,
wicked father, was torment enough, but she couldn't
change that. All she had been able to do was to say that
her inheritance was mine too, and that she would look after
me as long as she lived; her house would be my house, and
we would share everything.

She had not known or even guessed that Trevor had
been my beau. That Trevor had not indicated it to her distressed me, but one day, after he'd been calling regularly at
the house for two weeks, he took me for a drive in the park
and told me that he'd proposed marriage to Lucretia.

This crushed me. He said that even though he loved me
deeply, he would not marry me. "I have asked Lucretia to
be my wife, Roma. She is helpless, and needs a protector. I
want to be that protector." He looked at me, imploring me
to understand.

"I need the money, Roma," he said in a low, serious
voice. "Her fortune will keep Mullins for me, and I must
keep Mullins."

So the man I loved would be marrying my cousin for the
money that should have been mine. It was bitter to swallow. I said nothing. But he took me by my shoulders and
turned me around to face him. "You need not be at such a
loss, my love. I want you to come with us to Mullins, for
Lucretia herself has insisted that you make your home with
us. She cannot bear to be without you. And," he pulled me
to him, kissing my forehead, my hair, "I cannot bear to be
without you either. I want you to know Mullins. I will love
you. Lucretia—" he'd stopped, and regarded me with full
meaning in that moment between us.

I said haughtily, "And Lucretia? She will be your wife."

He took my hands in his and brought them to his lips,
his eyes never leaving mine. "She will be my wife, but you
will be my heartbeat. She is a child who will never grow
up. She needs protection, and you and I will protect her. I
want to have the wedding in the village church at Pelyn,
where all the St. Coryns have married. You must come and
attend my bride. She would soon perish, I think, if you did

not make your home at Mullins. Let us take what opportunities are offered us."

I threw away my hurt pride and, out of many reasons, I
accepted this offer. When I went to Lady Cecilia, this wonderful woman gave me sage advice. Be a mistress, she said,
but discreetly so. It would suit me far better than to accept
the menial labor of a "position." She affirmed Trevor's
great affection for me, and said that I could salve my conscience by being of help to my timid cousin while being
near the man I loved.

But this conscience of mine reared up often to mock me
during the weeks and months that followed. It gave me
grave cause to doubt that I should be able to lead such a
clandestine life. That Lucretia herself was frightened of becoming a wife to Trevor was apparent. She clung to me
and wanted me to be her strength during the ordeal. It was
ironic that when we were assembling her wedding trous-
seau, she insisted I have a new wardrobe too, and I sometimes despised myself as we prepared for the long journey
down to the West Country. Just how much was I going to
have to give of myself to protect her, I wondered now, as I
lay in this great deep bed waiting for morning to come?

And my thoughts kept alive the thing that had happened
to me. I would no longer be the same woman I'd been even
last night, because of Roc St. Coryn. Yes, I had suffered
what should have been Lucretia's fate at the hands of this
half-brother of Trevor's.

The man had certainly guessed the truth, I told myself. I
was the woman Trevor had chosen for himself; I was his
kind of woman and, had things been different, I would
have been his wife. And that horrible man would have had
his revenge. How I looked forward to seeing his face when
he learned the truth!

I wanted that more than anything.

I must have slept, for Pansy came in to wake me some
time later, smiling as she set down a tray with a pot of hot
chocolate beside my bed.

"It do be a lovely morning out, Miss, it do. We been
havin' a gale all week, and Cook do say 'ee and Miss Lucretia brought the good weather back, that 'ee have!" Her
dialect was as strong as old Combes', I thought, and
couldn't help smiling.

"Mister Trevor be home, too, Miss, and he do be askin'

for 'ee to join 'im in the breakfast room, if 'ee will, when
'ee be up and dressed. Tulip do say that Miss Lucretia took
a chill in the night and her won't be down, not now her
won't."

My heart stopped. Trevor home from Falmouth!

"What time did Mister Trevor return, Pansy?" I tried to
be casual as I yawned and sat up in bed, taking the cup of
chocolate she poured for me.

She turned and I noticed she'd brought in the hot water
for my bath. Her eyes were full of mischief, and her dark
hair was hidden under the white mobcap I was sure the
fastidious Mrs. Pascal made certain she wore.

"Oh, Mister Trevor he do come in not more than an
hour, Miss." As she said this, I saw by the small clock on
the mantelpiece that it was quarter past nine already.

"I see," I said, sipping the chocolate gratefully. "She isn't
ill, is she? Miss Lucretia, I mean."

"Oh no, Miss. My sister Tulip says her is such a frail
little thing anyway, and frightened as a little mouse, her do
be, and nothin' but Tulip must sleep in the room with her.
Tulip, her don't mind that, not one bit she don't!" She
paused, looking at me as she picked up the buckets of water. "And Miss Lucretia sent word for 'ee not to worry
none. Tulip be right there, lookin' after her needs, and it do
please me sister, it do. So 'ee are not to fret 'eeself, Miss,
her say, and to go down to breakfast with Mister Trevor if
'ee please."

So that was the way it was to be, I thought, my tongue in
my cheek. Lucretia would remain in bed until mid-day,
with Pansy's look-alike twin for company, postponing the
moment she would have to face Trevor, and giving me the
task of softening that moment for her. I heard Pansy filling
the bath with water, and I waited until she brought out my
clothes for the day before I slipped from the bed and hurried into the alcove behind the screen.

If she noticed the different chemise I threw across the
screen for her to take, or the absence of the peignoir she
herself had laid out last evening, she didn't let on, and, as I
lowered my body into the luxurious scented bath, I decided
she simply hadn't suspected a thing.

I could have wept in that moment. My encounter with
Roc St. Coryn, the nightmarish abduction, seemed so far
away, and I might have dreamed it all had it not been for
my sore body. I closed my eyes and gave myself to the

warmth, allowing the oils to penetrate, wishing I would wake up and discover none of it had happened. For a while, indeed, I gave myself to this moment, feeling my taut nerves relax, and then knowing a sense of well-being I never thought possible, for I had been aroused to something—a new emotion of sensuous joy—that could not be forgotten so lightly.

As I stepped from the bath some half-hour later, warmed, my skin glowed from rubbing it with the thick soft towel. I smoothed rose oil over my body, and then I stepped into fresh undergarments of finest muslin, the silky finish soft to my skin.

I considered the gown Pansy had laid out for me. Its shade was one of the most becoming to me, a pale pink which certainly highlighted my olive complexion to the best advantage. My hair was almost Egyptian black, and curled naturally. My eyes were like those of a doe, round and slightly slanted, and although I was considered striking in looks, I was not the least bit pretty by current standards, nor could I wear frills or the "baby-doll" gowns which were all the rage in London.

For me, the simple and beautiful tunic dress was best, and as Pansy helped me into this gown with the new demure neckline, high enough to be discreet, with the skirt smooth across the front and with the new fullness in back, I felt my self-confidence return to me. I loved the oyster-pink muslin, the sleeves long and full, with a series of puffs from shoulder to wrists, tied with dark brown velvet ribbon after each puff.

I had Lucretia to thank for my expensive new wardrobe. Miss Warren's House of Fashion in London had certainly outdone itself to create morning frocks such as this one, and the tea gowns and evening gowns in velvets and silks were even lovelier. Our portemanteaux had been packed solid with these latest fashions when we'd left London last week to travel to the Duchy of Cornwall. And certainly I could never complain of my cousin's lack of generosity. Both of us delighted in having such beautiful gowns; that Lucretia continued to provide my wardrobe now was proof of just how guileless her personality was.

I allowed Pansy to brush out my hair as I sat before the table mirror. I had not brought my own abigail with me to Mullins and I was doubtful that this gawky country maid could do my hair as I was accustomed to having it done. I glanced up to see the maid watching me, her eyes slyly going over my high full bosom, my neck, and my face. I had to bite my lower lip to keep from reaching out to slap her face.

She was a full-bosomed girl like her sister, her breasts almost bursting through her tight cotton bodice. Her dark blue woolen skirt was gathered over her too-full hips, but she was neat and clean, which was certainly Mrs. Pascal's doing.

Freckles stood out on her pinkish skin, and though I found no fault with her outwardly, there was a certain expectancy in her expression which unnerved me. I felt that she was studying me and could not help wondering if she had been the servant who had betrayed the presence of "Miss Kendal" in the Blue Boudoir, perhaps in return for favors?

My own color heightened with this rash thought, and I turned my head sharply, making Pansy spill out the hairpins on the table top. My voice was rather shaky as I said, "Miss Lucretia won't be down to breakfast then, did your sister say?"

I could very easily picture my cousin sitting up in bed in a dainty dressing gown tied prettily with blue ribbons, a lacy nightcap over her curls, which would peep out teasingly, allowing Tulip or anyone to fuss over her, babying her slightest whim. Because Trevor had warned us both that Mullins would be far too lonely and isolated for London maids, he'd insisted that we leave our abigails behind and promised us both our choice of maids at Mullins.

Now Pansy said cheerfully enough, "Aye, Miss, that do be so. Tulip do say her is such a dainty, fragile little thing, and she bain't like 'ee, no she bain't, Miss!" She shook her head and I winced inwardly at this lack of tact. But in her own way, I supposed, she was paying me a compliment.

"And it do seem like Mister Trevor's old aunt, Miss Phoebe, with her queer ways now has someone her can dote on, like her did on—" She stopped, and I saw her glance furtively around the room.

"Like what, Pansy?" I prompted, as she began brushing my hair again.

Her voice dropped to a whisper. "Like her did on Miss Kate, and so Mrs. Pascal do say, she do!"

"Miss Kate?" I frowned. "You mean the girl in the portrait there in the boudoir?" I couldn't help smiling, for Miss

Phoebe had mentioned her last night as we had dined. "Has Miss Phoebe been to my cousin's rooms already?"

"Aye, her do be the one, Miss." She held a pin in her mouth while she brushed a curl around her hand. "O' course, it were afore Tulip and I came up to the big house, but we do remember the talk, our mother tellin' us all. Tulip say Miss Phoebe came quite early to see little Miss, but that one do be frightened scairt of the old duck, queer that she be, and it bain't no wonder, it don't!"

I waited a moment, trying to digest what she was saying. "So Miss Phoebe took to my cousin like she did to Miss Kate," I said slowly. "I gather these were her rooms? Miss Kate's, I mean." I felt this maid could tell me something which might give me an insight into that secret past of the St. Coryn family.

" 'Ee wouldn't know now, would 'ee Miss? Why 'tis *her* ghost what haunts the boudoir. 'Tis a wonder to us all that 'ee were brave enough to come in here, what with her ghost about! My life, but 'ee do be a brave 'un, that's fer sure, Miss!"

"But if these rooms are haunted, Pansy, you too must be brave to come in here." I widened my eyes, and could have laughed at her comical expression in the mirror.

"That be so, Miss, it do. But it do stand to reason that if 'ee can be in here, then with the two of us, no ghost can walk!" She crossed herself, closing her eyes as if to ward off some evil spirit and muttered some chant to herself.

I was agitated. "But these rooms were ready for Miss Lucretia, were they not?" I persisted. "Surely, if they were haunted, no one would want to place a guest in them. Least of all a timid little mouse like Miss Lucretia. She would faint dead away—and did so last evening as everyone in the house now knows."

I watched her in the mirror as she wound my hair around her hand in a surprisingly deft manner, and I had the vague notion that I could teach her what my own abigail had been able to do for me in Chelsea. "Did the servants know Miss Kendal would have these very rooms?"

"Lawks, Miss, we didn't know her to be such a timid thing, now, did we? Why," she made a funny grimace, putting hairpins into her mouth again, puckering her lips in a manner that was almost hilarious, "them was none o' our doin's, no it were not! But that queer old duck herself, Miss Phoebe, it were hers. Harmless she be, but her do live in the past an' all, havin' that picture brought down from the attic, where it were all them years, and had it placed in the boudoir when Mister Trevor wrote that there were to be a new bride in the house." She took a pin from her mouth and stuck it into the curl.

"And her say to Mrs. Pascal—I heard her as did Tulip, we did—'The bride to be, Miss Kendal, shall have the Blue Boudoir, Mrs. Pascal, and make no mistake!' As if that one ever would, I tell 'ee! Oh but me'n Tulip did have a laugh over that one, that we did!" And she giggled, her breasts shaking as she did so. She enjoyed a good laugh, I could see, and I knew her sister was like her. I could visualize these twin sisters enjoying any mistake the efficient Mrs. Pascal could make, not to mention their mimicry of the aging Miss Phoebe with her strange, eccentric ways.

Trevor had tried to explain his great-aunt to both Lucretia and me. She lived in her own part of the house. "I never saw much of her, even when I was a boy, and I can't tell you what she does. Her old servant, Norie, as old as she is, I guess, attends her and lets no one into the old woman's rooms. But she's harmless, and you must not mind her when her talk wanders back to the past. I've never known her otherwise. She's my father's aunt, you see, and quite old. She keeps to her part of the house, so she won't bother either of you, I believe."

"So it was Miss Phoebe then, who wished Miss Kendal to have these rooms, Pansy?" I asked, as she picked up the brush and began on another curl.

"Oh yes, Miss. It were her all right, it were!" She pressed her lips together tightly, then pinned the curl in place.

"Why does Miss Kate's ghost haunt the boudoir, Pansy?"

She seemed surprised as she met my eyes in the mirror. "Don't 'ee know, Miss?"

"No." I said after a moment. "Tell me."

"Well, Miss," she began, loquacious as ever. "Her climbed right out of that window," she gestured towards the boudoir, "for this were hers then, 'ee see, to meet her lover who stood below in the courtyard, with a horse and trap waiting for her. Them two were eloping, 'ee see.

"And old Mister Edward, 'ee be angry and all, and he were deep in his cups that night, so our father, Tamblyn, says, Miss. 'Ee didn't meet Tam yesterday, Miss, but 'ee

will, that be fer sure." She stuck another pin in the cluster
of curls she was arranging.

"Well, our father tells us about that night. Me'n Tulip
were young then, to be at the great house and all, so he do
tell us. Mister Edward, he thought he heard a noise and
thinking it were the Revy men come to get him for the
dark deeds he do in his Lugger, *The Petroc*, Miss, as everyone *do* think that, Miss, and he took the gun down from
the chimney breast in the kitchen and shot them both dead.
It were awful, Miss, I tell 'ee, and so sad it were too. Mister Edward, when he saw what he did, poor thing, he
turned the gun on his self, they all say, and were found
dead next day right beside his Kate and her lover. That
were seven years ago, and Miss Phoebe, poor old soul, do
still carry on like her were acomin' back."

A faint tingling which began at the base of my spine
crept up my neck. This was what is known as making one's
flesh creep, I thought suddenly, and shivered. Seven years
ago . . . Something else touched the edges of my mind.
What was it? My heart almost stopped beating. "Kate?" I
asked, but almost to myself, so Pansy did not hear it. "How
tragic!" I said aloud.

She caught my expression and nodded her head. "Them
were buried, Miss, but not their souls, no." She sounded
bold in her prophetic words. "People who meet death that
way never rests. It were too violent, it were, and even Cook
says them can't stay buried, no. Too restless, adying that
way, and they . . . walk!" She gave a great shudder to
emphasize this doom.

"What nonsense, Pansy!" I heard myself cry too sharply.
"I thought it was supposed to be only Miss Kate's ghost
who haunts the place, not three people's!"

She stared at me as if offended that I had the audacity to
speak out against age-old superstition. "Them that knows
no better call wisdom nonsense, Cook says," she retorted,
piqued.

For more reasons than one, I too was piqued, yet Pansy
looked so hurt that I had derided her, that I asked in a
softer tone, "Who was Miss Kate, Pansy? Was she a part of
the family?"

In that moment, I saw that Pansy had a flair for cultivat-
ing the most dramatic expressions. She was shocked.
"Lawks, Miss! Don't 'ee know nothin' about her?" She regarded me with what could only be surprise. "Her were

Mister Edward's natural daughter, that's what, begat out of wedlock." At once, her black eyes gleamed and her mouth went a little slack. I could not hide my own surprise, and it all came back like one great jolt. But of course! Hadn't . . . *he* told me so? I only frowned, but I was shaken to the core. "A half-sister to Mister Trevor?"

She gave me a sudden wink in the mirror, a sly smile on her thin lips. "Oh my dear life, Miss, 'ee didn't know, did 'ee? That do be so, 'ee might say. Miss Kate and her brother, Mister Petroc, called Roc, he were, him being named fer Mister Edward's ship, 'ee see; them were that to Mister Trevor." Her eyes seemed beady and narrow, and suddenly I didn't want to hear any more. She placed the last pin in my hair, and I stood up. I couldn't help but remember what Roc St. Coryn had said of his sister, and I certainly didn't want to have it affirmed by Pansy.

I took great pains to study my hair in the mirror, and thanked her for dressing it, but since I could not for the life of me hide my disdain, I turned to leave the room. "I'll just go look in on my cousin now, Pansy. Thank you." I walked into the boudoir, and self-consciously I stopped in front of that portrait and stared up at it.

The young girl bore a faint resemblance to the man. There could be no doubt about it, I thought. But her eyes, as the artist had captured them on canvas, were merry and full of mischief, with none of her brother's cruelty in their expression.

No. There would be none, I told myself as I hurried from the Blue Boudoir, disturbed and terribly uncomfortable, my thoughts a jumble of accusations and superstitions.

I thought of what Pansy had confirmed about Miss Phoebe's insistence on installing "Miss Kendal" in that suite of rooms. Had *she* given Roc St. Coryn that information? And another distressing thought came to me. What if all Roc had said of Trevor and his business in the black slave market were true? I could not for one moment believe this, but all the same, the horror of it washed over me again.

That Trevor had not mentioned these relations of his seemed strange enough. Perhaps he felt they were of the past and best forgotten? But Roc St. Coryn was not only part of the past but a real threat in the present moment. He was full of vengeance, and had used that vengeance on me. I could not forget it, nor would I forgive it!

Lucretia was sitting up in her great, deep bed in a sunny room, her new satin morning robe tied with blue bows, a breakfast tray beside her bed with a silver teapot and delicate blue-bordered china on it. The maid was fussing over my cousin, just as I had imagined earlier.

She didn't look chilled; in fact, she looked in the best of health, all rosy and charmingly childlike. Sometimes I envied her this, for she had a sunny nature that no one could resist. I knew, too, just how innocent she was, so I could never be truly jealous, just amazed that she could remain untouched in our world of superficial personalities.

"Good morning, Lu," I smiled, hurrying over to her and leaning to touch her cheek with my cool kiss. "How lovely you look this morning, as if you did not stir the whole night. So what is this about your wanting to remain in bed and on such a glorious morning?"

I glanced about the room, which was newer than the old Solar room and somewhat larger. As it was on the east side of the house, the sunlight poured in. The rose-pink brocade bedhangings were bright, giving the room an airy look, lifting any shadow of the past which might haunt this old house.

"Oh Roma, you do tease, don't you?" she said, her eyes wide, like windows, I thought, to see down into her heart. She flushed and smiled.

"I came to see if you might need me, love," I laughed. "but I can see that you're well taken care of already." The maid, Tulip, exactly like her twin but dressed in a blue and white striped skirt with muslin panels and white stockings, looking proper enough to suit my cousin, reddened and turned to go into the dressing room.

"I am sorry to be so exhausted this morning. It was the journey down, of course, and I knew you wouldn't mind if I simply took this day to restore myself properly."

"Of course not, my pet. I shouldn't mind, but what of Trevor? He is back, and will be wanting to see you." It was then I noticed the beautiful single pink rose on the tray with a note beside it. She followed my gaze.

"Trevor sent it up to me. Wasn't it dear of him to think of it?"

"But of course," I said, my heart twisting treacherously.

A shadow passed over her face, I thought. "Oh, Roma, I do so hope I shall not fail him as a wife! I am so terrified!" Her voice lowered to a whisper.

So this was what it was all about, I thought. The chill was simply an excuse to put off seeing the man she was to marry.

"Don't be a ninny, Lu! Of course you'll not fail him. Why should you?"

"Oh, it's just that sometimes I think he might have preferred a strong woman, like you, Roma. You would never fail a man like Trevor!"

Treacherous, treacherous moment!

"Shall I tell you something?" I was impulsive, and I wanted to see her happy and unafraid. I could easily guess her fears, especially after my own interlude barely a few hours back. "You could never fail anyone. You simply capture their hearts and none can help themselves. The whole of this old manor and its servants adore you already as their new mistress. And even Miss Phoebe dotes on you!" I smiled, patting her soft hand.

She made a face, managing to smile, and looked more like an angel than anyone I ever knew. "But how fussy she is, Roma! She came into my rooms so very early, mind you, and routed poor Tulip to see to my every need. She is well meaning I know, but—" She stopped, and I saw something like fear flicker in her eyes.

"But what, Lu?" I prompted.

"Well, it's just that she keeps referring to me as . . . Miss Kate, whoever she is, and she speaks of the past as if it is still with us. She frightens me silly with all those ghost stories, about dead people who aren't really dead and haunt this old manor. She's not right, Roma. And she insists on calling me Kate. I don't like it."

I could guess at the fears in Lu's mind, being in this old shadowy house, but I could imagine too how the old woman would delight in scaring a timid child like Lucretia. I was faintly uneasy.

"Just as long as you know she is a confused old woman and, well, yes, a harmless lady who must be very lonely. And of course she would remember when other young people lived here at Mullins. But perhaps Trevor could speak to her. . . ."

"Oh no!" she cried, her hand going to her mouth. "I wouldn't *dream* of placing a burden so trite as that of my foolish fears on him! For they are simply foolish, I know. You must promise me not to say a word of this to him, or to anyone, Roma. He thinks I'm such a child as it is, without my little imaginary fears. I'm sure Miss Phoebe means well, and she's just as you say she is, a lonely old woman remembering when other young people were here. I shall just have to adjust to her eccentric ways, once I am mistress here."

It struck me then that Lucretia might have an inkling of the truth, but I shrugged off the feeling.

"There, you see? You've just made the first big attempt to be brave, Lu! You will be mistress here, and you've just said it to yourself as well as to me. Now, I'm going to run and allow Tulip to look after you. I must say, you do need to get some fresh country air. It will keep your cheeks rosy, and you must promise that you will not take to your rooms all day."

"Oh, Roma. You do know how to make things all right for me. I knew you wouldn't mind if you went down to Trevor alone this morning. He will feel all is right when he sees how you look."

"Oh la!" I cried, biting my lip to keep from chiding her, and to hide my own exasperation. "You know he will be counting the minutes until you are with him, so do promise to join us later in the morning. There is much to see and to do."

Again, I had the nagging thought that I was saving her from having to face up to her responsibilities. I despised myself at once for this uncharitable thought, so I leaned over and kissed her cheek fondly.

"Of course I promise. Besides, Trevor made me promise too. But I simply don't know how I should cope without you here with me in this scary old house!"

"Oh, cousin, really! It can't be all that scary. Besides. Look at all the attention given you, and you needn't worry over a shadow on the wall, if it comes down to that!" I laughed. But I knew now that there were indeed things for this timid heart to fear, for even the strongest heart would flutter at how I had been abducted. "But never mind, dear. We shall all of us look out for you. Believe that."

"You are a darling, Roma," she said, her eyes sparkling under the fringe of black, curling lashes. No one could ever resist such a smile as hers. "Do look after Trevor for me, will you?"

"Of course," I answered, and again my conscience mocked me, but I turned then and gave Tulip instructions to look after her mistress. The maid, already pleased at serving such a treasure as Lucretia, assured me she would do her best, and she gave me a polite half-curtsey. I left the room, confident but slightly disturbed for reasons I didn't dare admit, even to myself.

As I walked away, I again had the feeling I had been living in a fool's paradise to believe I could carry on this clandestine romance with Trevor while he was married to my sweet cousin. And then I remembered with unease as well as great excitement the man who had stirred me so but a few hours ago. It would be pleasant, I thought, to bring that man down a peg or two, when he learned the truth: that he had taken the wrong woman!

But even as I thought this, I forgot that life has more tricks than one in store for those who bargain on such ideas, and that revenge, though sweet-tasting, can turn bitter in a moment and not be what one bargained for at all.

Thus my mind was not on Trevor at all, but on Roc St. Coryn, as I went down a flight of stairs and came to the small but cozy dining room used only for the St. Coryn family.

CHAPTER THREE

Combes startled me as he met me at the door. I distrusted his pleasant smile and I was certain that he knew more than he showed in that pudgy face, now very pink in a shaft of sunlight which came through a window pane. He was looking at me with that curious smile.

For one moment, so brief it was, I thought we made a strange contrast; he in his sober, dark clothes, his inscrutable face, blue button eyes, and I in the fashionable pink gown, my hair caught back behind my ears in the ringlets Pansy had arranged.

The moment passed however, and he bowed to me. "Mister Trevor do be awaiting 'ee, Miss," he said with a twinkle in his eye, and I was suddenly sure that he was laughing at me, not openly, not with familiarity, but secretly, behind his shadowy eyes.

My color heightened, I knew, but I brushed past him, managing a polite, "Thank you, Combes," and entered the room, aware that he closed the door behind me. Again I

had the sudden thought that I looked somehow different
since last evening. Was it so obvious, then, even to a man-
servant? Then how should Trevor see me? It had been one
month since we'd last seen each other in London.

I found my pulse racing with this thought. Trevor stood
with his back to me, staring through the window flung
open to the sun. The delicate scents of clematis and mimosa filled the room, drifting in from the garden.

Yellow light poured in. Yellow damask curtains were
drawn back, and the carpet of soft rose and pale blues
lifted any gloom that could hover in a house like Mullins.
A fire, steady and low, burned in the hearth in spite of the
warmth of the September morning. The table was set for
two, silver candlesticks in the center with a bowl of purple
chrysanthemums between them. On a sideboard nearby,
dishes of food under heavy, silver-domed covers were kept
hot by spirit lamps. One helped oneself at breakfast, we had
been informed last evening.

Trevor turned in that moment. He was tall, his shoulders
broad, and my first thought was that he was not as tall as
Roc St. Coryn. It surprised me that I could compare them,
and I felt uneasy, as though I'd been caught doing something I shouldn't have done.

His eyes glinted blue-grey and, as they turned on me
now, they seemed curiously light. I had the impression that
they held resentment at my having kept him waiting, and I
searched his face for any sign that might betray he saw me
in a different light, or, heaven forbid, I thought with a sudden rush of fear, that Roc St. Coryn might have already
revealed the truth to him!

But with that tremor, I almost laughed. No, Roc St.
Coryn would never allow Trevor to know anything now. It
wasn't in his plans to reveal his diabolical revenge yet.

He moved swiftly across the room and took my hands in
his with a possessiveness I found oddly distasteful in this
moment. Without a word, he pulled me into his arms and
kissed me. It was not like the kiss I'd known under Roc St.
Coryn's lips, and I wasn't lost in that dark eternity. No.
There was passion in Trevor's kiss, but I felt none of the
excitement or even desire I now knew I could feel.

So even in this I found myself comparing the two men.
After a moment, Trevor stood back from me and regarded
me with a look that caused my heart to flutter. Had he
seen a change in me?

"You look different, sweetheart," he said in a low voice, because of the servants' listening, I supposed. "You are almost . . . well, glowing is the word, I suppose." And while my heart missed several beats, I did not meet his eyes lest he should guess the truth. "I thought you should never come down. I've been here over an hour, thinking of us. You mustn't ever keep me waiting like this again, my love, not when we have so few opportunities to be together and alone." He brought my hand up to his mouth and kissed it fervently.

A profound sense of relief swept over me while, at the same time, guilt was overpoweringly close, and I moved out of his hands. "I was extremely exhausted, I suppose, with the journey down," I lied, "and I must have overslept. And I was a little anxious for Lucretia." I met his glance.

"Yes," he said. "Combes did mention that he found you in the corridor very early this morning, and related the fainting spell Lucretia had last evening. You are so thoughtful of your little cousin. Too much so, I must say. But that is an endearing quality of yours which will save us much worry as time goes by."

He moved toward me again, but I went over to the sideboard and lifted a silver dome from a plate; scrambled eggs, bacon, chicken livers, and sausages, along with steaming tomatoes and scrambled brains filled these great silver dishes. There was freshly baked bread, crusty brown and crumbly inside, with mountains of fresh butter and strawberry jam. There were fresh berries too, with thick, rich cream and sugar, and plenty of hot brewed coffee. Immediately, I remembered the freshly baked bread and thick black coffee I'd shared in the cabin of *The Petroc,* hours ago on this same morning, and I was glad I had my back to Trevor at this moment.

When I turned, I found him watching me intently, and I felt the blood rush to my cheeks, but he brought the plates from the sideboard and I filled them.

Trevor was well-dressed in a dark blue riding jacket with high black velvet collar over a white frilled shirt. His tan buckskin breeches were tucked inside shiny black Hessian boots, and I could never imagine him dressed with the careless ease of Roc St. Coryn. He was clean-shaven, too, while his half-brother had a black beard and mustache, and he wore his hair short in the Roman style which was the rage of London now, and it was medium brown, not glossy black like Roc's.

I could not understand myself for making such comparisons between these two men! Trevor was the man I loved, the man I would have married had I not been cheated of my inheritance! And that odious pirate—that *blackguard* who had reduced me to some common wench—I despised with my whole being. There was something so wicked in his touch, even his dark looks, that spiraled my emotions to some peak I did not know.

Trevor came up behind me and I moved out of his embrace again, annoyed with myself as well as Trevor, and as he held the chair out for me to sit down at the table, I said, "I'm truly interested in your family, Trevor. You didn't tell me about your father. About his death, I mean. One of the servants, I forget just which one . . ." I tried to keep my voice level, very light, but I could not miss the scowl which formed on his face.

"Damn the servant, Roma!" he exploded, his face darkening. He was considered handsome and I had secretly prided myself that such a good-looking man had found me attractive. I'd even dared think to myself in the past year that we were well matched.

His square jawline was strong and his forehead high, the brown curls falling gently to his brow. Now, his eyes narrowed. "Servants will always talk, I suppose." He shook the large white linen cloth and placed it on his knee. "What have they been saying? But I will tell you. My father took his own life in one weak moment, for he was drunk like the old sea dog he was. Yes, he also shot and killed my half-sister Kate as she was eloping with her lover, Phillip Wilkes, from Wilkes Reach, our closest neighbors. He thought them to be the Revenue Men, for he had that guilty conscience, you see, and was always expecting them to come and take him unawares." He laughed harshly, without compassion. "He couldn't see properly in the moonlight, drunk as he was, and when he discovered what he'd done, well, we all assume he turned the gun on himself, right there beside Kate."

He looked at me unemotionally. "There you have the not-so-nice story, but it's the full story. That's why Kate's so-called ghost haunts the Blue Boudoir, as all the servants here would have you believe." He smiled warily, but the smile did not reach his eyes.

My mouth was dry, and I could think of nothing to say.

He continued, "I suspect Miss Phoebe has been doing her share in keeping that ghost alive, Roma, and I did learn she was responsible for Lucretia's uncomfortable night, frightened as she must have been by 'ghost stories'!" He smiled, the amusement now seeming genuine. "She is a strange old woman, as I'm sure you both have noticed by now, and as I've told you before. I do dislike her meddling in the past as she seems to do. Let's just hope that she keeps to her part of the house. I can't turn her out, nor do I want to. It is her home as much as it is mine. We shall just have to accept her, I suppose."

"She must have been overly fond of your half-sister, Kate," I said. "She keeps referring to Kate when she is with Lu, confusing the two, but for the life of me I can see no resemblance, from the portrait of Kate hanging in the Blue Boudoir." I said this lightly, but although the food had been tempting but a moment ago, I now could find no appetite to touch what was on my plate. But Trevor was eating heartily, and didn't answer immediately.

I cleared my throat and said, "Tell me about your half-brother, Petroc St. Coryn, Trevor. He was Kate's own brother, was he not?" I met his eyes then, as his head jerked up.

In that moment, I saw a fury I'd never seen in him before rise just to the surface, while a strange little tick jumped at the corner of his right eye. For the first time, I realized I didn't know Trevor as well as I had thought I did. A muscle in his cheek tightened, and I believed he was just barely checking that fury which possessed him.

But he spoke calmly enough, though there was anger in his voice. "So you have heard of that scoundrel too, have you? From what servant? I'll have him or her flogged! I won't have a servant at Mullins who even mentions the name of that scourge of the St. Coryns! A pirate of the worst kind, his name is black on the Spanish Main, as well as all along the Cornish coast."

Naturally, I felt all he was saying of Roc St. Coryn was true, but it somehow distressed me to hear the truth from Trevor's lips. I ignored his tirade and asked, "So, he is your half-brother? As Kate was your half-sister?"

"And how I wish I could deny *that* truth!" He thundered, then seemed to collect himself and began to eat deliberately and slowly. Ironically, I recalled that Roc said he wasn't blood-kin at all, though now I thought Trevor did not know of this. As he ate, he told me about his father's mistress, Katherine, and all he could remember of how his own mother had been heartbroken to learn of her husband's illicit "love nest," as the servants had been wont to refer to the affair Edward St. Coryn had nourished for all those years in secret.

"I was away at school from the age of seven, mind you, and never knew about it until my mother's death," he said darkly. "My father was always sailing off somewhere in his lugger, *The Petroc,* carrying on his smuggling in his swaggering buccaneer manner, so I suppose it was easy enough for him to have a mistress somewhere. One would have thought he'd have had several, but no, it was this one woman named Katherine he lived for, loved, and kept with him even after he married my mother."

I studied the food in front of me, but Trevor seemed not to notice me as he went on. "When my mother died suddenly, and I was called back to Mullins, I found my father had brought his children of that love affair to live here, because Katherine had died six months before my mother. It was his bringing of those bastards to be brought up here and to be recognized as his heirs that actually caused my mother's death, Roma. She was frail, and she couldn't take his effrontery. The sight of them reminded her of what he'd been doing, and it killed her to see the way he doted on their every need. Especially Roc, whom he favored and spoiled with affection he would never show me, you see."

And of course I saw all too clearly.

Trevor's hatred of the past and this one person obsessed him. "We never got on. We couldn't, you see. Roc, whom my father called his bastard son, was the most despicable, hot-tempered character I'd ever known, and I resented him and the fact that my father favored him so by naming him Petroc after his ship. He had never taken enough interest in me to allow me to go on even one voyage in his lugger, or to go aboard her. My God, how I resented that, and those two bastards!" All the old emotions now came to the surface. I had heard Roc's story, and now Trevor was telling me his.

"I was but a boy of fifteen and didn't know how to curb my resentment, I suppose. I saw only what they represented, and what I felt they were doing to my place as my father's legal son. He was partial to them, and made no effort to hide the fact. I hated it all, and was miserable. Thankfully, I was sent back to my school and never saw much of them, but I knew they were there, and that was enough to kindle my hatred."

I sipped the hot coffee and it burned my tongue. I mulled over what Roc had told me of Trevor's birth and wondered which account was true. I was uneasy and more disquieted than ever.

Trevor, too, took a deep swallow of coffee, and continued. "When I did return at last, about seven years ago, I found my father was a ruined man. He'd gone overboard in giving those bastard kids of his an education, and the money he'd poured out on Kate was staggering, to say the least. Anything she fancied, he saw to it she had. She was always going into St. Austell, or even to Plymouth, bringing her bright friends home with her, and they stayed weeks on end, partying and never giving the cost a thought.

"Father had sent Roc to a school especially to learn the sea and ships and by the time I arrived home, the boy had already been to sea on *The Petroc* as bold as any *man* I'd ever seen! By God, but I was sickened by his boasting, swaggering manner! He needed cutting down, and I knew I was going to do it!" His knuckles as he clutched the cup were white.

"We're just simple farmers here, Roma, with no claim to aristocracy, but my mother was genteel, and of course, the St. Coryns are classed with the local gentry. My father was drinking heavily, and had been caught by the Revenue Men for smuggling contraband. Someone had paid his fine, of course, so he didn't have to go to prison. In general, the manor was going to seed, my father having no interest in it any more. I suppose, had it not been for Jake Polden down at Barton Farms, the manor would have been lost." His eyes blazed with the anger he felt even now, and something cold touched my heart.

"But it was rumored that my father had given Mullins, the whole of the estate, to this bastard son of his, not to mention the lugger! Can you, of all people, understand what I felt when I heard this? To be cheated out of my rightful ownership of Mullins was not to be borne on any terms. That was the state of affairs when I came home that summer seven years ago."

His voice lowered, became deceptively quiet, and his eyes

were steely as he regarded me over the brim of his cup.
"But that is exactly what my father did, Roma. His will
had been changed that summer my mother died, only I
never knew. I only learned of it when Nick Seaton read the
will after father's death. It was gall, I can tell you. But I
took measures to change it at once. I had the law on my
side, you see, as I was father's legal son. Oh yes. I simply
took the matter to court and had it all restored to me.

"Roc was a stubborn youth of twenty then. He had
stormed out of the church at the funeral, and had taken
The Petroc back to the Spanish Main, I was told. Although
the ship is legally mine, I didn't pursue him as some believed I should under the circumstances, but rather allowed
him the right to use the ship as long as he stayed away
from Mullins and never showed his face again. But there is
no question; Mullins is mine. If he shows his face here but
once, I will find it just cause to claim *The Petroc* as my
property too." His voice carried the full weight of bitterness, I thought, and I too felt the sour taste of what all this
hostility had done to alter my life. It seemed unfair. Had I,
too, been a man, I might have reacted as Trevor had, in
order to regain what I believed to be mine. But now I had
the misfortune to have been abducted, ravished by a venge-
ful St. Coryn, and all because of a murderous intent upon
revenge.

Trevor pushed his plate back, and looked at me with less
hatred than I'd seen a brief moment ago. "It was a nasty
affair in some people's eyes, Roma. There was talk, as there
always is in a small village and among manor servants. My
father hurt my mother deeply, and I could find no pity for
those bastard children he brought here to raise as his heirs.
But it is over now, and what's done is done. I feel justified
in that Roc took *The Petroc*. We're even, so to speak." He
covered my hand with his, but I pulled it away.

"And, what of our situation, Trevor? Surely, you mean
to . . . hurt my cousin, your wife, as your father did your
mother?" I could not keep the sting of contempt from my
voice and it seemed to echo in the room.

He laughed as if he would banish from the moment all
the sordidness of the life we'd decided to embark upon.
"Roma, my love, my dearest. It will never come to that.
We both know it never could. We'll be sensible."

It made me want to laugh. However, I lifted my brows
and said, coolly "What would happen if Roc St. Coryn

came back to Mullins? Would he not want what he feels to be justly his?" I couldn't control the strange pulse which began to throb in my throat, and I placed my hand there to hide it as well as I could.

Trevor regarded me warily. "I've told you. I shall make it so hard for him that he'll wish he hadn't. I'll catch him at his own game. I have alerted the Revenue Men down at St. Austell, just as an extra precaution, and I've warned the servants that anyone caught aiding the smugglers in a run will pay the stiffest fine of his life, or be hung on the spot. And I am a man of my word."

In the strained silence which hung between us, I thought of that run I'd witnessed a few hours ago in the moonlight, and knew at least one servant was betraying Trevor. I thought of the ship hidden in the creek, and of the man who was her captain, and now of these threats Trevor was prepared to carry out.

I wanted nothing more than to bring Roc St. Coryn to his knees, and I smarted under my own desire to get revenge, especially to see his face when he learned he'd taken the wrong woman.

"Then you think he might just try to do a 'run' as you call it, here at Mullins? Has he done it before?" I poured more coffee into our cups, and knew my eyes were flashing, my heart beating heavily.

Trevor seemed self-assured. "I have no doubt that my unscrupulous half-brother will return some dark night to Mullins with a cargo of illicit brandy or the like, Roma. So far, I do not think he's had the nerve to come here, or I would have somehow known about it. One of the servants would have made it known, for they always do, you see." He smiled confidently.

So Roc St. Coryn was several jumps ahead of Trevor, I thought. He would be, for he was like a fox in his cunning, diabolical plans. That he had already won the servants' loyalty was clear enough, and that he'd been here more than a few times during the past seven years was evident. I couldn't help but feel the fear of excitement mount within me. I could say nothing. Now was the time to tell him of what I'd endured and of the humiliation he would soon face, but I knew I could not. It seemed I would be Roc St. Coryn's unwilling accomplice.

I picked up the cup of coffee and brought it to my lips.

Trevor caught my expression and laughed in a deep, confident manner.

"You must not worry about Roc St. Coryn, Roma, or think that he will come back and abduct you, or Lucretia for that matter, as has been done in the past at Mullins. Before that happens, I will have him in chains and hung by the neck, and be justified in doing so." Smug satisfaction was written all over his face.

My cup clattered into the saucer and shattered into fragments, coffee spilling out, staining the cloth and running down onto my gown. My cheeks flamed and my hands trembled violently as I stood up and wiped at my skirt.

Trevor reached for the bell, and Mrs. Pascal entered almost immediately through the green baize door that separated this part of the house from the servants' wing. It was as if she had been waiting there for the summons.

"Oh!" I exclaimed in confusion, and to my annoyance. "It was so careless of me!" I tried valiantly to remain calm, for I could see the surprise on the housekeeper's face, her concern over the broken china.

"It's all right," Trevor said. "I believe there are replacements to the set, but Mrs. Pascal will know that, won't you? Please send in a maid."

Mrs. Pascal was a tall spare women, with a hook nose and a domineering manner. With a white mobcap over her grey hair, and a crisply starched white linen apron over a plain black gown, she was as fastidious a woman as ever I'd seen. Not much escaped Mrs. Pascal, I thought, and I guessed she kept a tight reign over all the servants under her supervision. She rang the bell for Daisy, the maid who helped Cook in the kitchen, and then eyed my gown.

"It do be the cream in it what sets the stain, Miss Roma," she said, wiping at it with a clean cloth. "If 'ee can change it, I'll see to it the gown be properly looked after at once."

"Thank you, Mrs. Pascal," I said, grateful to be able to hide my own confusion at the accident in all the fuss, as Daisy came in and began to remove the table cloth and broken china. I agreed to go at once and change my gown.

"We do have extra of these pieces, Miss, so 'ee aren't to worry none. 'Hap 'ee didn't burn 'eeself? That were hot coffee."

"Oh, no. I'm quite all right. It was just clumsy of me.

Thank you." I turned to Trevor, who seemed amused by all this. "I'll leave you now," I said, knowing my face betrayed my embarrassment. I looked away and started to leave.

He came with me to the door. "Perhaps we can take a ride out around the grounds this morning, before Lucretia joins us," he said. "Dress in something suitable, and I'll have Jeffers saddle some horses for us. I'll see you in the Bower in a short while." He spoke decisively, yet I didn't mind, for I knew I needed a breath of fresh air.

"Very well," I said, and I felt his eyes upon me when I turned to go. I glanced at the housekeeper. Was there speculation in her eagle eyes? But I heard her say as I left the room, "Mister Trevor, Tamblyn brought a message for 'ee, he did, not five minutes back . . ." I didn't wait to hear more, but hurried back to the Blue Boudoir.

What a strange turn of events, I thought wildly, as I closed the door behind me and made my way up the stairs. Roc St. Coryn had returned to Mullins time and again without Trevor actually knowing it, had abducted me on my first night in the house, believing me to be the heiress and bride-to-be, and had carried out the first part of his revenge in a manner that changed my life, even before Trevor knew the man was close by and hidden in that creek! That I had come so close to losing my honor—and so easily!—and that Trevor should now be unknowingly open to disgrace because of it, was too apalling for me to contemplate.

I was still in a state of shock at Trevor's laughing remark about abduction, and I knew that Roc St. Coryn was far more crafty than Trevor gave him credit for. I felt an hysterical urge to cry out at the horror of it all, for I had been a pawn in their deadly game and had suffered a humiliation which still infuriated me.

Had my maid been in the rooms, I might have taken all my fury out on her, but fortunately for poor Pansy, she was not there, and I didn't ring for her. I hurried into the dressing room and removed the stained gown with trembling fingers and in angry jerks, and flung it aside.

I searched through the wardrobe and pulled out the beautiful amber velvet riding dress, the russet beaver hat and soft leather boots. Yes, I told myself, these would do most definitely. I needed to be out on good horseflesh, with the sea air on my face, so that I might forget even for a while how I had been used, and perhaps was even still a victim in the battle between these two men who hated each other.

With a renewed sense of frustration, I smoothed cool lavender water over my hot skin before I began to dress in the modish new habit. The skirt was full in back, smooth in front, and shorter so that the boots could be seen; the fitted jacket had the new frog closings with a pert Cossack-look collar, and as I viewed myself in the mirror, I was satisfied with the effect, especially when I set the beaver hat at a tilt over one eye. I noticed, too, the defiant gleam in my eyes. I would meet the challenge, and I would fight back in my own way, I told myself, thinking of Roc St. Coryn instead of Trevor.

Nearly three-quarters of an hour had passed, I saw by the mantel clock, and I rang then for Pansy. In the minutes before she came, I took time to look over some notes I had placed in the drawer of the secretary in the boudoir, notes about wedding plans which Lucretia could never take care of.

Certainly, Trevor had implied there would be several dinner parties and an announcement ball, and these would be left up to me and the housekeeper. I had not yet approached her, but would do so during the course of this day, I decided. She would have the wedding-guests list, Trevor had informed me by letter when he'd left Lu and me in London, and now I thought about his reasons for going. That Trevor had had to go abroad hadn't seemed significant at that time, for he'd said he had business on the Ivory Coast. He had never explained his business there, I thought now, frowning, and placed my notes beside a quill to remind me later in the day to take care of them.

It was just that I was remembering that Roc St. Coryn had accused Trevor of being in the slave trade, and I wondered if it was true. How much more did Roc St. Coryn know about Trevor's movements, if not everything? And why, I thought, bewildered, hadn't Trevor known the whereabouts of the man he most despised?

I suddenly recalled that Roc had said he'd seen Trevor with me, and that was how he knew I was the right woman, though I tried to deny it. How much did he know, if he'd been spying on Trevor? And was there any truth behind what he'd said about using Mullins as a slaver base?

Thus I was engrossed in disturbing thoughts when Pansy

entered, and I saw at once she had a smug, almost guilty, look about her. It annoyed me and I spoke too sharply.

"Please see that my gown," I gestured towards the pale muslin thrown across the chair, "is taken down at once to Mrs. Pascal, Pansy." I could guess that she had already been informed of the accident at breakfast, but I continued in a haughty voice, "I spilled hot coffee on it accidentally, and it must not be allowed to set. See to it at once."

The maid swallowed hard and glanced at the gown. I immediately regretted my tone with her, and reminded myself that I had always prided myself on being above those women who considered their servants beneath them.

But today I was quite different. Pansy's face was blotched, her eyes were like slits, and it seemed difficult for her to speak. But she said, "Yes, Miss. I'll see to it."

It occurred to me that she was holding something back, but I was so preoccupied with my own problems that I didn't stop to apologize or to find out what the girl was concealing. I hurried from the room, my glance just flickering across the portrait of Kate St. Coryn.

In the corridor, I hesitated for a fraction of a second before making up my mind not to look in on my cousin. I had neither time nor patience for her now, and I wanted to be out in the fresh morning air with the wind and sun on my skin, and the feel of a horse beneath me.

I didn't want my conscience to nag at me either, for being at the side of the man Lucretia was going to marry. I turned deliberately and descended the spiral staircase which took me down to the entry hall below.

Once downstairs, I looked out upon a walled garden, past the peach trees and beyond, to a wicket gate and dovecote where white doves fluttered their wings and cooed softly in melodic song.

Old Soady, who was deaf, kept this garden and the one behind the kitchens. Here the earthy scents of late summer and early autumn mingled with the sea, spicy and tangy, and I knew that nowhere had I ever seen plants as rare or late-blooming as those of Cornwall. Camellia and pink azalea thrived, but there were also the more common, and what were thought of as medieval, flowers which Old Soady seemed especially fond of. Just looking at them and breathing in their scents had a soothing effect on my frayed nerves.

I was tempted to go out into that garden, but I hesitated.

If the people of this house felt this room to be its most livable one, I thought it to be the most serene. It was a comfortable room, with a quiet feeling about it. Books lined the walls to the ceiling on one side, and plush velvet chairs were arranged under the windows and near the massive open fireplace; the huge oriental vases in the corners were filled with Michaelmas daisies and blue delphiniums Old Soady brought in from his gardens.

Trevor wasn't around, and I started for the open door, unaware of the woman until she moved slightly at the far end of the room, replacing a small china shepherdess on the table she'd taken it from. She apparently had seen me, for she was not startled, as I was. She had had time to study me before I'd been warned of her presence.

For one awkward moment, we seemed to measure each other. She was a young woman, a year or two older than mysef, I judged, and one of the most attractive women I'd ever seen. The simple grey gown she wore, unadorned, with a long grey cape thrown back over her shoulders, seemed to enhance her beautiful figure and bring out the rich highlights of her dark auburn hair.

Then she smiled, her wide mouth friendly, and the smile touched her very blue eyes. She came over to me.

"You must be Miss Kendall," she said in a positive but melodious voice. "Trevor's bride-to-be." Her glance went over my clothes and then came back to meet my eyes.

"No," I said, feeling awkward. "It is my cousin you're referring to. I am Roma Kendal. Lucretia is Trevor's bride-to-be."

I saw the speculation touch her eyes, and she seemed suddenly relieved as if she had harbored a wariness behind the friendliness of that smile. She was indeed beautiful.

"Then I'm happy to meet you, Miss Kendal," she said after a moment. "I'm Taryn Wilkes, from Wilkes Reach. You mayn't have heard of us as yet. My brother is the local doctor, and we are Mullins' nearest neighbors. Welcome to Cornwell."

At once, I recalled what Trevor had said of Wilkes Reach, and that it was Phillip Wilkes from Wilkes Reach that Kate St. Coryn had been eloping with. For a second I was silent, and then I said, rather too quickly, "Thank you," to her welcome. She sensed my surprise and then spoke candidly.

"We heard that Trevor was bringing his bride-to-be

down to Mullins—Hadrian and I, that is. And since my brother had to make a call at Barton Farms, he decided it was time to look in on Miss Phoebe too. He worries about her, you see. She has a stiffness in her back, which comes with her advanced age and the poor old dear does suffer occasionally. So Hadrian comes in once or twice a week just to make sure she is comfortable."

"How good of your brother to take such an interest in his patients," I said, and found myself wondering if it was her curiosity about Trevor's bride-to-be that had caused her to accompany the doctor. She answered my unasked question quite simply in another moment.

"I sometimes help Hadrian when someone breaks an arm or leg, which did happen at Barton Farms late last night, or rather early this morning." She chuckled, her eyes full of light and secret laughter. "So I came along."

"Why, what happened?" I asked.

"Jake Polden's young brother, the one that ran away to sea a year ago, returned, it seems, and when he came in long after midnight, he stumbled in the dark down a flight of stairs and broke his leg. We've been quite busy since dawn, for it was a nasty break."

"Is he all right? The brother, I mean?" I was certain I should meet these people, perhaps today.

"Yes. Arnie is in great pain, of course, but Hadrian gave him an opiate to keep him sedated for a few days. He is young enough for the breaks to heal well, if he keeps off the leg." She seemed knowledgeable in this line.

"You help your brother, then, with his doctoring?"

She inclined her head gracefully. "Yes, as much as I can with the small things, and in making plaster for casts."

I suspected then that she and her brother were part of the local gentry and regular visitors at Mullins. "Is your brother with Miss Phoebe now? She seemed quite agile last night. She took to my cousin uncommonly," I offered.

"I'm glad to hear it," Taryn said. "Miss Phoebe needs someone to dote on. It's been only in the past two months that the dear women has seemed to sag under the weight of her years. So Hadrian makes a point of coming to see her, for he is rather fond of her." She laughed again with the candor I found attractive. "And unless I miss my guess, he is with her now, having bribed old Norie to let him into her rooms, as he must do, usually with a box of French bonbons. Miss Phoebe is an eccentric who won't budge from her part of the house until tea time, and Hadrian, so far as I know, is the only outsider ever permitted into her rooms."

We fell silent for a moment, then she spoke. "I think perhaps I'd best give you the message I was to relay to you," she said slowly. "Trevor had to hurry out to Barton Farms with Tamblyn and I suspect it has to do with Arnie Polden. Anyway, he left a message with Jeffers, who relayed to me, mind you, that Miss Kendal would be riding, and that her mount was ready for her. I assumed, of course, he meant Trevor's bride-to-be." She looked at me questioningly.

This startled me. "Oh, Lucretia doesn't ride very often, and she is still tired from the journey down from London." I frowned, finding myself forced to explain Lu's not riding with me. Taryn Wilkes could guess that Trevor and I were going for a ride together, and I was suddenly irritated that I should have to explain this to such an attractive woman, one who apparently knew Trevor quite well. I was uncomfortable for a moment or two, but then she spoke to me again.

"I believe he meant that you should go on with your planned ride. You will probably be able to get more information from Jeffers than he gave me." She laughed in her attractive manner.

"Thank you. Yes, of course," I said, quickly agreeing with her, and we fell silent again, the moment somehow strained.

"I should like to meet your cousin, Miss Kendal," she said frankly. "To be honest, we all here have wondered why he would choose to settle at Mullins now, knowing he has had interests outside Cornwall for years." She lifted her elegant silky brows. "I suppose his other business will take him away for long stretches. Do you know?"

It was my turn to be surprised. "I'm sure I can't answer that, Miss Wilkes—" I was more annoyed than I cared to admit.

"Please do call me Taryn. May I call you Roma? After all, we'll be neighbors."

"Yes. Please do." I said.

She accepted this. "Perhaps I am speaking out of turn. Trevor was never one for the quiet farm life." She seemed amused.

"You know him . . . well, then?" I was uneasy, though I couldn't say why.

"Well enough. Of course, our families didn't always get on. My father and Mister Edward, Trevor's father, never liked each other, and it didn't set well when Phillip, my oldest brother, decided to elope with Kate. You've heard about their tragic deaths, haven't you?" I acknowledged that I had heard of the triple tragedy and she went on.

"It's been seven years, long enough to be talked about without all the upsetting emotions it brought then. Heaven knows how many scars it left, but they are but scars, now that the healing has taken place. Our father died shortly after Phillip was buried in the churchyard, there beside Kate and near Edward St. Coryn. All things end with the grave, I've heard it said. But breaches heal, and that is what was important." She smiled, and again I was aware of how that smile came through her eyes, enhancing her beauty.

"It must have been a double tragedy for you and your brother Hadrian," I ventured, for I wanted her to tell me more.

"Oh it was, then. But our father, had he lived, would never have accepted any apology, either from Trevor or Roc, or even an emissary from Mullins. He hated the whole household, servants and all. But since his death, there has been peace between the estranged houses of Mullins and Wilkes Reach. And Hadrian does his best to make that peace possible, I can assure you." I heard the note of sisterly praise in her voice for this brother I was yet to meet.

"You must be proud of him," I offered.

She smiled, her teeth white and even. "For a younger brother, he does all right."

"You . . . knew Roc St. Coryn too," I said evenly, my heart skipping a beat. "The brother of Kate. I understand he went off in his father's ship? Shortly after the tragedy occurred?" Why did my hands go cold with moisture, my cheeks hot?

She didn't seem the least perturbed. "Roc St. Coryn was a hot-blooded young fool," she said boldly, knowingly, "but terribly handsome. Yes, I knew him and all too well." Her words had a secretive inflection that gave me a second's unrest, yet she went on and I listened, amazed.

"He left Mullins quite unexpectedly, but with a threat

which hung over all our heads for months and even years afterwards!" She shuddered visibly, but then shrugged her shoulders, as if she harbored no great fear of this man's threats.

"What sort of threat did he make?" I persisted. We were still standing, facing each other, and I was startled to see the slow blush which began to stain her creamy, almost flawless, skin. A strange pang of envy stirred within me as I had the sudden thought that he had used this beautiful woman as he used me. That struck the core of my being, and I hated the thought. What a despicable man!

She shrugged her shoulders again and I found myself evaluating her. She was about my height, rather tall, but she somehow made herself look soft and feminine, without seeming vulnerable; for all her soft appearance, there was a singular hardness beneath that smile and gentle exterior which frightened even me. She would be used only when she agreed to it, I decided.

"Well, Roc had some definitely strange and rather harsh ideas about the deaths of his sister and his father. He was all set to tear into the inquest and get his revenge, and of course it was Trevor he blamed. He had a truly misguided conception of his sister, whom he adored and thought no one should touch.

"Kate, of course, had a stubborn streak, and had Roc stopped to see it all, instead of being blind with rage, he'd have known that she even . . . invited suspicion on herself and Trevor. She was a little flirt, to be truthful, even though she was supposed to be crazy about Phillip. Poor Phillip. I remember how he lived for just a glimpse of her." She sighed, then laughed.

"That was the setting for the quarrel between the two brothers. Roc accused Trevor of being too . . . familiar with Kate, you see. It was all so mixed up when the murders were discovered that no one had any sense of how it all could have happened, except that the inquest did come to the verdict we have all accepted; that Mister Edward did shoot Kate and Phillip, thinking they were the Revenue Men, and then turned the gun on himself."

She looked at me with an appeal to see the irony inherent in the logic everyone had accepted of that long-ago tragedy. "It's all over, and Trevor, thank God, is doing the most sensible thing for Mullins, as everyone believes."

"And what is that?"

"Saving it from Roc, of course. He has threatened to come back and make it his." She spoke without fear or malice in her voice. She was unaffected by the calamity of that past, it seemed, at least outwardly so.

"Has he returned since that time? Roc St. Coryn?" I tried not to betray my interest. I suppose I was testing her, but it was evident that she was not aware of the presence of *The Petroc* or its captain hidden in that creek.

"One cannot be certain, of course, that he has not at times been back at Mullins. Servants have a way of believing what they want to believe, and some of them around here swear that Roc has returned from the Spanish Main on several occasions since he took *The Petroc* down the estuary seven years ago."

She could not know my feelings for this man, or that I knew without a doubt he was back and hiding. Apparently, she had not seen him herself during these years, I thought.

"But you don't believe it yourself, then?" I pursued.

Perhaps it was just a flicker of her eyelids, but I believed I saw a wariness in her eyes. For a moment she was silent, as if she had come to a decision, and she said in a rather amusing manner, "I wouldn't put it past Roc, to sneak in here anytime he pleased. He has that way about him. No, I would not be surprised to learn Roc St. Coryn comes to Mullins, or that he could be here even now, hiding in some creek. It's done often, ships coming up the estuary to hide in some little-known creek, and Cornwall seems to be getting its share of raids, from foreign ships as well as our own. I overheard Hadrian and Jake saying only this morning that the days of privateering have reopened. Word has it the government is even commissioning those ships with guns to catch the French vessels that slip in and raid our coastline. It's becoming unsafe."

I could say nothing to this for I knew I couldn't trust my voice. It occurred to me to ring for coffee, but Taryn saw my movement toward the bell and put up her hand.

"Please don't bother. Hadrian won't be long and we both must be getting back to Wilkes Reach. But I suspect we shall be seeing much of each other, Roma. I shall like that. Perhaps when we meet again your cousin will be rested from her long journey. I should like to meet her."

She was sincere, and I felt more comfortable. "And Lucretia will want to meet you, I'm sure," I said easily. "It takes her quite a while to adjust to being in the country, you see. She is quite sensitive."

She smiled at this, as though she understood without further explanation. The door opened and it was Daisy, reporting that Miss Wilkes was wanted in the kitchens, if she were free, for Cook wanted to speak to her on an urgent matter. When she saw me, the maid bobbed a half-curtsey.

"Very well, Daisy. I'll come with you now. How is your little brother, Toby? Has his ear healed?"

"O lawks, but yes, Miss Wilkes, and me Mum do think it were that salve 'ee rubbed on it right away, her do! And not a scab it brought, no it didn't. Cook do say it were a matter of 'ee being there at the right time, her do. Toby do be all right now, thanks to 'ee, Miss." She blushed with gratitude, and felt shy in front of me, I suspected.

Taryn turned to me and explained, "Toby, Jeffers' little boy of four, fell on an open flame in the blacksmithy a fortnight ago, burning his right ear. As luck would have it, Hadrian and I had just come over, and I was right on the spot. I suppose you've met Mary Jeffers? She's Jeffers' wife and she works in the dairy room. Daisy and Toby are their children."

"Yes, I met them yesterday," I said, regarding Taryn in a new light. How easy she was with these people. "Then, the little boy is not hurt seriously?"

Taryn laughed again. "No, he just has a burn, which of course could have been more serious. Anyway, Roma, Jeffers did send in word that your mount was ready. Do enjoy your ride."

"Thank you," I said. "I shall, I'm sure." And she left the room with Daisy. I made my way out through the garden and walked towards the stables, somehow at cross purposes with myself, as a strange uneasiness began to take possession of me.

CHAPTER FOUR

Jeffers was mending a broken harness when I arrived at the stables. He looked up and saw me, and jumped up, an able-bodied man somewhere in his late thirties, I guessed. He smelled of tobacco and leather, a man used to the out-of-doors, and friendly enough in his manners. This was Daisy's father, and I could see the resemblance at once in their coloring, although Daisy would be plump like her mother in a few years, I thought. It shocked me to think that I might even be here at Mullins to see the changes that were to come, even in the servants.

More than anything, I wanted to belong to a house like Mullins, to know the true feeling of having roots, and I knew these very people were the heart and soul of this beautiful old manor. They belonged here, as I wanted to, and strangely enough, I felt strongly attached already.

"Good mornin', Miss," he said, and I caught the scent of hay and pitch behind him in the barn, a strong clean smell, and I liked it. I suspected then that he'd been expecting Lucretia instead of me. "Mister Trevor he do give orders to saddle 'ee a mount and I reckon 'ee might like our Neptune, now might 'ee? He said to tell 'ee he wouldn't be long, but for 'ee to take 'ee time."

"Thank you, Jeffers. Yes, I'd like that. I was hoping there'd be some good saddle horses here."

"Aye, and that we do, Miss, that we do. The finest, we have. But Neptune, he be extra special, 'ee wait!" And he went inside and brought out the most beautiful black horse I'd ever seen, his coat glossy and sleek as he came out into the sun, already saddled. Jeffers, in his pride, spat tobacco juice as he watched my expression.

My eyes glistened at sight of the magnificent animal, and I touched his lovely neck fondly. The sensitive creature seemed to understand. "He's magnificent!" I cried, unable to hide my joy.

This impressed Jeffers. "Why, 'ee's taken to 'ee already, Miss. That one do be more than sensitive-like. It's as if he could understand. Now if'n that don't beat all I ever see!"

Excitement raced through me as he brought the mounting block and I stepped up into the saddle. Then he said, "It do be a good mornin' for a ride and all, Miss. But 'ee not to go far, Mister Trevor do give orders for 'ee. Unsafe, it be, but there be a bridle path after 'ee reach the paddock, in them copper beeches and what brings 'ee out on the promontory. A nice hour's ride, I should judge. 'Ee can't miss 'em."

That he was not worried about my ability to handle Neptune was evident as he watched me. I saw something like admiration in his eyes as I said, "Thank you, Jeffers.

I'm sure I shall be all right, and if Mister Trevor does return before I do, feel free to say I can look after myself,
and not to worry."

"Aye. That I will, Miss. That I will."

I touched Neptune's flanks and rode out of the stableyard, knowing Jeffers was watching me, and I passed under
the clock tower and cantered down a path toward the paddock he'd directed me to.

The feel of a horse beneath me always brought ecstasy
to my blood, and Neptune reacted as though he knew this,
responding to my lightest touch.

I was exhilarated as I took him across the paddock and
down another path, passing through an open gate into the
copper beeches, red in the sunlight. As we entered the gold
and green woods, the scent of moss and pine was pungent
and strong to my nostrils, and it brought back all too vividly my early morning escapade.

However, I was determined to put from my mind that
unfortunate encounter, and I allowed Neptune to find the
path which wound through the trees and rustic bracken
and fern alongside the estuary until we came out onto a
higher flatland, where, in the distance, men were piling
corn into wagons in the fields. They did not take notice of
me, for we skirted these fields and followed one that led to
the sea.

The sky was clear and bright. It was the third week in
September, and there was a soft east wind blowing in from
the sea. Only yesterday, Hamilton the coachman had said a
squall of rain from the southwest had blown itself up to the
north the night before we'd come, and that we should have
some rather fine weather for the next week or so.

I had every reason to believe him as I felt the sun on my
face now. The sea was very blue, a deep aquamarine color
where it touched the rocks and reflected the glorious sky.

Looking into the waves, I thought of *The Petroc* and
how it lay at anchor in the creek, tucked away and
shrouded by trees so that no one would ever suspect it was
there.

I thought of its captain as I stared at the horizon, then
watched how the tide was rippling in toward the estuary
which bounded the land on the east. I wondered if he was
sleeping now, after his long night of black deeds. Did he
know that Trevor was back from Falmouth, where he'd
been for a full week? Was he brooding about the future,

with his hands behind his head as he lay on the bunk? And was he satisfied now that he had started on his wild revenge?

A wretchedness and discontent came over me. All the things I'd felt about that man were backed up by what others said of him, and I suspected Roc had had his way with Taryn Wilkes. It even occurred to me that she might not have spurned his advances, and then immediately I chided myself for that thought.

Just how well, then, did she know Trevor? It surprised me to realize that her knowing Trevor did not disturb me, or not as much as the thought of Taryn and Roc St. Coryn. I couldn't understand myself.

My spirits dampened, I turned Neptune and for a while, with the wind cool on my skin, I pushed it all from my mind, and felt the glow of both nature and beast, that proud animal beneath me.

Given the lead, Neptune moved with ease and grace over the uneven field where the corn had already been gathered, as if he knew every foot of ground beneath him. We came to the other side of the east paddock, and I walked Neptune over this last stretch, savoring the precious moments. Sea pinks and red and white valeria mingled with the rich purple heather dotted over the paddock. There was something spicy in the air, and somewhere a linnet trilled. Sea gulls, feeding near the edge of the copse, rose suddenly, their cries melancholy, and I felt a touch of loneliness I couldn't explain. I was totally caught in a web of deceit and treachery. More than that, I knew no sense of peace, or belonging. In a few weeks, Lucretia would be the wife of the man I'd set my heart on. For her, I'd had to suffer a loss of personal pride, and yet I could not stop thinking of the man who had brought it about.

I knew with a frightening certainty that something inside me had responded instantly to Roc St. Coryn, despite my utter dislike for him, and it would be hard to kill it. Just thinking about it left me weak, and a new surge of anger welled up and took precedence over everything I felt for that man. I spurred Neptune's flanks and he cantered under the tower clock and into the stableyard.

Since Jeffers was nowhere in sight, I dismounted and led Neptune into the barn. For a long moment, I stood beside him stroking his long silky mane, and fed him an apple from the big barrel near the stall. The animal was gorgeous, and I wondered where Trevor had purchased him or if he'd been foaled on the estate.

A few moments passed and Jeffers hurried inside, with a little boy running in after him. Jeffers apologized for not being there to help me dismount. The little boy came up and stood shyly beside the man's legs, his large round eyes bright in a chubby face.

I smiled and said, "I didn't mind, Jeffers. Neptune is a wonderful animal. How long have you had him?"

"Oh, he do be a good 'un, Miss. We not have 'im long, and it do be a good long while that we had such horseflesh as Neptune here. Mister Trevor, 'e brought 'im in from Araby, as 'ee can see 'im do be of Araby stock. Nothin' like 'im, no there bain't, except Neptune's mate, the mare the Master rides hisself. Want to see her, Miss?" He spat out another stream of tobacco juice. I, of course, could think of nothing I wanted to see more, and followed him and the little boy inside the stables where the box stalls were, leading Neptune behind me.

The other beast was just as exquisite, black and glistening like silk. "Venus, this one is called, Miss. Bain't she somethin' though?"

I couldn't hide my admiration. "Venus. But what a lovely name for an exquisite animal!" I cried.

"Aye. I thought 'ee would like her, Miss." He suddenly swept the little boy up in his arms and held him close to the mare's beautiful head. "Mister Trevor do like good horseflesh, that's fer sure, he do."

For a while, I could think of nothing more to say, and stroked the lovely, long neck. As she nibbled at the little boy's outstretched hand, the child's laughter rang out.

"This is your son Toby?" I asked politely, remembering what Taryn had said of the child.

He seemed surprised that I should know the child's name, and he was pleased, I thought. With the pride of a father for son, he nodded.

"Aye, and this do be so, Miss." He looked at the boy fondly. The boy's eyes were beautiful, and he was but a baby, for all the four years I knew him to be.

"Miss Wilkes spoke of his accident, Jeffers. And Daisy said the burn on his ear was quite well healed." I suspected this was the reason he'd not been inside the stables when I returned with Neptune, that he brought the child with him often to the stables. "You must be quite pleased to know you can rely upon Doctor Wilkes and his sister in case of accidents."

"Aye, Miss," he said, pleased because I had taken such notice of his family. "We all do be grateful to the doctor and his kind sister. Why this little'un of mine do be so full o' mischief at times, 'tis a wonder to us all he bain't afallen on that fire-iron afore now! But 'ee now't little 'uns. And Miss Wilkes havin' one of t'her own, like, well." He shook his head. "Her did take all precaution with that burnt ear, and with our own Toby." He placed a rough brown hand on the child's head to brush back the soft brown hair, and Toby hid his face in his father's shoulder. "Her do be wiser than most, Miss Wilkes do, fer her age." He inclined his head, giving all the credit to the good doctor's sister.

"Miss Wilkes has a child of her own, Jeffers?" I asked in surprise. "She is married then? I had no idea. . . ." I stopped, seeing the surprise on the stableman's face.

He was staring at me strangely, then reddened under the deep tan of his skin. "Her not be married, Miss, not her. Never married, that is." He closed his mouth tightly, and I felt uncomfortable because he was uncomfortable. Neptune gave me a gentle nudge with his great head.

"How old is her . . . child then?" I could think of nothing more to say, but I somehow felt I should ask.

"The boy be but two'n half year older than our own Toby, he do, I reckun. He do be lucky to have Doctor Hadrian for his Uncle, we all say. Like a father to the little boy, taking him all about the place with 'im. We take kindly towards them what cares fer the weak and sick alike, we do. No tain't or stain on them or their past. What is, is, we all do say here at Mullins."

He was telling me to mind my own business, and that to speak ill of Hadrian and Taryn Wilkes, no matter what had occurred in their past lives, would be a sacrilege on my part.

I met his eyes, giving him the leather reins, then said softly, "Is Mister Trevor back from Barton Farms?"

For a moment, there was regret in the deep grey eyes. I knew he was a proud man, loyal in his duties, but then I had an absurd thought. To *which* master was he most loyal? Roc St. Coryn, or Trevor? I turned away, not wanting Jeffers to guess at my thoughts.

"Oh, yes, Miss, not half hour since. And I did plum forget to tell 'ee, I did. 'Ee are to go to the Bower. Mister

Trevor do be anxious fer 'ee, but I tell 'im 'ee could look after 'eeself. I did. A fine horsewoman that 'ee be. Then he say, 'Ee can't be too careful here. It not be like in London ridin' in Rotten Row, so make sure her do be sent right in when Miss Kendal do come back.' And I plum forgot."

I laughed. "You were quite right to assure Mister Trevor I'd be all right, Jeffers. Thank you. Goodbye, Toby," I said, but the little boy hid his face again. I left the stables, crossed the yard, and entered the house through a side door. I was disquieted by what Jeffers had told me of Taryn Wilkes. Still, I knew it was none of my business. It was just that she'd been so open and I hadn't even suspected that she had a son. And who was the father of her child?

It was only when I was inside the house that the thought struck me. Could it be possible that Roc St. Coryn was the child's father? And why not? Two and a half years older than Toby, who was four? That would indeed add up to seven years, wouldn't it? Of course! How blind I'd been, how stupidly blind! And how many more bastards had the man left in his wake, taking women as he chose, bending them to his will, reducing them to helpless creatures with his sweet, brutal advances?

This thought brought a scowl to my face, and I was more miserable than ever. In that moment, I glanced up and saw Mrs. Pascal coming towards me.

"Oh, Miss Roma," she said. "Mister Trevor and Miss Lucretia do be anxious about 'ee. Them be awaiting 'ee in the Bower, and 'ee are to go right in." I thought she looked at me rather suspiciously, but I ignored it by holding my head high.

"My cousin is with Mister Trevor, then?" I asked, glad that I should not have to face him alone. He just might see too much, and for no reason at all I was at odds with myself.

"Yes, Miss. And Doctor Hadrian and his sister be with them. I've brought coffee in, and there's a cup for 'ee." She smiled affably.

I said nothing to this information that the Wilkeses were still here but a mumbled "thank you," and turned away. I found my way slowly to the Bower, not stopping to change my habit, only to glance in a mirror in the corridor to straighten my hat and give my curls a pat. I knew my eyes were too bright, my skin glowing and my lips much too pink, but it didn't concern me.

When I saw Combes, I simply handed him my riding

crop and gloves, but I saw that secret amusement in his merry eyes as he opened the door and made his polite little bow.

"Them be a'waiting 'ee, Miss."

They did not seem aware of my entrance when Combes closed the door softly behind me, and for one moment I had the advantage of observing them before attention was called to me. Trevor and the other man stood facing each other, engrossed in a subject all four seemed to be interested in. My cousin was her usual gay self, her lilac muslin very correct under the paisley shawl she wore over her shoulders. I fancied her grey eyes were turned on the handsome man who now looked down at her, a light shining in them as they widened at what he had been saying.

The man, Hadrian Wilkes, looked up first and saw me. He and Trevor both held cups of coffee in their hands, and as Hadrian's glance warned him I was in the room, Trevor turned and came forward, setting his cup down on the table.

His eyes went all over my face and person, and I was glad his back was to the others, for anyone who was even casually looking on could not mistake what was in that look.

"We've been concerned and anxious for you, Roma. I must have been out of my mind to allow you to go off on your own. But Jeffers did tell me you took such a delight in Neptune, and I should've guessed that you would be out longer than usual on him. You did like him, I can tell." He smiled.

"Oh yes. What a gorgeous animal! Both of them are!" I exclaimed, and told him how Jeffers had insisted I see Venus when I returned.

He laughed and took my arm, and brought me to be introduced. "You have already met Taryn," he said. "And this is Hadrian, her brother. Hadrian, Lucretia's cousin, Roma Kendal. You must be friends. The Wilkeses are our closest neighbors."

"How do you do, Miss Roma?" Hadrian said, and I liked him at once, with his easy, unaffected manner. He was dressed in a casual way that suggested he did not care a fig for style: his rumpled buckskin breeches of dark brown were tucked into unpolished leather boots; the dark, rough tweed coat with leather patches sewn on the elbows looked as if it had had much wear. His hair was ruddy

brown and sprang up from his wide, high forehead like
springs of curled wire, and it was collar length, rather long
and unruly compared to Trevor's short locks.

I found his eyes were quieter than his sister's, with easy
laughter lines creasing the tanned skin around them. He
was tall, although a little stooped. His hands, too, were
long and slender and his manner was warm when he took
my hand and shook it politely.

"Welcome to Cornwall and to Mullins, Miss Roma," he
said, smiling down into my eyes. "I can see that you're
already learning to be a true Cornishwoman. You've no
doubt found our part of the world something to explore,
riding out so early." He regarded me with his smoky hazel
eyes.

"Yes, thank you," I answered, warming to this friendly
man. "I certainly find it most exhilarating to be out in the
country. But Mullins especially is lovely. It's all and more
than I'd been told it was."

He stood back and regarded Lucretia then, and she
blushed like a rose as she poured coffee into a cup and
passed it on to me. I took the offered chair Hadrian so
obediently held for me. Taryn's eyes were on Lu, and then
on Trevor, and I had the impression she had guessed the
truth of the situation and found it amusing, which I did
not. Not much could be hidden from this young woman, I
thought, again more disturbed than I cared to show.

There were little spiced cakes interlaced with thick clot-
ted cream which Lu passed to me on a plate, saying Cook
had sent them in and that they were one of her many spe-
cialties. At this moment, a young boy ran in through the
open door from the garden. He was a slender child of six
or so, and he carried a bouquet of purple Michaelmas
daisies and a bunch of lavender in his arms.

He came to stand beside Hadrian after handing Taryn
the flowers. But I could tell the boy was shy; there was an
expression of undue repression in his eyes, and no smile on
his face. So this was her child, I thought, and I felt awkward inside, for I believed I had guessed the truth about
Taryn and the notorious Roc.

Hadrian introduced the boy not as Taryn's son, but as his
nephew Jonathan.. He placed a fond arm about the boy as
he did so, then after the introduction, which was to both
Lucretia and myself, he looked down at the child and said,
"So Old Soady gave you the flowers, Jon? How very good

of him to remember we needed lavender for the lotion we are making, don't you think? I hope you thanked him properly?"

The boy nodded and placed his hand in Hadrian's, and when Lu passed the cakes to him, he took them gratefully, with a small "thank you." Lu smiled gently at him.

It was then that the subject of Jake Polden's brother Arnie came up in the conversation and Trevor, a dark scowl on his face stated, "Of course the young fellow is lying. It's clear as anything that he came off a shipload of smugglers, and it wouldn't surprise me at all if that ship is hidden somewhere along this estuary! You can bet too that an illegal run took place somewhere nearby. But by heaven, it had better not happen on my estate! I warned Jake, and I warn only once!"

I could feel myself shaking, and I had to place the cup down on the table beside my chair. It angered me that I should be so upset whenever Trevor guessed at the truth, making me tremble inside like a frightened child. I could not suppress my guilt for not revealing all I knew to Trevor, but neither could I confess to him so belatedly.

Lucretia sat where the sun coming through the window made a halo around her light brown hair and gave her such an ethereal beauty that I found Hadrian gazing at her as if he were spellbound and hadn't heard a word of what Trevor had said. But I was wrong. He had heard.

"There's every reason to believe that these smugglers are now legal, Trevor, or haven't you heard?" What a good-looking young man he is, I realized, and I noticed the way Lucretia was staring at him. But he was saying, "The government is backing up these fair traders of ours, especially those whose luggers are equipped with guns, and their captains are being commissioned to catch any foreign ships raiding our coast. Indeed, there's even talk of having seen slavers steal into our own creeks. We're not safe, none of us."

Lucretia paled, and I glanced at Trevor. His face was a mask and I knew a moment of uneasiness. Had the rumors been true? But if he were involved, then wouldn't Hadrian have known of it?

I let my glance wander to Taryn and saw that her eyes were fixed on Trevor's face, and I wondered what she was thinking. Because I didn't know her well, I couldn't guess. She was intelligent, I knew, and she might well know more about Trevor than I did. I turned my attention to Hadrian.

"One would surely think the days of privateering were over, but this new war with the French is creating havoc. We simply don't have the time or the energy to waste on blocking the coastal smuggling."

Taryn spoke up then, and I noticed how her son, Jon, was listening as if he understood the conversation. "Well, Trevor," she said, "I do hope you won't be too hard on Arnie Polden. After all, who are we to condemn these people for earning extra money by smuggling? Tobacco and silks, not to mention the brandy and gin, bring in a considerable sum to these people."

Hadrian said quickly, "I should judge more than 50,000 pounds have been made in and around St. Austell alone in the past six months, just on single runs, for the Revenue Men are scarce in these parts and people will pay dearly for that much-sought-after brandy. And to be sure, these people will not turn informer on one of their own. But as far as Arnie Polden is concerned, Trevor," Hadrian said sincerely, "I'm more inclined to believe his story of having come in off a merchant ship bound for Plymouth. On the other hand, if what you think is true, then he would be a first offender, I should think. It might not go in your favor to be too hard on him."

There was a warning suggested in his voice and manner, but Trevor was adamant. He said, "I will not have anyone harboring or aiding a smuggler on my land, and I have given Jake my warning. I shall look into the matter, and by heaven, if I find him guilty, that young man will either pay a stiff fine or be transported. I am making that the law here on my estates!"

It sounded sinister, and Hadrian looked grim, but I noticed Taryn's eyes were full of secret amusement. Lucretia paled, and for a moment I thought she might faint during the heavy silence which followed.

In spite of my own anger against Roc St. Coryn, I couldn't help but hope his presence went detected, and this strange emotion left me with a wretched sense of doubt and confusion in my feelings toward Trevor. It maddened me to feel so completely at odds with myself, and why I did not speak up in this moment to reveal all I knew was beyond my comprehension.

I waited to see what other plans Roc had for Trevor's fiancée. I suppose that was the answer; I wanted to see his face when he learned the truth, and it could only be to my advantage to keep silent. Besides, I thought, looking anxiously at my cousin who I was sure never looked so utterly feminine and helpless as she did now, there was just a chance that, should Roc St. Coryn know the truth, he might try to harm Lucretia, and I knew that should never be risked.

In the ensuing silence, I suspected the brother and sister were wise to keep their own counsel, and shortly afterwards they took their leave, promising to come to dinner the following evening and to discuss at length the wedding plans. Trevor thought Taryn would be a great help to me.

Hadrian promised to ride over to look in on Miss Phoebe, for he'd found her more excited than usual in his visit this morning. "I suppose it is your coming," he said to Lucretia and me, smilingly. "But one can never be certain with people of such an age as hers. Mind you, I gave Norie explicit instructions to see that Miss Phoebe rests as much as possible in the next weeks, for it seems she is excited about the wedding. You'd think it was her own, the way she talks about it." He laughed, as we walked together out into the hall. But even as we watched them take their leave, my mind chased after Roc St. Coryn, thinking that if he had indeed been in contact with his great-aunt, it would certainly be cause for her agitation. If she had doted so on Kate St. Coryn, then would she not have felt the same toward Roc?

After Hadrian and Taryn left with her son, I begged to be excused. I wanted to change my riding habit before luncheon, and this apparently satisfied Trevor who wanted to show Lucretia the quay along the estuary, which bordered the gardens. She sent Tulip for her parasol, and I watched them walk off together, managing to avoid Trevor's eyes.

I returned to the Blue Boudoir, somehow unhappy.

For luncheon, we had lamb cutlets garnished with mushrooms and a meat pie with crust so tender it almost melted on the tongue. There was a green salad and afterwards cheese and fruit, and a blackberry tart with cream. I found I was indeed hungry and I ate heartily, doing justice to Cook's labors in the kitchen. I mentally noted I would go into the kitchen very soon and pay my compliments to her. We spoke very little while we ate, but discussed the small dinner party Trevor felt we should have before the announcement ball, which was to take place one week before the wedding in the Plyn church.

"There will be a second ball for the servants, who, according to tradition, will toast the bridegroom and bride on the wedding day. We shall keep that old custom, I think," Trevor said as we finished eating. "But for now, I want to take you both out to Barton Farms this afternoon. I'm certain you will enjoy seeing the view from Poppy Meadows on the promontory." His eyes were sparkling and he seemed pleased.

"I should like very much to meet Jake Polden and his family, Trevor, and perhaps we can arrange to meet Tamblyn at North Lodge. They weren't here yesterday," Lucretia suggested. I could see she didn't feel timid about this.

"And so you shall, my dear Lucretia," Trevor answered her. "We'll begin our pilgrimage to meet all these people this afternoon. There's quite a lot to see, so I suggest we start soon. While you both ready yourselves, I'll have Hamilton bring out the open carriage." He seemed excited, and I could see he meant to please her as well as myself.

Barton Farms formed a peninsula, with Poppy Meadows at the far end of it and the sea running into bays, east and west on either side. It was bounded on the western side by the estuary, some four or five miles in length, and on the east by the great stretch of sandy bay. The Barton Farms faced the bay, while the manor house itself sheltered by the beeches faced the estuary.

All this Trevor repeated for Lucretia's benefit. When we skirted the fields where the corn was still being loaded into the wagons I'd seen earlier, she seemed to take an undue interest.

"The corn has been carried in already. But most of Barton is grazing land now. We're taking the long way around. Look," Trevor added as he pointed toward the bay. We came out on the upward slope toward the Poppy Meadow, which gave us a tremendous view. "There's the sea."

I remembered how the sea had been aquamarine that morning, but now it was a deep Chinese jade. Tall waves crested and broke, the water crashing on the beach below. A salty breeze tugged at our shawls, and the pink sea thrift were thick along the lane we'd stopped to view. The low-flying gulls soared and wheeled and cried downshore. Far out on the horizon, the white sails of a three-rigged ship billowed in the breeze.

Again, unwillingly, my thoughts jumped to Roc St. Coryn. Where was he this golden afternoon? Of course, it was only that passing ship that brought these unwanted thoughts, and when I glanced up, I found Trevor's eyes were on my face. There were questions in those eyes. I knew I had been unusually silent since I had returned from the morning's ride on Neptune, and he appeared to have noticed.

Lucretia broke the silence. "I don't quite like the idea of those ships stealing up into the rivers and hiding, and all that smuggling talk! It unnerves me." She shivered visibly, her eyes on the ship, and then she regarded Trevor. "I do hope you can prevent such things as that at Mullins, Trevor. I wouldn't want any of the servants to get involved and have to be transported. What a horrendous fate for some poor unsuspecting young man!" Her gaze rested on the fisherman's cottage on the beach.

"Why, I do believe that is where Mrs. Pascal's nephew Cal lives, is it not? She was very concerned about him, even this morning. Perhaps we could stop in and say hello to him, can we not, Trevor? I do not want to slight anyone on the manor."

This exclamation and her previous one had brought an unusual glint of steel to Trevor's eyes, but he only nodded and said, "No, we must not slight anyone, Lucretia. This is as good as any time to look in on Cal Pascal." There was a deadly serious note in his voice as he flicked the reins and started down a steep path which led through gorse and heather and pink sea thrift. Beyond, in the bay, were small fishing boats, all tied up on the little quay where the nets hung to dry. Smoke curled from the low chimney pot of the cottage, but there was no sign of anyone about as we came down into the yard.

Trevor stepped down from the carriage, walked over to the door, and knocked. It didn't open, and though he waited some minutes there was no answer. As he started to return to the carriage, however, someone appeared from behind the cottage. An old man with a pipe in his mouth, a strange little three-cornered hat pushed back on his head, came into view. His dark blue breeches billowed out in the wind as he hailed Trevor.

"Aye, there, Mister St. Coryn!" He said in the Cornish dialect. "Hap' 'ee lookin' for Cal, like, eh?" As he neared, I could see he was having difficulty walking.

Trevor turned. "Oh. Hello, Danny. Yes, as a matter of fact, I was. I knocked but there was no answer."

"Hap' Cal be a'restin, he do, Mister St. Coryn," the old man said, holding on to the corner of the building. "Sleep, I should think, he do. 'Im hurt 'is back more'n a fortnight ago, and laid up in the bed like." He puffed on the pipe and smoke curled up and trailed away.

"Sorry to hear about that, Danny. Where's Dolly?"

"Oh, Dolly. Her t'went in to Plyn with Nell but this here morn'. Back afore sunset, her do be, aye."

"Well, Danny. Do come and meet my bride-to-be, and her cousin, who've come to live at Mullins," Trevor said, and waited for the old man to hobble over the cobblestone courtyard before he took his arm and helped him.

"Danny is Mrs. Pascal's father, Roma, Lucretia. He's always lived here on the beach, in charge of the fishing fleet when the herring run, and the like. Now Cal has taken over. Dolly is his wife. Danny, meet the Misses Kendal—Lucretia, my bride-to-be, and her cousin, Roma Kendal."

The old man squinted up at the sun as I shook hands with him. "How-do-'ee do, Miss?" he inquired and I smiled. "Thank you, Danny," I said to his "Welcome 'ee to Mullins. Hope 'ee'll both be happy." Lucretia, too, seemed pleased to meet him and said so in her most charming manner, which made the old man smile pleasantly at her.

"Well, I won't disturb Cal, Danny. Do tell him we came. I'll send Doctor Wilkes down to look in on him."

"Aye. 'Ee do be kind, 'ee do, Mister St. Coryn. Hap' I won't forget to tell me grandson thet, no." And he stood back as Trevor stepped up into the carriage.

Thus we left the sea-side cottage, with the old man looking after us, and then we left the promontory and turned eastward, past the byre and the midden and into the courtyard of a low-built farm house, its ancient grey stones almost amethyst in the clear afternoon sun.

It seemed the Poldens were awaiting us, and I felt sure this was no surprise visit, but one purposely arranged. Mrs. Polden, a comely woman with wheat-colored hair and a pleasant face, wearing a fresh white apron over her brown muslin, stood beside her husband, Jake. There were several small children about, sturdy boys and girls who were, like their parents, comely and friendly, and I imagined their household to be as warm as their greeting to us.

They invited us at once into the beautiful old house, into the great kitchen where we were offered cakes and cream, and Lucretia and I were delighted to accept.

I had never been in such a comfortable kitchen. It was low, with heavy dark beams overhead. On the low window casement, where the latticed panes were thrown back to allow the strong sun to stream in unchecked, was a large pewter pot filled with fresh Michaelmas daisies. A long refectory table of polished wood stood to one side, with pewter plates and a few blue-and-white willow-patterned plates and cups, rare indeed and beautiful. One end of the room was taken up by a huge fireplace and cloam ovens and a large brightly colored hooked rug covered a great portion of the smooth stone floor. There were two rocking chairs and several other chairs with cushions, and through a Dutch door I caught a glimpse of the scullery where dried herbs and spices were strung up, and the buttery where great cheeses were stacked in a blue-tiled room. It all smelled clean and wholesome.

I should have suspected how well Lucretia would be accepted, and although it pleased me, it annoyed me too. I somehow felt my situation more than ever in that sunny farmhouse kitchen. I didn't belong anywhere, I had no role to play, and for all the Poldens' efforts to include me I somehow couldn't relax.

Trevor went out with Jake after the introduction, and Lu and I sat down. After our cakes and cream, we were asked if we'd like to try their cider, which of course we accepted politely.

"And how is your brother-in-law, Arnie, Mrs. Polden? We heard from Doctor Wilkes that his leg had been broken in several places. What pain he must be suffering! It must be a great worry," said Lucretia.

I fancied I saw something like surprise mingled with fear in her pleasant face. That she seemed tense when Arnie's name was mentioned there was no doubt, but the good lady said, "Arnie is doing well enough, Miss Kendal. Poor lad. Doctor Wilkes did give him opium and he hasn't yet wakened. It gave us all quite a turn but he's young and the bones of the young mend well enough. Thank you for asking."

Lucretia smiled. "Not at all, Mrs. Polden. I am deeply

interested in everyone connected with Mullins. I promise to
pay a visit to your brother-in-law when he is able to receive
visitors."

"That is very kind of you, Miss Kendal," she answered,
her own deep grey eyes crinkling around the corners, and
then I said, "Miss Wilkes was saying only this morning that
young Arnie left Cornwall about a year ago. I suppose the
sea does lure most young men at one time or another. It is
true that you and your husband had no idea where he went
off to? That must have been a worry."

She turned her eyes on me, a hesitation in her manner.
One of the children, a little girl of perhaps five or six, went
over and picked up the old grey tabby cat near the fireside
and sat down in the rocking chair. The woman's eyes followed her absently and then came back to me, as if she did
not know what to answer.

"Why yes. 'Twas indeed a hard thing for Jake and me,
not knowing where Arnie went off to, and it took us by
surprise when he did come home late last night, Miss Kendal. But Jake knows how young boys must get out on their
own sometime in life, and the way of the sea was always a
yearning for Arnie, even as a young lad." She inclined her
head to one side.

I agreed. "Then he will go back to the sea again?" I met
her gaze, and she suddenly seemed embarrassed and looked
away. I suspected again that the only ship he could have
come in on was *The Petróc,* that he had been part of that
crew who had brought in the contraband and smuggled it
into the manor house. I wondered, then, just exactly where
the goods were hidden so that Trevor wouldn't come upon
them before they were carried away to Exeter or London.

"If his leg mends he'll go back. But he won't be going for
a long time, I suspect," the woman answered slowly.

"The same . . . merchant ship won't wait for him,
then?" I pursued, and then added, "But then, I suppose he
can always get aboard just any ship, so it won't truly matter, will it?"

Her eyes widened. I believed she wanted to discontinue
talking of Arnie, for I felt she was very apprehensive over
what Trevor had warned them of only this morning. And it
was then a sudden misgiving struck me. Surely this visit
had not been arranged out of consideration on Trevor's
part? For now, as Lucretia was making friends with the
little girl Sally, and the old tabby cat, I heard Trevor's

voice outside in the courtyard with Jake. I fancied too, that Mrs. Polden heard them, for our eyes met as we heard Trevor speaking.

"Nineteen or twenty, Jake, it doesn't matter. Arnie is old enough to answer for himself. And don't mistake me; I mean to investigate. I believe he is lying. You make sure he is telling the truth."

Jake answered, but I didn't hear it, for he turned away, but I could tell from Mrs. Polden's expression she was frightened.

We didn't stay long after that. When Jake and Trevor came into the kitchen, I noticed Jake's closed face. Trevor had been too adamant and unbending, I thought, and the tense moment was relieved only by the easiness with which Lucretia talked with the children and Mrs. Polden during those remaining few minutes before we climbed back into the carriage.

It was a marvel that Mrs. Polden extended her invitation to Lucretia to come again, and as often as she liked, but I felt she was wary of me.

"I certainly shall return, Mrs. Polden," Lucretia said, "and you must come to the house when there is need to discuss Jamie's and Sally's schooling." At this I was surprised, and realized now that for the past ten minutes or so this was exactly what Lu and Letty Polden had been talking of, while I had been dreaming in my own little world.

Letty smiled affectionately at Lucretia and promised, and the family stood together and watched as Trevor drove the carriage out of the farmyard, but I could not help noticing the grim look about Jake's mouth and the blanched look of his usually ruddy skin.

Trevor spoke very little during the ride back to the manor house. Instead, it was Lucretia who talked with me about the dinner party we were to have the following week, the Wilkeses coming on the morrow eve, what gowns we both should wear, if they were much too pretentious for country dinner gatherings, and if Mrs. Pascal would have enough help in the house to accommodate all the guests she felt certain would have to stay overnight when the announcement ball was given.

These little things, so unimportant, provided the best cover-up for my own growing apprehension. When we reached the pony paddock, midway between the house and the sloping fields, I glanced back and saw the wagons piled

high with grain silhouetted on the hill in the red setting
sun. The shocks of corn were golden in those last rays, and
the sea was a deeper blue than I'd ever seen before, but there
was no ship on the horizon now.

The manor house was still in a sun-trap, designed, I
imagined, in that long-ago day to catch as much sun as
possible. The stones caught the sun, so rosy and warm, and
a little twist of pain came upon me with startling force as I
realized for the first time that I could never hope to be
mistress of this lovely old house. It would be Lucretia who
would have that title, not I.

I looked at her, and she seemed to have changed as we
approached the house. She had a wan, tight look on her
face, once again the frightened cousin I knew her to be,
and she pulled the shawl around her shoulders as if to protect herself from what lay hidden in that house.

We had not returned in time for tea, but Mrs. Pascal
informed us that Miss Phoebe had taken hers in her rooms,
and it was I who asked after the old woman.

"Oh, there bain't nothin' wrong with her, Miss, no I
should say not. But since the family were away, old Norie
just thought to treat her, and them two had their tea in
Miss Phoebe's rooms."

Miss Phoebe joined us for dinner, however, much later.
She came to the Bower while I sat at the pianoforte playing
a cadenza from Mister Beethoven's *Concerto No. 1 in C,
Rondo, Allegro Scherzando*. I could always lose myself in
my music, and tonight I did so, as Lucretia and Trevor sat
close to the glowing fire on the hearth. Miss Phoebe sat
across from Lucretia, and stared at her in a most unusual
way.

She was a tall, very thin woman, dressed in an old-
fashioned gown of puce silk, with a panniered skirt and a
large white fichu criss-crossed over her front, very quaint
with silver-buckled shoes that peeped out from beneath the
voluminous skirts. She lacked the white wig of that "other
day," but the frilled lace cap did just as well and covered
her stringy grey hair. Her pale tea-color eyes seemed ever
more alert than I remembered them yesterday.

Now and then, her eyes would go to Trevor's face, lingering there, and it looked as if the old woman was keeping
a secret to herself, something that would make her smile
but not with great certainty.

When I finished playing, and just before we were called in to dinner, I sat down facing Miss Phoebe. "I say, Miss Kendal," she said in a pleasing voice, "I had no idea you were so accomplished on the pianoforte. Not many young ladies today take the time and the interest to be so. Have you studied long? Oh, to be sure, you must have, for that was most excellent. Did you study abroad?"

Her questions, which brought a dark scowl to Trevor's face, amused as well as pleased me, and I answered. "Thank you, Miss Phoebe. No, I didn't go abroad, but studied in London. I had an excellent instructor. I'm glad you enjoyed it."

She nodded her head, smiling still. "Yes, I have always been fond of music, and that was Mister Beethoven, was it not? To be sure, he is a gifted man, and after Mister Mozart, I find him even better than most."

I'd had no idea she was as knowledgeable on this subject as she now appeared to be, and I was pleased that she could appreciate good music.

"Music is like pictures, Miss Kendal," she said softly, her eyes never wavering from mine. "One must work hard. I, too, am an artist." Her smile suggested she and I enjoyed a certain intimacy neither Lucretia nor Trevor could share.

Trevor said, "Why, Miss Phoebe!" His voice was gruff, I thought, annoyed because he seemed to slight this lonely old woman. "I never knew you could paint. Is that what you do in your part of the house?" He was not smiling, and even Lucretia sat huddled into herself.

She seemed to take offense, and replied, "No. I do not paint, although I do pictures. They are of tapestry, and tell more than portraits ever could. I have a tapestry gallery, Miss Kendal. My gallery . . . tells all. Though it is remiss of you, Trevor, not to know."

"Of course," Trevor exclaimed. "I recall now. The tapestry hanging in the Great Hall was done by you, was it not?" He lifted his brows, and somehow his interest picked up, his humor restored.

"Yes. Edward always said that one did our house honor. I worked on it while he was away at sea for the first time. Have you seen it, Miss Kendal?" She smiled, vaguely boasting, and did not wait for my reply. "It is *our* part in the Civil Wars. Did you know that the St. Coryns here at Mullins did not make history in the sense that other great houses do? But they *lived* it, suffered under it, and profited by it.

"Yet the Civil Wars proved too much, for it was then they took active part, and by siding with Charles I, they were nearly ruined—the St. Coryns, I mean. Not that they were of nobility, or even received a knighthood at any time, no, and this is what is most surprising and interesting about Mullins." I was astonished at her memory. Apparently, she delved into their family history to know all this.

"It was built, Miss Kendal, Mullins was, slowly, gradually, by ordinary gentry, to live in and to bring up their families in, and to die in. This house has witnessed dark deeds, but what house has not, pray tell?" She lifted her thin light brows, and I murmured my own surprise, then asked if I might see her gallery of tapestries.

The old woman looked at me, her face almost smooth, and happy that someone had mentioned such a desire. "You are interested in what I do, Miss Kendal?" That she did not call me Miss Roma seemed strange, but I felt that in due time she would get used to me.

"But of course I am interested, Miss Phoebe. It must be very intricate work and time-consuming as well."

"Then by all means I do invite you to come to see my gallery." Her smile was almost gleeful, as though she'd snared the choicest prey. "I show it only to those who are interested." It was a very haughty invitation, but I noticed she was looking at me as though she were having difficulty placing me in her mind.

"I shall be honored," I said, and meant it.

She seemed almost girlish and had a wish to please, I thought, and I was disturbed that Trevor was scowling darkly, as silent as poor Lucretia. Miss Phoebe, however, darted her eyes from me to Lu, then back, restlessly.

"It is time that a member of the family," she looked reproachfully at Lucretia, "takes an interest in the history of the St. Coryns. Mind you, Kate, you should have taken more time, I always told you. You simply won't learn unless you take more care and time and do your stitches in even tiny rows. I know you are anxious to get out and go riding with Roc. . . ."

Lucretia's eyes darkened in her already pale face and, for a moment, her lips trembled. But it was Trevor who stood up suddenly, almost angrily, and without a word left the room.

I spoke gently. "You forget, Miss Phoebe. Lucretia is not Kate. She is Lucretia Kendal. She is to marry Trevor."

Her eyes wandered over to me, and I knew her mind was confused. "Ah yes, Miss Kendal. It *is* Miss Kendal, is it not?"

"Yes, of course. I am Miss Roma Kendal. And this is Lucretia Kendal."

She nodded her head, but already I could see she had somehow made up her confused mind that Lucretia was Kate. It seemed ludicrous, for Lu did not in the least resemble the dark-haired girl of that portrait.

Miss Phoebe looked frightened, every bit as much as Lu did. "I . . . made him upset, did I not? Trevor? I hadn't supposed he would be angry—" she stopped, appealing to me, but Combes entered then to say dinner was being served, and Trevor came in directly. He took Lucretia's hand, nodded to us, and then led the way into the dining room.

CHAPTER FIVE

The dining room was intimate and cozy, with warm firelight and candlelight flickering over the polished dark woods of the table and chairs. A bowl of fruit was placed between the silver candlesticks on the table, instead of the usual bowl of flowers. What should have been an easy time between the four of us was tense, the atmosphere very strained, for it was clear that Trevor was displeased with what his great-aunt had said.

Miss Phoebe seemed uncertain and vague during the whole dinner, her animation gone, and I felt quite sorry for her. It was obvious that her mind wandered in and out of the past and present like a strange colorless moth fluttering from dark to light, and this was upsetting to poor Lucretia.

When Combes began to pour the wine into the cups, I could not help but remember the sweet golden wine from Burgundy I had tasted in the cabin of *The Petroc.* I kept hearing Roc St. Coryn's words: "This is sweet wine from Burgundy, Miss Kendal, smuggled into Mullins for its great wine cellar . . ." And these unwanted thoughts brought a strange flutter to my heart, making me self-conscious as I met the old steward's eyes. I had the sensation that this old man was laughing, amused, but *with* me, instead of *at* me, as if we were conspirators in some dark deed.

The dinner was superbly cooked. Combes did the serving from a large tureen of a rich thick soup, which was spicy as well as hot. This removed, we were served a white fish, baked with a lemon and butter sauce; following, a stuffed duckling with orange sauce and small green peas done somehow in pastry shells that made the mouth water. This finished, we were served Chantilly cake and cream, with coffee in tiny cups afterwards for the ladies, served in the Bower, while Trevor sat alone with his brandy.

Miss Phoebe did not stay for coffee. She rang for old Norie, and when she stood to leave us, she whispered to me in a conspiratorial manner, "Remember, Miss Kendal. We have an engagement. You must come to my gallery, and I will show you all of Mullins. We will learn much together, you and I."

"Yes," I agreed. "I am sure you have much to tell me, Miss Phoebe. I am very much interested."

"Then you must not delay too long. I will wait for you. Goodnight, my dears." She looked at Lucretia, and for a moment I thought she might call her her beloved Kate, but she did not. Then Norie came, and it was apparent this old servant was still in control of her own faculties, for she took charge of Miss Phoebe as she would a child, and they left the room together.

Trevor did not join us. He sent Combes in to say he had to go out, and thus both Lucretia and I left the Bower with our lighted candles to make our way to our rooms. I believed I saw relief on Lu's face as we parted for the night.

Impulsively, I said, "Please don't be frightened tonight, pet. Tulip will be with you, and there are other servants who are most willing to help you. I'll have Cook send you some warm milk again, and tonight Trevor's presence in the house should give you a warm sense of security." I didn't like the deep shadows I saw around her eyes, or the way all her color had vanished since coming back to the manor earlier in the day. "What is it, Lu?" I whispered, touching her arm.

We were standing at the top of the old spiral staircase. Her rooms lay across this landing and to the east side of the house. From here, we both could look down into the entry hall below, the candles still glowing in the huge chandelier throwing eerie shadows around us. Lucretia was ghostly white.

She shivered, her lips trembling, then shook her head, closing her eyes for a brief second as if to shrug off some great fear.

"Look," I said, taking her arm and turning with her down the hall. "I'll walk with you to your rooms. And Lu," I said frowning. "You simply must not mind anything Miss Phoebe seems to . . . connect you with. She does live in the past, it is true, and I've long since learned that Kate was none other than Trevor's half-sister. She lived here at Mullins, and Miss Phoebe was very partial to her, I'm told. She can't mean any harm toward you." I stopped myself from telling her that Kate's lover was the brother of Hadrian and Taryn Wilkes. That would surely send her into a swoon, I felt.

"You are right, I know, Roma," Lu said in a faint voice. "I know I must . . . adjust. Oh, here's Tulip now." She looked relieved. "Tulip will ring for my warm drink. You are so brave, dear cousin. I can't think what I would do without you. But there. If I've said that once, I've said it ten times, or more. But thank you. You are such a comfort to me." She kissed my cheek.

I relinquished her into the maid's keeping for the night, and returned to my own rooms, exhausted.

While I brushed my hair the usual one hundred strokes, I thought that so much had happened to me that it seemed days rather than just hours since I'd gone to bed in this very room last evening.

When I blew out the candles and climbed into bed between the soft silky sheets, my last thoughts were of Roc St. Coryn, and it was his face and voice which hovered teasingly before me all night, the black hair and merry eyes haunting my dreams.

In the days that followed, I went over the house and got to know it better. Lucretia went with me on these tours, with Mrs. Pascal in tow, while Trevor was busy about the estate. He was usually up long before I rose, and it was I who had breakfast with him and a morning ride about the estate, which always lifted my spirits and gave me a certain exhilaration nothing else could do. Afterwards, Lucretia would join me in the Bower and we both would go over the house.

In the afternoons, Trevor would take Lucretia and me out in the open carriage, for the weather held beautifully, and we made the rounds of the estate, meeting the people, the Tamblyns at North Lodge, and Cal Pascal on our second trip down to his cottage, and again to Barton Farms. Lucretia was always most relaxed away from the house, and more than once we met Hadrian Wilkes traveling about.

The evening the Wilkeses came to dinner was what one would call a success. They came rather early, and sat pleasantly in the old Bower, Taryn, Lucretia and myself, while Trevor took Hadrian aside and discussed, as I was to learn afterwards, Arnie Polden.

The little boy, Jon, stayed at his Uncle's side, and we saw very little of him, for he had dinner in the kitchen, where Cook insisted on spoiling him. This seemed to make little difference to Taryn, I thought, and it puzzled me.

However, Taryn was talkative and came up with surprising suggestions to Mrs. Pascal about the parties we were soon to be having. "There's no doubt about it, Roma," she laughed. "Everyone in these parts loves an excuse for a masquerade ball, and I do believe it would be exciting. It would enhance the occasion as well."

Lucretia looked surprised. "But what on earth could we masquerade as?"

Taryn shrugged her shoulders. She was wearing a very attractive gown of beige muslin, similar to the one she'd worn when we first met, this one just as simple, fitting her figure to perfection.

"Anyone, I should think. But there are vast chests in Mullins, I'm sure, and one could simply choose a costume from the St. Coryns' ancestry, shouldn't you think so, Mrs. Pascal?"

Mrs. Pascal, delighted that she should be called upon to have an opinion, inclined her head and echoed Taryn's own suggestions. "Why, I do expect so, Miss Taryn, that I do. 'Ee do remember now, don't 'ee, when Miss Kate gave that costume ball, and used all them old clothes stashed away in the cupboards, I dare say."

To this, Taryn laughed happily. "But yes, wasn't that a mixed-up affair, if ever, Mrs. Pascal? Phillip came dressed as Cromwell, and Kate had the audacity to dress up as Prince Charles. What a night that was, with old Mister Edward furious at Phillip!"

"If I recall rightly, yes. That were the time and the case, Miss, it were," Mrs. Pascal said. A small silence left them both remembering, and it was another moment or so later that, while trying not to show too much interest, I turned to Taryn.

"Was Roc St. Coryn at this particular ball?"

Taryn's smile did not betray anything she might have felt, but it was the housekeeper who answered fervently.

"Oh, my land yes, Miss, that he were, if I recollect, I do. And he were like Satan hisself, he were, all mean like, that he could be, weren't he, Miss Taryn?" Now as loquacious as could be, she went on without waiting for the answer.

"All mean and black he were, over Mister Trevor's attentions to Miss Kate. It took no masking to know who them two were, no not by a long shot it didn't! Oh but what a stew that one were in, I can but tell 'ee! Why, had us all but known what was to come about the very next night, what with them two at each other's throats like it were!" She clacked her teeth, then said with a heavy sigh, "But none of us could guess that, now, could we? And it do be all in the past now, yes. Best forgotten about, I say."

So it was the night before that tragic time, I thought. I glanced at Lucretia, who sat twisting her lace-edged handkerchief in her lap. She didn't ask questions, nor did Taryn volunteer to carry on. I suspected Lucretia didn't want to know anything more about Kate St. Coryn or that dark past, so I made a mental note that I would protect her as much as I could, to spare her this dreaded truth.

But as in everything, had I foreseen the events myself, I should have known I could not protect her from the truth, and had she known it then, the outcome might have been different. But little did I suspect the outcome of all this as we sat in the Bower, turning the conversation back to the present and the coming dinner party and ball, and the wedding itself.

It was decided, then, that we should have a masquerade ball. As for the dinner party, there would be a select group of people of the local gentry, those on intimate terms with the St. Coryns.

Miss Phoebe joined us shortly before we were to go into the dining room, and I thought she seemed different from last night, almost withered. Her eyes were vacant and she seemed strained, as if she was trying hard to grasp what was going on about her and could not. Her eyes lit up, but only vaguely so, when she saw Hadrian.

The smile she gave him was sweet, and it was his arm she leaned on when we went to the dining room. There were six of us, with Taryn beside me on Trevor's right, and Hadrian on Lucretia's. It was a cozy, intimate room, with soft candlelight, but tonight promised to be gayer and this gladdened me. To see my cousin so light-hearted lifted my spirits too, but as the dinner went on, I saw the reason for it. She was charming, and had a powerful effect on Hadrian.

"Is Wilkes Reach as old a manor as Mullins?" Lucretia asked. She was beautiful in the simple blue velvet gown, with a strand of pearls around her neck. A matching blue ribbon was threaded through her curls, and the dimple near the corner of her mouth was like a charm itself. I knew her smile was enchanting this young man seated across from me, for he could not keep his eyes from her face.

I glanced down at Trevor from time to time to see if he noticed, but he was already engrossed in a whispered conversation with Taryn, and didn't appear to see anything remiss in Lucretia's manner, or Hadrian's for all that. I couldn't hear what either Trevor or Taryn were saying, so I gave my attention to what Hadrian said about his home.

"By no means, Wilkes Reach is far from that antiquated beginning, Miss Lucretia," he chuckled. "The Reach came into being after the Reformation. It is nowhere near as large or as impressive as Mullins, but it is comfortable enough. We now have very little land, for most of it has been sold in the past twenty years to keep the house and grounds from actually going to decay. My forebears were, alas, doctors such as myself, and had very little interest in keeping up with the repairs. Once, and that was a long time ago, I suspect," he said with a twinkle in his hazel eyes, "the Wilkeses were rated with the best families in Cornwall, and in the local gentry. Now, we're merely comfortable, earning a living by the same traditions as the past four generations."

Lucretia smiled. "But you do so much for humanity, Doctor Hadrian. That must be rewarding, knowing people rely upon your attentions, your . . . caring for their well-being. A life of servitude, which somehow excels that word by far. I would call that the most rewarding of anything in life, to know you are helping others, by healing their bodies."

I had never heard Lu talk this way and I would have thought she might have been frightened by the prospect of human suffering and pain and death. I found myself being constantly surprised.

A very flustered Combes hurried into the room and poured the wine into beautiful goblets. He did not meet my eyes and when Trevor questioned his manner, he seemed to take offense and muttered, "Oh, 'twas only that Mrs. Combes sent me t'last minute to fetch the cider down from the Farms, sir, thet do be so, and I just got back. Sorry about thet, thet's fer sure." He apologized and Trevor turned his attention back to Taryn.

The dinner this night was exceptionally elaborate; course followed course, beginning with a fish soup. There was pink salmon with lemon, roast pheasant as succulent as any I'd ever tasted, in its own savory sauce, and a stuffing of wild rice and chestnuts; slices of thick ham with pineapple, a rarity, I knew, followed this course, with small potatoes in cream and a green salad sprinkled with garlic. The dessert was a light peach tricol with French sweet cream and tiny cups of thick black coffee.

After dinner, the ladies retired to the Bower so the men could have their port. They did not stay long, but joined us shortly. The Wilkeses left a few minutes afterwards, however, for Hadrian had been handed a message that he was needed immediately at Barton Farms. Arnie Polden, it seems, had tried to get up, and the plaster had broken.

It was then that Trevor and Hadrian had words, which surprised me. Trevor had insisted that he go along, but Hadrian was opposed.

"No. This is my patient, Trevor. I cannot allow you to interfere on any pretext." He was scowling, but adamant in his protection of his patient.

"Stop it, Hadrian," Trevor said harshly. "You know very well you're protecting him! You know he was trying to leave Barton Farms. It's as plain as the nose on your face! I tell you, I won't stand for it! Arnie Polden is as guilty as sin!"

"Nevertheless, I cannot allow you to interfere!" He looked at Taryn, who was already in her cloak. "If you're ready, Taryn, we'd best be going. Fortunately, we didn't remove the plaster mixture from the carriage." It was as if he were talking to himself.

Trevor was enraged. I could see the fury just barely checked behind those light eyes and the nervous tic near the corner of one. His face became dark and clouded with a look of distrust. I suspected that Trevor was not used to having someone like Hadrian defy him, but Hadrian stood his ground as he ignored Trevor and went to Lucretia.

"Thank you for a most delightful evening, Miss Lucretia." He took her small hand into his, looking directly into her eyes. They were wide, darkened now with some emotion she was feeling. "I am sorry to leave such pleasant company," he said and glanced at me, his eyes almost sparkling. "It is seldom that I get this opportunity, but I do hope you and Miss Roma here will indeed forgive a very busy man for having to leave so early? Perhaps there may come another invitation?"

Lucretia smiled, that dimple near her full pink mouth bewitching as she said, "You will always be welcome, Doctor Hadrian, at Mullins. Your work comes first, and I am to be included among those who know just how important you are to your many patients." There was an expression in her eyes as if she had stumbled upon something intimate and secret. I myself was discovering much about my cousin which amazed me. "Isn't that so, Roma?" She turned her gaze on me.

"Of course, we all do understand and appreciate your work, Doctor Hadrian, and I am certain Jake Polden appreciates you and Taryn more than ever just now. You must let us know just how serious an injury Arnie Polden has done himself."

"What's this?" cried Miss Phoebe, suddenly perking up, and her birdlike eyes darted from Hadrian to me. "Arnie Polden? The young lad of Barton Farms? Didn't he run away to sea last year? What happened to him? Norie said he broke his leg coming off the ship. What has he done now, Hadrian?"

I saw a look pass between Hadrian and Taryn, and I felt a tremor inside me. What truth did they know? And indeed, how much did Miss Phoebe know of *The Petroc* and its whereabouts? It occurred to me that Hadrian knew far more than he let on, and that he was alarmed that this old woman might reveal that truth as she wandered in and out of the past and present.

"Now, Miss Phoebe," he said, placing his arm about her, and silently signaling his sister with his eyes that they had best get on their way. "Norie really didn't tell it right, but yes, Arnie Polden did break his leg the other night, and he just stood upon it too soon, so there's nothing for you to worry about. Let me see you to your rooms now, for it is quite late, and I insist that you take this mild sedative I shall instruct Norie to give you. We want you to be at your best when the wedding march is played in the village church, now, don't we?"

"The wedding march? Oh. Yes, of course." She seemed doubtful, and for a moment faltered on the brink between past and present again, but Hadrian didn't allow her to stay there for long, and took immediate charge of her.

He rang for Norie, and when she came, he and Miss Phoebe left us, and Taryn made her leave-taking simple.

"I'll ride over to the Reach, perhaps within the next day or so, Taryn, to see into that little matter we were discussing," Trevor said quietly.

She only smiled, inclining her head, and then went out of the room with Trevor beside her as they went toward the kitchens to fetch her son. Lucretia and I were left to ourselves, each silent in our own thoughts. It seemed that Trevor and Taryn had a lot to say to each other, and I wondered just what was that little matter they had been discussing?

For no reason at all, I found myself irritated, but I knew then that it did not stem from what they had to say to each other. Rather, it was because I suspected Taryn had been the mistress of Roc St. Coryn, a suspicion that had been with me all evening, and I was angry with myself for allowing it to bother me. I could not explain why I was tormented so.

Combes came in to tell us that Mister Trevor had ridden off, and that Lucretia and I were not to wait up for him, and he then inquired if he might light our candles for us if we wished to retire.

Lucretia smiled at the old steward and said, "Yes, I believe so, Combes. Thank you. But first I should like to go to the kitchens and express my thanks to Cook for such a lovely dinner. Roma dear, will you come with me?"

I said I should like nothing better, and Combes was delighted with this, for his face shone and his eyes twinkled.

"Let's hope we shan't be interfering with the staff's evening," I said, but he assured us we would not be doing anything of the kind.

"Now't bain't nothin' to int'rupt like, no. 'Ee be more'n welcome, 'ee both are. Me Missus be pleased, 'er would." And he opened the door for us as we left the Bower, leading the way with lighted candles.

The kitchens were two long rooms, with an archway between them heavily beamed, a step separating one from the other. The lower was the cook room, the higher one was where the servants ate their meals at a long trestle table.

The cook room was large with two long latticed windows which I knew would let in much sunlight in the mornings. At one end was an open fireplace with spits and a cloam oven where Cook made her delicious bread three times a week. From the oak beams hung large hams, several butchered lambs, sides of bacon, and a few large hens already plucked, and in a smaller room beyond I noticed the inevitable small bundles of herbs and strings of bulbous onions and garlic, and brown earthen tubs of fresh vegetables.

Mrs. Combes now sat at a small table shelling peas, her pink face shiny and free of wrinkles, and so much like her husband's that it was amusing. I suddenly thought of that old saying that two people could actually begin to grow to look alike if they lived long enough and close enough, and I could quite believe it true, as I looked at both of them now.

"An' a good ev'nin' to 'ee, m'ladies!" Cook said, beaming at us both. I was aware of the comfortable atmosphere in the room, my eyes wandering to the bright hooked rug before the hearth and the two rocking chairs with side baskets holding red and black wool in bright balls, with knitting needles stuck inside them; a beautiful large grey cat with her five baby kittens held the honor place near the hearth in a wicker basket, and I suspected this was what had drawn the little boy, Jon, to eat his dinner in the kitchen.

She invited us both to take a chair by the hearth, and because the night had brought a certain chill, it was pleasant to accept her offer. "Hap' 'ee both might like a cup o' hot cider to warm 'ee up a bit, I reckun', m'ladies," Cook said, smiling as we took our chairs. "An' a'fore 'ee go to bed?"

Remembering the good cider we'd had in the Polden's farmhouse kitchen, I was more than pleased and said so. "Thank you, yes," I said, holding a soft little kitten close to me, and watching Combes stir the blazing logs in the fireplace. A long tongue of fire leapt up and curled around the logs and up into the dark wide chimney.

There comes a time in one's hectic life when the small, pleasant, simple joys seem by-passed; the smell of a cozy kitchen, the crackle of a wood fire, baby kittens, and the autumn chill of the night kept at bay by the warmth and security in the congenial company of people like Combes and his jolly wife. It made me feel contented just to sit there in comparative quietness of spirit, as Cook went to fetch some pewter mugs from a dark polished oak cupboard, and began to fill them from the copper pot which hung from an iron hook within the hearth.

I wondered idly where Mrs. Pascal was, but I didn't inquire. I glanced at Lucretia, and in the flickering firelight she too had that appreciative look about her, with not a trace of timidity as she accepted the mug of hot cider.

They seated themselves near us, and for the next half hour, we could not have been more at peace. I sometimes marvel as I look back now on that evening with the Combeses that neither Lucretia nor I could guess the anxiety that was burning through these people, as they sat there, detached as it were, from the drama being played down at Barton Farms.

When we parted company, Lu and I, to go to our separate rooms, I could see she was as deep in thought as I was. I could not sleep easily, for my mind was on Trevor's harsh words, and I was sure there would be a search, and then a discovery of *The Petroc*. And it would be Roc St. Coryn's undoing.

There was excitement throughout the house because there was to be a ball—the first since that time seven years ago, and for a week there was little talk of anything else, except of course the dinner party to be given, and then the wedding itself. Pansy and Tulip were hysterical with delight, for it would be their first social occasion at the manor house.

The ballroom was to be decorated with old Soady's flowers brought in from the greenhouse he kept, and Mrs. Pascal was kept busy seeing to the many details. I supervised old Soady's decorating of the Great Hall, and the entwining of ivy leaves around the beams, which was an old Cornish custom. Pots of deep purple and gold hothouse blooms were brought in and placed around the Hall and in the Bower, and along the steps of the Elizabethan staircase; great wax candles filled the sconces, and I imagined that when they were lighted for the great occasion, there should be nothing like it. It made me proud, yet I ached inside that it was not for my wedding, but for someone else's.

It was Lucretia who decided that she didn't want a costume for the masquerade ball from the trunks of Mullins, which Mrs. Pascal had brought out of storage. I came upon my cousin in the garden one morning, and found her with a strange expression on her face, as if she'd been caught doing something she shouldn't have been doing. She stammered a bit and then told me that she wanted to go into Fowey town to look for her own costume.

"Hadrian told me there was such a shop in Fowey port, run by a distant relation of his, Roma," she said after an embarrassed silence between us. She met my inquisitive glance, but turned her face away after a moment, and I could say nothing.

After all, I told myself with a defensive swallow, I had been riding every day with the man she was going to marry. Why then, could she not be in another man's company if she chose? Yet I was uneasy as I agreed that I should accompany her into Fowey town in the next day or two.

That Hadrian had been at Mullins during these past days had been necessary, we all knew, because of Arnie Polden. The doctor had remained in constant attendance, for the young man had suffered a severe setback. Hadrian came every day to the manor, and I knew he sought Lucretia's company.

Trevor had been unduly silent on the matter. It was understood between us that we would ride every morning before breakfast, while the good weather continued. On these occasions, Trevor had been affectionate, more so than before, and it had been all I could do to keep him at arm's length.

So it seemed ironic that I should be the one to watch Lucretia find pleasure in another man's company, as I made arrangements for her wedding.

However, as I rummaged through the trunks Mrs. Pascal had placed in one of the convenient bedrooms in the east wing of the house, I found to my delight several choices of costume. I did not have an occasion to discuss any of these

with Taryn Wilkes, for she had not been able to come over
to Mullins, not until the night of the dinner party.

It was only after I went to see Miss Phoebe's gallery that I
made up my mind what I should wear that evening of the
masquerade. When Miss Phoebe learned we were having a
masquerade ball, she was more than enthusiastic, like a
child, I thought as I watched her at tea in the afternoon.

Trevor was out on the manor estates and I had a suspicion that he was conducting an investigation with Tamblyn,
who, according to Pansy, was reluctant to ". . . turn tail
on any of the manor folk, for it were like puttin' the noose
around his own neck." But when she saw my interest, she
turned red in the face and stopped talking.

Lucretia and I had our tea with Miss Phoebe. It was one
of those warm, lingering autumnal days, hazy and still, and
the doors were open in the Bower to allow the late afternoon sun and the smell of the garden to drift in. Mrs. Pascal, busy as she was with getting the house ready for the
merrymaking, brought in an elaborate tea service of silver
and placed it on the table nearest the windows. I caught
Miss Phoebe eyeing it with an avaricious gleam like an expectant child. She had been hardly more than a vague
shadow during the past few days, always mumbling about
the Polden lad who'd run away and whom Norie had kept
her informed about.

There was a silver kettle over a spirit lamp, and a tea
pot, cream jug and sugar bowl, all of gleaming silver, beside it, with delicate china cups and plates which Mrs. Pascal handled with pride. I knew these were the heirlooms of
the St. Coryn family, and I remembered the cup and saucer
I'd accidentally broken on that first morning in the dining
room. How glad I was that it hadn't been one of these.

Mrs. Pascal left us, and Lucretia, feigning a slight headache, asked me to pour. She was lost in her own thoughts,
hiding under the soft blue paisley shawl she wore about her
shoulders, and it seemed to me her voice, too, was exceptionally soft.

"Yes, of course," I said, and I, too, touched the treas-
ured heirloom china and the silver, appreciating the preciousness of it with longing in my heart.

I poured the tea, and passed a cup to Miss Phoebe first.
There were cucumber sandwiches, thinly sliced bread, both
dark and light, a seedcake and a variety of small pastries
laced with cream. The old woman helped herself liberally

to the sandwiches and sliced bread, and she contented herself with munching on these as Lucretia was served, and then myself.

We ate in a congenial silence, but from time to time Miss Phoebe's eyes darted from me to Lucretia, just as I recalled they had done each time we'd been together, as if she were making comparisons for future use, yet not quite deciding where she would place us in her plans.

When the last crumb on her plate was eaten, she turned to me.

"You promised to visit my wing of the house, Miss Kendal. I show it only to those who are interested. You spoke as if you were indeed interested." It was a haughty reminder of her own invitation a few nights ago.

"But of course! I would love to see your gallery, Miss Phoebe. Both Lucretia and I would, wouldn't we, Lu?" I looked to my cousin, who turned a ghastly shade of gray. "Lu? Are you alright?" I placed my cup down and started to rise, but she suddenly seemed to regain her composure and shook her head, then gestured with a faint wave of her hand that she was perfectly well. "We'd love to see her wing, don't you agree?" I persisted.

"Oh, I . . . should indeed . . . agree," she said haltingly, but I guessed wild horses could not drag her to Miss Phoebe's rooms. Her eyes looked dilated, so large and full of fear in her pale face.

The old woman didn't notice. She laughed gleefully, as though she'd snared the choicest prey. "Then I invite you both to come to my part of the house, when we are finished."

We had finished, but Lucretia was biting her lip in a nervous way. She caught my eye. "I shan't go with you, Roma. Do be a dear and go without me, please. I find I have a most . . . nagging headache, and I shall ring for my maid." She glanced out into the sunny garden. "Tulip shall accompany me into the garden. Yes. I do think I shall . . . recover in all that sunlight."

She stood up then, and pulled the bell rope for Mrs. Pascal, who came in almost immediately. Lucretia asked her to summon Tulip, and then to take the tea things.

"It's all right, Mrs. Pascal," she said in her sweetest voice. "I should like to have Tulip with me in the garden, while my cousin looks in on Miss Phoebe's art."

This sounded completely reasonable to Mrs. Pascal, who

immediately sent for the maid. When Tulip came, I watched the two of them leave the room, going through the opened doors into the garden, and I marveled at the devotion with which Tulip waited upon my cousin. But I knew too that Lucretia would do anything to stay out of Miss Phoebe's reach.

The old woman had sat in a confused silence as Lu and the maid left, and then Mrs. Pascal began clearing the tea things. "Shall 'ee show Miss Kendal your part of the house now, Miss Phoebe?" She looked inquisitive. "Norie be down in the kitchens with Cook havin' her tea. Will 'ee want her?"

Miss Phoebe suddenly came alert. "No. Norie can have her tea, Mrs. Pascal. I shall take Miss Kendal up to my gallery now, if she is ready." She looked to me, and I nodded.

I went over to her chair and helped her to her feet. She laughed and put out a thin hand with which she clutched my arm. Her fingers were callused and scratchy, like talons on my skin.

"Come," she said eagerly, as if she were afraid I might change my mind and escape her. "We shan't mind that naughty Kate for running off and not minding her lessons. She will be disobedient. I've told Edward time and time again not to spoil that child. But he will not listen, no."

Mrs. Pascal looked at me and shrugged, and I led the old woman from the room, saying chidingly, "Lucretia is not Miss Kate, Miss Phoebe, but Miss Kendal. You must remember that." I kept my voice soft.

She brightened up. "So you are coming to see my tapestry, Miss Kendal. It is time you did, you see. I know you will like it. You, more than anybody." She stood close to me and stared into my face. "You will figure in my work. But first, we must learn the secret. You and I will discover the truth."

"I?" I was bewildered. "What truth?"

"You'll see," she said almost smugly. "Come. Let us seek it together."

We went up the main staircase which led past the old minstrels' gallery and entered into the east wing of the house, then up another flight of stairs to the third floor and down a corridor I was not familiar with. The vastness of the house astounded me still, as well as the antiquity, and it was into one of these vast rooms that the old woman brought me, quickly closing the door behind her.

Of course it was perfectly obvious that she flitted in and out between past and present, and I might have been at a loss with her had we come into an ordinary room where we would have had to sit and chat on ordinary matters. But this room was different, as I saw at once.

The room was large, and hung with tapestry, exquisitely worked in vibrant colors of silken thread. I stared in utter fascination. Although I had seen the tapestry in the Great Hall, that of the scenes depicting the Great Rebellion and the Restoration, I was quite unprepared for this gallery of art.

She saw my expression and chuckled with delight. "There. You do like my work. You, Miss Kendal, can appreciate true art. I knew you would. It is like your music, do you not agree? This is my tapestry. I tell my story in these pictures."

"It's incredibly beautiful," I said in a hushed voice.

"You see what a large space it covers," she said as she led me over toward the first section of her work. "Come closer, and I will tell you about it."

She took my hand, her fingers restless and moving continually; I thought again they felt like claws.

"Here. Look. Do you recognize this?"

"It's the manor house—"

She nodded, still holding my hand. "When Mullins was first in the St. Coryn family." She chuckled, pulling me on to another and another, each telling a story of Mullins or the St. Coryn family, and I was impressed more than ever.

"But it looks so real, and all those tiny stitches! You have made it so perfect." We stopped in front of one that had several people in it. "Who are all those people?" I asked, excited.

She caught my excitement and her face creased into a childlike smile. "This is my father and mother, and this is my brother, Edward's father. They are all gone now, and I alone remain to tell their story."

"What a wonderful talent you have," I cried, awed as I stared at the scenes we came to stand in front of. There was one of the house and of a ship tied up at the quay. "Why, this is *The Petroc*," I exclaimed, my pulse racing. "Who are all those people?"

"Yes," she said, smiling and stroking the velvet work

fondly. "That is Edward's ship when it was first built. Those men are his crew, the smugglers he hired to bring in the contraband, hiding it until it could be distributed. Oh, Edward was clever but a real rascal! He knew how to outfox those clumsy Revenue Men. He brought Miss Katharine to Mullins too. See?" She pointed with a thin finger to a young woman nearer the house.

"Miss Katherine?" And I frowned, recalling what Trevor had said of his father's mistress.

"Oh, yes. Edward wanted to marry Katherine, and I suppose he did marry her in his heart and spirit. He loved her. But she had no dowry." Her expression was sad, almost tearful.

"He had to marry the woman my brother arranged for him to marry. They weren't suited, as anyone could see. I knew Edward's feelings, you see. He always came to me, even when he was a boy, to tell me what he felt about things. He didn't love or even like Sarah, but the wedding took place all the same."

"Sarah. That would be Trevor's mother?"

She nodded, leading me to the next scene. "This is the death of Edward's beloved Katherine, only six months before Sarah's. Roc and young Kate are kneeling at their mother's deathbed, and Edward," she said sadly, "poor Edward's heart was broken. I think he died with her then. Part of him did. But he had the children, and he kept his promise to her, and brought them to live at Mullins." She was almost tearful as she looked at her own work, reliving the memory of that day.

I marveled at how she had managed to capture perfect likenesses with all those tiny stitches. My heartbeat quickened as I recognized Roc St. Coryn as a boy of twelve or thirteen kneeling at his mother's bedside.

In a few moments, she said, "And here is Sarah's death. Her son is standing in the doorway. She was already gone, three days before Trevor came home."

I recognized Trevor, and again found the likeness astonishing. "Here is Edward's death, only it is not yet finished. I cannot finish it until I know the answer." I was puzzled by the strange look that had come into her eyes as she stared at the unfinished portion.

"What answer, Miss Phoebe?" The pictures had aroused my interest and I was looking at the scene she had stitched so carefully of that tragic moonlit night in the courtyard, of Kate St. Coryn and Phillip Wilkes where they lay fallen.

There was another panel of two young men facing each other across that courtyard, and I knew at once they were Trevor and Roc St. Coryn.

"How did Edward die?" She spoke near my ear, and I almost jumped, turning to her. Her words startled me.

"But wasn't it . . . suicide?" I said, my heart fluttering wildly.

She shook her head, her face altering again into a frown. "It was not like Edward. No. I do not believe he could have done it."

"Then how did he die?"

"I do not know. I only sense within me that he could not have taken his life. So you see, I have had to stop my story. I must find the answer first." And as she had done once before, she looked at me conspiratorially. "We must discover the truth, Miss Kendal. You and I."

I knew she knew far more than her wandering mind betrayed.

"Perhaps if Roc St. Coryn came back with *The Petroc*, Miss Phoebe, you would have your answer," I suggested.

She looked at me with sharp awareness. "So you believe that naughty boy had a hand in it, do you? He was always impetuous, hot-tempered, and I told Edward he'd better take that young scamp in hand or there would be trouble, but Edward always laughed and said, 'Leave the boy alone. It's good for him to feel his freedom.' He was not easy to get on with, yet I warmed to him for he was Edward's son. He wasn't like Sarah's son, always so quiet. Trevor always thought out his actions before he did them. A strange lad, even when he was just a small babe."

"You keep referring to 'Edward's son and Sarah's son', Miss Phoebe. I . . . . I thought they, the two sons I mean, were half-brothers." *I* kept my voice low, playing her game and hoping she would disclose something of interest.

She looked at me, then glanced around her in a furtive manner. "Miss Kendal, can you keep a secret?" she whispered.

I inclined my head towards her. "And what is the secret?"

"We here at Mullins don't know who is the true master of the house. It is yet to be decided. That is why I must wait for the answer to finish my story." That she hadn't directly answered my question annoyed me, and I looked at her in feigned surprise.

"I understood the master of Mullins is none other than Trevor, Mister Edward's true and legal son. How else can it be?"

She eyed me warily. "Two sons—one Edward's and one Sarah's. Who knows the answer? There were two sons. Edward could not make up his mind. But we are going to learn, are we not, Miss Kendal? Yes, I know you are going to help me. You will figure in the key picture." She led me to the unfinished work. "Kate just didn't have the time, naughty child that she is. Young children must be so naughty, I suppose. Will you tell Kate that I forgive her, Miss Kendal?" Tears now brimmed in the old woman's eyes as she looked up at me. Her mind was wandering, and I was suddenly weary of her senseless talk.

I began to walk around the room, looking at the scenes she had drawn and stitched with patience throughout the long years, of those who'd lived at Mullins. She was a true artist, I thought as I stood in front of her portrayal of the Blue Boudoir.

It was done in shades of blue and green, and as I looked at it, I noticed she had pictured what was an apparition— the ghost of Kate—in that boudoir. It seemed almost bizarre, if not truly eerie, and it occurred to me then that she probably would delight in frightening someone as sensitive as my cousin, or one of the superstitious servant girls.

I turned to her as I reached the door.

"There are rumors that Roc St. Coryn will come back and claim Mullins as his rightful inheritance, Miss Phoebe. He could be here now, with his ship, hiding in one of the creeks. Do you think he will do this? Will you accept him in your part of the house?" I was bold with my words, and I was gratified in seeing her expression change once more to that look of conspiracy.

She smiled almost greedily, but sobered quickly and I noticed her eyes go beyond me. I turned quickly.

Norie stood in the door. How long had she stood there, listening? I was annoyed for no reason, except that she had a look of total distrust on her face, and was displeased to find me there with Miss Phoebe.

For a full minute we stood there in an awkward silence, and then I made the first move. "It is growing late, Miss

Phoebe, and I must now go. Thank you very much for showing me your tapestries. I have enjoyed this very much."

Her face brightened, but Norie's scowl deepened, and Miss Phoebe seemed to wilt back into uncertainty. "You must promise to come again, Miss Kendal."

"I shall, I promise," I said, but I too was not certain I would be allowed to come in, if I were faced with Norie. She stood aside as I pushed my way through the door, and then she turned and watched as I walked away.

I was angry as well as disturbed, yet I knew without a doubt that old Norie must have been the one who had given the information to Roc St. Coryn's man. She knew Roc St. Coryn was hiding his ship in the creek.

I felt as though a strong, invisible net was being spun around me, around Trevor and Lucretia, and that we were the victims of Roc St. Coryn's mad plan of vengeance. And somehow because of it, my feelings toward Trevor were changing. I told myself that I loved him, that he was the man I wanted more than anything, but I knew this was a lie even before I admitted it. It caused me more anguish than I ever dreamed possible during the long, sleepless nights I spent sitting at the open window, my thoughts ever upon Roc St. Coryn.

Several days later, Lucretia and I went into Fowey town with Trevor, who said he had business there and would leave us to shop around. The day began with a rosy sunrise, veiled by mists that Pansy informed me always came in autumn and would vanish by midday. The smell of burning leaves from the orchards was in the air, and along with it a nip which made my skin tingle.

As we drove along the road through the estates, I noticed the blond, dry stubble in the fields, and how gold the lime trees were beside the copper beeches. As we passed through the North Lodge gates, Tamblyn came out to meet us. This was Pansy and Tulip's father, a big red-faced man whose eyes were dark and alert.

He tipped his hat to Lucretia and myself, then spoke firmly to Trevor. "Aye, sir. I'll keep an eye out fer what 'ee want. Me'n Hamilton'll scout around. Not much'll get past us, I'll warrant."

"Very good, Tamblyn," Trevor said.

In the distance, I glimpsed the brilliant colors of zinnias, marigolds, petunias and dahlias, lovely enough to vie with old Soady's gardens at the manor. This was the last bloom of color, of heat, of the summer sun, but I knew more exotic blooms would take the place of these hearty summer flowers, and camellias, magnolia, azaleas and mimosa would bloom all winter in this mild Cornish clime.

Trevor drove on, and a heavy silence settled upon us as we traveled into Fowey town. It was a busy market town and a flourishing seaport, with beautiful old buildings of brick and stone, and a fine center street climbing from the quay to the marketplace halfway up the hill. Fowey, with its deep-water harbor, had ships of every description anchored there on this day, and it was a handsome sight we saw as the fishing boats were lined up, already in with their catch of fish for the day.

Trevor took the chaise around to the town stables, and suggested that he meet us at the Gold Florin Inn, which faced the sea front, at midday. "I must look into some business," he said, and both Lucretia and I were aware of his ominous mood and were thankful he did not want to accompany us as we browsed through the different shops.

Lucretia murmured, "If this pleases you, Trevor, then Roma and I will do our shopping so it won't tire you to wait upon us. We'll meet later, then, at the Gold Florin Inn." She smiled, the tiny dimple near the corner of her mouth showing. She was beautiful in a flowing frock of pale blue, and her bonnet was trimmed with tiny rosebuds which also graced the blue parasol she held above her head.

He nodded his head in agreement and walked off hurriedly.

This was market day, a gay affair by the looks of all that was going on around us. Up the hill, I noticed the old market house where farmers and their wives were gathered on the steps. The fisherwomen, wearing scarlet cloaks and broad felt hats, began to call out their wares in loud chants to all passers-by, and for a moment both Lu and I were reluctant to leave this colorful scene.

But hardly had we taken a step in the direction we wanted to go, when a voice behind us called out, "Why, Miss Lucretia and Miss Roma! May I be of assistance to you?"

We turned, startled. It was Hadrian Wilkes, a smile creasing his tan face, the hazel eyes gleaming with the light of laughter in them.

CHAPTER SIX

This was no mere coincidence, I guessed at once. I looked over at Lucretia, saw the rush of pink come to her skin, and that secret smile in her eyes.

"Good morning, Doctor Hadrian," I said, with surprise in my voice, but Lucretia said prettily, "Oh la! How nice to see you here, Doctor Hadrian. Pray do show us to the shop your cousin owns. I declare, I simply feel lost already, what with seeing all those merchant ships and the market. Is it far from here?" She looked up at him with such adoring helplessness that I wondered how anyone could resist her, and Hadrian fell under the spell of her charm immediately.

"I will take you there myself, if you will allow me. It is down from here, and along a narrow street on a hill overlooking the harbor. I should be happy to introduce you to my relation. Fanny was my mother's second cousin, and she was an actress years ago. A fascinating old woman, truly." His eyes almost danced with the laughter that was never far from their surface.

"Then it should make our visit quite worthwhile," Lucretia said, and looked at me. "I should like that very much, wouldn't you, Roma?" Her own smile was as disarming as Hadrian's, and I had the feeling that neither of them truly cared what I thought. That they both had discussed the masquerade costumes at length was equally obvious, even though she went on with her explanation.

"We both want to acquire a costume for the masquerade, although Roma, I believe, has already decided upon one from the trunks of Mullins, haven't you, dear?"

I nodded, aware of the look which passed between them, and managed to say, "Those beautiful old clothes cannot be improved upon for a masquerade ball. But I shall need a mask. I suppose your cousin has such items in her shop?"

But Hadrian was gazing down into Lucretia's eyes, oblivious to what I had said. I certainly was not wanted here, but I had to find some way to transcend the awkward moment and, I hoped, to leave them.

"And how is your patient Arnie Polden, Doctor Hadrian?" I asked, placing myself between the two of them in order to get his attention. "The servants have been quite worried about his condition, and I believe there is general alarm among them. I understand his situation has worsened." I implied that I was indeed surprised his doctor could leave him.

The hazel eyes were grave as he looked down at me. "Arnie will lose his leg, Miss Roma. Of that I am positive, for it is doubtful that he will pay attention to the wisdom of his brother and myself to stay off it until it can heal. He is frightened, and it is all we can do to try and quiet those fears that one man only is responsible for. I came into Fowey to consult another surgeon." The anger in his voice startled me.

That he blamed Trevor for this fearful situation was clear enough, and I too felt that Trevor had been too rash and unfeeling in making such threats.

"Trevor believes Arnie was with a smuggler crew. I think he is having the estates searched for possible evidence." I knew I was too direct, but I met his gaze steadily. He stopped, and looked down at me. I was vaguely aware of the blue sky and the harbor below us, of the crying, swooping gulls, of the fisherwomen's cries nearby, and all I could think of was the strange silence between the three of us standing there.

"For what evidence, Miss Roma?" Hadrian said a moment later.

I glanced at Lucretia; her face had blanched and she was unsmiling, the old fear in her eyes.

"For acts of . . . smuggling, I am sure," I said. "A ship, perhaps, in hiding along one of the many creeks." I remembered the talk I'd had with Trevor only yesterday morning when we were out riding and had come upon Cal Pascal's cottage. Trevor's eyes had narrowed as he had stared down at it, and he'd said, "There are some things I find very strange indeed, Roma. Cal Pascal, for instance. I'd give anything to know how he injured his back, and why he wasn't around three nights ago, the night Arnie Polden tried to get out of bed. I am beginning to suspect something is very wrong here, and what's more, I intend to find out exactly what that might be."

It had been another chance for me to tell what I knew, but Trevor had turned his horse and had raced with the wind across the uneven turf, and the moment was lost.

How I had despised myself in that moment, for I knew I was betraying Trevor and my love for him.

Now I kept my eyes even with Hadrian's, my voice as level as I could make it. Hadrian spoke softly, but in a controlled manner, like a warning, I thought.

"It would be best for him and for everyone concerned, Miss Roma, if Trevor did not meddle in something which he may come to regret, should he drive these people too far. Look," he turned and pointed out to the harbor, to where a three-masted ship lay at anchor, away from the other ships crowded along the quay. "See that ship? She is a slaver, one of the few we've been seeing lately in these waters, along the coast of Cornwall. Many a decent, hard-working man has been taken aboard just such a ship, and transported from his home and family to either the Spanish Americas or to the slave pits of Australia. What Trevor has threatened to do to Arnie Polden is such an act, Miss Roma, that brings fear to everyone on the Mullins estate."

Yes, Trevor would see justice in that punishment, I thought bitterly. I had quite forgotten Lucretia until I saw that look on Hadrian's face, his gaze going beyond me, and he reached out quickly and caught her before she could fall. It startled me, and I was sure she would have gone into a dead faint had he not caught her in time.

It happened so quickly. His arms were about her, and she leaned against him, pale as death. Without a word, he guided her across the street toward the Falcon Inn. In another moment, we found ourselves in a small secluded alcove at a table, with Lucretia leaning back against the cushioned seat and Hadrian quietly ordering refreshments. His concern for her was touching, and I thought of how it was Trevor's place, not Hadrian's, to attend to her.

I was uncomfortable, and a bit annoyed. I wondered what Trevor would think if he knew his fiancée had fallen in love with Doctor Hadrian Wilkes?

When Hadrian left us for a moment, I touched Lucretia's very cool hand, and leaned close to her. "Should I not send for Trevor, Lu? If you are—" She lifted her hand and silenced me.

"No. Please, no. I am all right, Roma, truly so. It was all that talk. . . ." She looked at me with pleading eyes, color returning to her cheeks, her eyes lit with a glow behind them. "Roma," she whispered. "Please do understand. Will you mind so very much if you went on alone to look into the shop? I shall be all right, I promise, for I shall sit right here for awhile with Hadrian to look after me. Please don't mention it to Trevor. He mightn't understand."

So this was the way it was to be, I thought, and for no reason at all, I felt annoyed. If I stayed with her, I would be an absurd third party to a blossoming romance, and I wondered at the outcome of such a ridiculous situation as I pressed her hand and stood up.

"I shan't mind, Lu. I know you'll be in good hands, so I'll just hurry along to the shop before Hadrian returns, and you can make my excuses." I tried not to let her see that I understood everything that was happening, for she would deny it, I was sure. She said nothing now, but smiled, and I turned and left the inn quickly and stood outside on the narrow crooked street for a moment before I started the descent toward the harbor front.

What a fine kettle of fish this was turning out to be, I thought as I crossed the street, out of the path of a small cart laden with farm produce for the market, and I found myself walking down a very steep and narrow lane. The half-timbered cottages bulged out above the shops beneath them, some narrow and others large.

Suddenly, a hand grabbed my arm from the doorway of one of these narrow shops, yanking me inside. My heart dipped into a great spasm of fear, and I cried out, "Oh!"

Yet before I could say another word, I was inside, the door closed, and I was staring up into the face of Roc St. Coryn!

For a moment, I was too stunned to speak. Surely, I thought, he would not dare to abduct me again, in broad daylight?

He seemed amused, and I was certain he'd guessed my thoughts. He was much too close to me, and I smelled brandy on his breath. He raised his black brows and my face went hot, for I remembered . . . *everything!*

"No, Miss Kendal. I shall not abduct you," he said in that strong voice. "I only want to talk to you, to warn you, if I may." His hands were like steel on my arm where he still held it; I tried to wrench free, but I could not.

"I see that we have nothing to talk about, Captain St. Coryn," I said haughtily, angry at him for giving me such a fright. "Please let me go." I met his dark eyes with a challenge.

He laughed in a low satanic manner, and I despised him

all over again. I wanted to slap that evil smile off his face, but of course I could not even move out of his grip, let alone try to defend myself.

"Come, let me take you up into the parlor of this shop, Miss Kendal, and I will show you a view, and you may have a cup of good cider as I tell you about your future husband."

I gasped. He still believed I was the bride intended!

It was only when he stood back, and turned towards a staircase that wound up into the house that I actually saw we stood within the narrow foyer of a private house. Up these stairs Roc St. Coryn led me, and I found myself being ushered into a room where dark, heavy wooden tables and high-backed benches were placed before the curved windows of leaded glass that gleamed from the sun pouring through. The room was crowded with sailors and merchants, alike talking shop, and a few women were there with their men from the sea.

"This is Tom's Place, Miss Kendal. Tom is a very smart and proper-like citizen, who knows his trade very well, and keeps his place. Come, let's sit here." And he ushered me into a small alcove, with dark red curtains pushed aside on polished brass rods.

Through the window one could view the whole of the harbor, and it came to me suddenly that Roc had most likely seen me from this very spot.

It was on the tip of my tongue to lash out at him, but a waiter appeared and Roc ordered two mugs of cider and, for a moment, I could study him closely in the bright morning light.

His skin was bronzed like some sea god, and his teeth flashed white and strong in that handsome face, the mouth sensuous and full under the black mustache. I could see that he was respected here, and probably well-known, though how could his presence be so well-kept a secret if this were true? Surely, word would get back to Trevor that his half-brother was seen in Fowey daily?

The waiter left and Roc turned his eyes on me. He grinned in that devilish manner of his, and I had to look away to keep from erupting with pent-up vehemence.

"You did not . . . confide in your future husband, Miss Kendal?" He laughed. "I thought as much. Trevor would not have believed you. But, I can see that you are not convinced either that what I tell you of him is true."

"And what is that, pray tell?" I could not hide the scorn in my voice, even had I wanted to, which I didn't. What audacity the man had, and yet, there was a certain undeniable magnetism about him, and a shiver of excitement pulsed through my whole being just being near him.

His eyes narrowed, and something like a chill of horror washed over me when he said, "He deals in slavery, Miss Kendal. But not only black slavery. Look," he pointed out the window toward the harbor. "See that lone ship anchored off to herself there? She's a slaver, and no one enjoys seeing her in these waters."

As he spoke, I sensed something evil; the ship was the same vessel that Hadrian had pointed out to Lu and me not more than a quarter of an hour past.

The waiter brought the mugs of cider and placed them in front of us. Roc waited until the man left before he spoke.

"There will be more than black slaves from the Ivory Coast on that one. Did you not know that Trevor ships out poor French refugees to the slave markets in the Spanish Americas? Those who could not raise the sum of money to pay for his helping them get out of France, those poor aristocratic aliens who knew no better than to trust this man, with their very lives at stake!" His voice was like a whip cutting across the table at me, and I shuddered in horror.

"What are you suggesting?" I cried in a voice not quite my own.

He laughed. It was a wicked laugh, harsh, without mirth. "I am suggesting that he plans to have some good Cornish men thrown into her bowels before she sails West. My guess is that he is making the transactions this very moment."

I thought I hadn't heard right. A tremor shook my voice as I said, "You believe that ship is under Trevor's supervision?" I hadn't been brave enough to confront Trevor with what had been suggested, either by Roc or by Taryn Wilkes. Could it be true then? But I didn't want to believe it.

"No. He owns the line of slavers, Miss Kendal, bought by the fortune he has gained from his victims." He seemed to mock me as his lips curled into a satirical smile. "Have you not wondered where he is this morning, while you shop around alone and unescorted?"

"I do not make it my business to spy!" I retorted, uncomfortable, and for a while we sat in silence, sipping the cold cider.

A nagging fear roused its ugly head inside me, a fear that what this man was telling me could be true. Hadn't Lady Cecilia confirmed Trevor's usefulness in helping to locate the families of the unfortunate victims of the guillotine, and in helping them establish a new life in England?

Dread filled my heart, and I could make no reply to this man who seemed to know more than anyone of Trevor's affairs. I was, at the same time, conscious of Roc's eyes on my face. That he still believed me to be the woman who was to marry Trevor was evident, and I again thought of old Norie, Miss Phoebe's maid. She had given the information that "Miss Kendal" was lodged in the Blue Boudoir to this man's own servant, Robin. But, I thought, with my tongue in my cheek, did she not know it was Lucretia rather than myself whom Roc St. Coryn had wanted?

He said, "I will tell you where Trevor is this very moment, Miss Kendal. He is aboard that slaver. And perhaps from my warning you will benefit. For if that vessel moves up the estuary toward Mullins, there will be all hell to pay!"

"Then, why are you telling me this?" I asked, with a manner of mocking remorse to match is own anger. "If you know him so well, you must know I could not persuade Trevor to change his line of business. Why not warn him yourself?" Sarcasm stung the air between us as I spoke.

For one moment, he was taken off guard, and then he smiled that leering smile I had come to despise. "You are so right, Miss Kendal. He would never listen. He is too intent on trying to get revenge and is greedy for wealth. Your own life would be in jeopardy should you even suggest such a thing."

"Have you the right to talk, Captain St. Coryn? You talk of revenge! Your own greed for revenge is like a festered sore, for you *see* people, destroy them as you destroyed. . . ." I didn't finish my sentence, because fury was rising inside me against this man, though I knew he had far from destroyed me, and this thought burned in me like a scorching flame. My face went hot with embarrassment and humiliation.

He regarded me with dark amusement, and he resembled a satyr with that strange light in his eyes tilted in that dark face.

"You were not destroyed, Miss Kendal. Anyone can see that. I did you a service, shall we say. An enjoyable service, I might add, for me as well as yourself. It makes you more desirable, if anything."

I was so angry that for a moment I was unable to speak, and he chose this moment to antagonize me further. "Your eyes have a certain fire in them when you are angry, Miss Kendal. They are like twin topaz gems. I like women with fire in them."

"Such as Taryn Wilkes, no doubt?" I could not for the life of me hold my tongue.

He lifted those silky brows, surprise in his eyes. "Taryn Wilkes? But of course you have met her. She would be at Mullins as often as she could get the chance. So you are jealous of her?" He laughed, and I trembled with rage that he should have that impression. What an insufferable creature he was!

"Jealous, Captain St. Coryn?" I feigned a mockery I did not feel. "I can assure you, jealousy of Taryn is farthest from my feelings toward her. She is a remarkable woman, considering what she must have had to suffer from the . . . company forced upon her. She bore it quite well, I should think." Why was it that this man aroused so easily both my passion and my hate?

He laughed again, at my expense, and I fumed, not trusting myself to speak out for fear of giving him the truth. I could not jeopardize poor Lucretia by subjecting her to this man. It would mean her death, and I was immediately strengthened by this thought. It alone brought sanity back to me and I composed myself to play this man's game to the end.

He challenged me then. "I dare you to speak to Trevor about this business, Miss Kendal. You of all people should learn the truth before you tie the bonds of matrimony with such a man. This comes as a friendly warning," he lowered his voice, and for a second so brief I might have imagined it, I believed it held tenderness. "You could prevent a tragedy by simply discovering how he plans to use your wealth. Probe into the matter, Roma, for all our sakes."

So he knew my name too, I thought, disturbed, and he dared to use it. But I liked the way his voice softened when he said it, and felt a bond between us.

He stood up then before I had the opportunity to question him. "You must go now. But this will not be the last meeting, I can assure you. Think over what I have said. You will be surprised, I think."

He took my arm and pulled me up from the bench quite suddenly. My flesh beneath the pale amber velvet felt the hardness of his touch, and it sent a wild flame coursing through me, as I feared it would.

As we walked down the stairs, and before he opened the door for me, he bowed gallantly and kissed my hand. "Make no mistake about it, Roma Kendal," he used my name frequently now, "we shall meet again, and sooner than you expect."

"Good day, Captain St. Coryn!" I was defiant, but he only laughed and opened the door onto the sun dazzled street, and stood there watching me as I turned my back to him and walked away, hardly knowing where I was going.

I knew I was angry at the manner in which he handled me, but I was also excited, and my eyes were flashing as I walked down the crooked, narrow street toward the waterfront. I could still feel the warmth of the kiss on my hand, and it unnerved me. Thus, when I turned a corner in the street and saw Trevor, I was startled back to reality.

His face was a dark scowl, and I wondered if he would smell the cider on my breath and I would have to make up some excuse for it. I stood where I was and waited until he made his way over to me.

"My dearest Roma. Where is Lucretia?" His eyes lightened, and the scowl was gone. He was pleased to see me, and guilt rushed forward, making it hard for me to defend poor Lu as well as check my own emotions.

"Oh la!" I cried, unlike myself, dazzling him with a coy smile. "You know Lu, and how faint she sometimes becomes, just shopping around! I left her in a shop, with the attendant there being very kind and giving us both a glass of cool cider. She insisted I go out on my own, and she said she would meet us at the Gold Florin. I am sure she is all right, and she wanted me to give you assurance that she was so, if I should see you beforehand." I lied with a boldness unlike myself, and I was disturbed to see that he accepted my excuses so readily.

He took my arm and turned me in another direction, his face close to mine. "Then, my dear Roma, we shall have this time for ourselves, which is what I wanted. Oh, that we could be together always, without our little *ninny* to keep me from loving you so the whole world could see it!"

For one moment, my heartbeat quickened with hope, but I knew all too well that Lucretia would always be between us.

"But, we could have it like that, Trevor. We could. You could marry me, you could give up Lu and the wealth, for me. Your . . . business should be enough to keep Mullins safe, and we both could face the world in honesty."

He stopped and looked down at me, his eyes piercing mine.

"And what do you know of my business, Roma?"

I met his gaze challengingly, remembering the dare Roc had thrust at me only minutes before. "That's just it, Trevor. I know nothing about your business, except that you go to the Ivory Coast often enough, and there are rumors you are connected with slavers." My gaze was as direct as was my statement. "Is this true?"

I saw the muscles in his jaws flexing, and the small nervous tic at the corner of his right eye I'd noticed before. He was measuring me, searching my face for some light of understanding, as though he didn't trust me, demanding to know from what source I'd heard this ugly rumor.

I defied him with this challenge, however, not wavering. "You must tell me, Trevor. Are you responsible for that slaver anchored there in Fowey Harbor?"

For a long moment, he could only stare at me, his face tense and dark, and then, as if he made a decision, he sighed heavily and placed one hand on my shoulder, the other taking my hand and pressing it firmly.

"Yes, you would hear from someone, wouldn't you?" He lifted his brows anxiously and cautiously went on. "My dear Roma. I do have a business, dealing in slavery, because it brings in good money. Slaves are needed as manpower in the Americas, and I am but one of thousands who dabble in such trade. It is nothing to be ashamed of or frightened of, for that matter. I want you to know you have nothing to be afraid of." He kissed my hand, his mouth cool and somehow passionless.

I pressed my cause. "Then you wouldn't need my cousin's wealth to keep Mullins safe, as you had me believe when you proposed marriage to her. You and I could marry, without her wealth, and be very comfortably settled at Mullins." I thought of Lu and Hadrian. They were well-suited to each other, and certainly they were in love. I was determined that Trevor should see the folly in his proposed alliance with my cousin. I wanted to be his wife, and the mistress of Mullins, and I wanted the world to know this. It had been my dream for so long.

He took my shoulders with both hands, and smiled down into my face. "Sweetheart, you must not be blind. I know you are in love with me, and that you want to be my wife more than anything. I want that too, but we both must be realistic. We shall have each other, for better or for worse, even if Lucretia is my wife. You know she is much too delicate, and for this cause her money will be an asset to my business. See that ship? Yes, you guessed right. I own a line of slavers, and I want more, for there is a demand for slaves. In a few years, with the investment of my wife's money, I shall be rich, my sweet, darling Roma, and you shall share it with me. We shall take a voyage in grand style to the Far East, or to the Spice Islands. I even have plans of investing in a diamond mine. But all this must come with carefully laid plans, and I have them."

How could Trevor be involved in something as sinister as this? I could not trust myself to speak of what mattered most to me: that he, the man I had wanted to be my husband, who even now could make me his honorable wife without a fortune behind me, was set to take all he could gain from a woman he didn't love, so that he could invest in selling human lives!

A dark cloud of despair seemed to settle upon me as Trevor placed my hand through his arm, believing perhaps that my silence betokened agreement to what he'd said and, as we walked slowly down the street, he was smiling.

"I am glad it's out in the open now, sweetheart," he said. "I wanted you to know, but you are so close to Lucretia, and I felt she just might not be able to cope with knowing everything about me. You are strong and that is what I most admire about you. Lucretia need never know; you and I will protect her." This sounded like an echo from the past, and a shudder of revulsion made me cold inside.

"No, she would not marry you, if she knew all this, Trevor." I was hurt and bewildered, and I knew this stung him.

"Nonsense. I would make her marry me by giving her no chance to refuse, my dear. But she mustn't know, you see. You and I will be partners in this, and we shall keep it from her. She is not strong enough even to leave the shores of England, but you and I can travel, as long as we provide her a safe and comfortable life." He was boasting, and my conscience smarted as I thought of the life of deception he wanted to live with my cousin—and with me.

"We must plan carefully. The wedding will be an elegant affair for her, and will give her an introduction to all the local gentry. The dinner party we are giving will allow the best of them to meet my bride-to-be, and they will be the ones who will forever look after my timid little wife, while you and I, my love, will see the world together." He looked down at me, his eyes afire with excitement.

I thought of Lu, now keeping a tryst with the one man she loved, and I could hardly hide my contempt or my fears, which were beginning to mount.

White gulls flew up from the harbor-front like bits of paper in the distance, only to settle again on a fishing vessel as we descended onto the wharf. For a while, I gave myself to the color of the waterfront; chestnuts roasting over glowing hot coals, tended by old men or women in strange, out-of-date costumes, fisherwomen in their bright cloaks selling their wares. Other women had baskets of gaily colored ribbons and laces, tortoise-shell combs and cases. Gypsies sold huge paper roses of saffron and crimson, and swarthy sailors in striped shirts thronged the piers, with monkeys on their shoulders or huge colored birds from the West Indies in cages.

Then Trevor led me to the Gold Florin to wait for Lucretia. Once inside, I went to the small powder room, while Trevor arranged for our alcove and table. I was glad for this moment alone, for I was greatly disturbed by all that he'd said to me.

I washed my hands, then removed my bonnet and smoothed my curls. My face was flushed, my eyes too bright—glittering, I thought angrily, from all the excitement of the morning. My thoughts should have been on Trevor, I knew, and the wild proposal he'd made to me, but as I stared at my reflection in the small mirror above the washstand, I was remembering Roc St. Coryn and the way his eyes had flashed at me, challenging me to learn from Trevor himself what Roc had known all along.

A new dread gripped me like bands of steel around my heart, and I trembled with it. What would happen when those two half-brothers met?—Or were they brothers? Hadn't old Miss Phoebe herself suggested what Roc had warned me was the truth? Was there any positive proof that Trevor might not be the blood son of old Edward St. Coryn?

I tried hard to shrug off that sense of evil, but I could not. I was deeply concerned over Lu's situation with Hadrian Wilkes, knowing that it was so unlike her to be nurturing a forbidden romance practically on the eve of her wedding day. But then my own guilt rose on the crest of that indignation, and I wondered what Trevor would do if he ever suspected that Lucretia was betraying him.

Where was she now? Would she have the sense to keep the rendezvous with Trevor and myself? Deep in thought, I placed my bonnet back on my head and returned to the lounge where, to my relief, Lucretia was sitting, flushed and smiling, with her purchases in ribbon-tied boxes beside her. She had a secretive smile on her lovely face, a light in her eyes that no shopping spree could have been responsible for.

She would not reveal her costume to either Trevor or myself, and I concluded this was just as well, for I too was being secretive, taking only Pansy into my confidence.

Our ride back to Mullins was pleasant, for Lucretia seemed content and gay, agreeing with everything Trevor said, and I could hardly wait to learn just what was in her mind behind that secretive smile.

But there was no chance whatever to learn that, for when we'd reached the house, Trevor whisked Lucretia down through the gardens toward the quay. I stood at the window of the Bower and watched them, while my own disquieted heart gave me no peace. He had his arm about her slender waist, and as I watched them, I could see they were deep in conversation. I moved over to the piano, and began to play at random, wondering just what it was they were discussing so intently.

It was late when they returned to the house, and Lucretia immediately went to her rooms. I could tell she was quite upset, but I did not follow her. I glanced at Trevor, but he did not seem bothered, and asked me if I would care to take a stroll about the gardens with him.

"I need to talk with you, Roma. We are going to make a few changes, which I am setting into motion at once, but now I want to discuss these changes with you."

I lifted my brows. "Did you discuss these changes with Lu?"

He glared at me, but a smile touched his lips. "You must

not allow your heart to suffer so, my darling Roma," he said in a low, cautious voice, taking my arm firmly and guiding me into the sun-filled garden.

"Yes, my dearest Roma," Trevor said, as we walked through the wicket gate. "I have told her of the changes. It did upset her, of course, and that is what I want to discuss with you. I want you to talk some sense into her pretty little brainless head."

We took the path which led towards the quay on the estuary, where I'd seen them walking earlier, and Trevor waited until we were quite alone before he began to elaborate.

"The plans for the ball and wedding have been changed, Roma," he began, and my heart quickened strangely. "I want the wedding to take place as quickly as possible, so I've arranged for the banns to be cried this Sunday in the village. The wedding will be Tuesday week, and the ball immediately afterwards."

I stared at him in utter amazement. "But, how on earth . . . ?" I stopped, and turned as he looked down at me. "Is this what you did in Fowey? You made no mention of it to me. Why the sudden change?"

He shrugged his shoulders. "It is all for the best, I think, and naturally, time is now of the essence. Mrs. Pascal has agreed that it can be arranged, and in the morning I shall send Hamilton out with special notes to the wedding guests. Tomorrow's guests will be notified. It shan't be too difficult, and most likely less trouble for all."

"Lucretia's solicitor, Sir George Thorpe, has written to say he will be our guest, and will be here in Cornwall tomorrow. He will tie up all the loose ends of this business in the marriage settlement. I'm learning that she is a spoiled child and I intend to assert my authority now. Sir George will set her straight."

I was filled with bitterness. I still smarted from Sir George's unfair and unkind words to me after Uncle's death. He was a man completely without compassion, and the scorn I had in my heart for him burned deeply; I could not forget nor forgive my Uncle Doyle's injustice to me in robbing me of my inheritance, and Sir George, I believed, had been his advocate in all of it.

"And why does Lucretia object?"

I already knew full well why my cousin was holding back, the love of another man in her heart. I wanted to

laugh at the absurdity of it all. She was giving away her
fortune in a marriage she now did not want while I would,
according to Trevor's plans, reap the pleasures her money
would bring. Poor dear Lucretia! Upset? She had every
right to be.

Trevor answered my question briskly and confidently.
"She needs you to convince her, Roma, and assure her it is
all for the best that we get it settled. She will come out of
it, once things get moving. I'm going into Plymouth early
in the morning, to meet Sir George, and I shall expect to
see Lucretia all soft and submissive when we return." We
had resumed our walk. The beeches glowed dark red in
the late sun, like deep stains of color on the jewel-green
lawn which old Soady kept so beautiful. The river moved
slowly as we came out onto the quay, and I turned back to
stare at the manor.

I was suddenly reminded of the beautiful tapestry I'd
seen in Miss Phoebe's gallery, the one of the ship, Edward
St. Coryn's *Petroc*, designed with her silken threads and
imagination. She had used an autumnal setting in her color
scheme, and the likeness of the trees and the old quay here
was astonishingly real. A shiver of uneasiness touched me.

"I am counting on you, my sweet," Trevor said, his
hand on my arm, "to work on your pretty cousin while I
am gone. We must make an impression on our guests, and
I want my bride-to-be in her sweetest frame of mind."

"You seem sure that I can achieve what you could not
do," I taunted, now irritable. But he took that in a far different manner, and chuckled, his hand pulling me closer to
him.

"I do like it, sweetheart, that you are jealous, even of
your timid little cousin. It makes me feel you want me, and
I like that. I should feel the same way if you were ever to
look at another man. I can assure you, I would not allow
it."

I could not help the rush of words. "I believe I should
welcome the interest of another man, since you will be so
busy being a bridegroom to another woman," I said teasingly, but meaning every word of it.

His hands closed on my wrists and turned me about to
face him. They were like steel, and hurt me painfully. "I
will *kill* any man that you ever show an interest in, Roma.
Believe that. You are my possession, and I will make you
know it, even before my marriage to your cousin is con-

summated. Yes, even on that wedding night, it will be you who will belong to me. Don't ever doubt this, and don't you tempt me!"

In spite of myself, a chilling sensation of sheer horror moved over my whole being, and I began to tremble. What would he do when he learned what his half-brother had done to me? Something told me then I should leave, run away before Roc St. Coryn carried out his diabolical plot to ruin Trevor. I could not still the growing fear that I would be caught between these two men when they met, and not Lucretia.

So I didn't answer Trevor, but lowered my eyes, afraid that they would reveal the truth of my encounter with Roc, and he took that to be the submission he wanted. His voice was soft and low as I turned from him, and we continued strolling along the old quay, but I still felt the pain where his hands had bruised my wrists.

"Sweetheart, you know how I love you, and our life will surely be different after a few years. Believe me. I want you by my side." We walked on for some minutes in silence, and then he continued, "You will try to persuade Lucretia, Roma, that once we are married, her own life will be settled. I see no reason to delay it now. For such a timid creature, she certainly has the characteristics of a very spoiled rich child, and I feel she must be treated as such. But I warn you now, I will take certain measures if, after indulging some of her whims, she continues to pout. . . ." He stopped, for one of the stableboys was coming towards us. He called out to Trevor, saying Jeffers needed his help.

Trevor looked at me. "All right, Sid," he said. "I'll be right there." Then he lowered his voice and said to me, "Trust me to do what is right for Lucretia and for you. Talk to her, make her see some sense if you can."

I watched him walk away in long strides, across the green turf towards the house and stables. I was annoyed, because in my mind I knew Trevor was playing a hard and fast game, using Lucretia and me as pawns for his own selfish pleasure. My emotions were a jumble of pity and remorse, mixed with another sensation I did not dare to admit to myself.

I glanced at the old manor house. Its lines were gracious, those of a house meant to be lived in, full of love, warmth and children. I wanted these things, I thought, as I looked at the mullioned window of the Bower catching the last rays of sunlight. My eyes stung suddenly with tears, knowing I should never be mistress of this manor. If Trevor had his way, I would remain at his side but never enjoy this house as its hostess and chatelaine, or raise the children I so longed to have. It hurt me deeply.

I knew I was being greedy and yet, was it greed to want an honorable name and a home like this one? My wealth had been taken from me and given to my cousin, along with the right to live in this lovely house where centuries of St. Coryns were born and lived and died. It seemed unfair and I wanted to avenge the injustice.

Revenge. Roc St. Coryn's revenge, I thought angrily, would hardly touch Trevor, until Trevor learned it was I whom Roc had taken. Then what good would that revenge be to Roc? I could imagine the black anger of both men once they met face to face, and I couldn't help but shiver with apprehension, recalling Roc's last words to me:

"Make no mistake about it, Roma Kendal. We shall meet again, and sooner than you expect."

In this frame of mind, I saw sense in moving up the date of the wedding. There would be less chance of Roc St. Coryn learning that he had taken the wrong Miss Kendal, and Lu would be safely married, unharmed.

I was always placing Lu's own safety above everything else; I was always protecting her. Wasn't it time that *she* suffered something? Even as this thought came to me, I knew guilt, for indeed she would be the sufferer in this loveless marriage to Trevor. She had not been able to hide the fact that she'd lost her heart, even in so short a time, to Hadrian, and marriage to another would not be easy.

As I made my way slowly back to the house, I could not throw off that sense of evil which, like a cloud darkening a bright day, now darkened my spirit. It seemed like an omen, and often, afterwards, I knew I had felt that uncanny sense that some tragic drama was about to take place in this old manor and in my life.

I went to Lu's rooms as soon as I could, and found her more irritable than I could ever remember. She was having her bath readied, and at once I knew she was in no frame of mind to talk with me.

But she looked at me and stated, "You may tell Trevor that he can carry out his latest plans for the wedding, Roma. But, I shan't be down to dinner. I am quite exhausted by this day and . . . other matters. Be a darling and leave me now, Roma. Please. Please don't ask questions." I saw the pucker between her brows, and knew just how hard she was straining to keep her mouth from quivering.

"All right, Lu," I said, and pretended that I was not surprised by her annoyance. It was most unlike her submissive self. "I'll come up later to say good night."

She only nodded, and I left her then, feeling worse than I had all day.

It was the day of the dinner party.

The house was freshened with banks of flowers from old Soady's greenhouse, and the Bower as well as the Great Hall was garlanded with leaves entwined about the dark wooden bannisters and posts. Everything was sparkling clean and smelled of lemon and beeswax, due to the diligence of Mrs. Pascal. I fancied I saw a strained look on the housekeeper's face, and I was reminded of how restless the whole household staff had seemed since yesterday.

I asked her about her nephew Cal. This seemed to upset her more.

"Oh he do be so much better now, Miss, he do. He be back in the boats now, didn't 'ee know?" She gave me a look that suggested I knew all about the matter. Hadn't I been with Trevor on that day he'd gone down to the cottage on the beach and taken Cal by surprise? The man had been lifting one of the boats off the rack where he had mended it, and looked as healthy as a young lion, as Trevor had said, doubting that the man had indeed been injured.

I knew the servants were frightened by the threats, by the warnings Trevor had given them about smuggling contraband, or even helping a smuggler. And my own suspicions mounted every hour as I came to think the servants were more involved than they had led me to believe.

Trevor had left early, shortly after breakfast, to ride to Plymouth to meet Sir George Thorpe. I had given him Lu's message, and he'd only said, "I was certain she would see the logic of it, Roma. Look after her while I'm gone this day. She is a frail woman, we both know, and she will no doubt need all the rest and support you can offer her. I should be back before the guests begin to arrive."

But I did not see my cousin during the day. She left strict orders with Tulip that she wanted to see no one, and that she was indeed resting and preparing for the dinner party. I abided by her wishes, for I knew Lu was not thinking so much of the party as of her own situation, and I felt I understood. So I went for my morning ride on Neptune, enjoying it even more than usual, as it helped me forget my tense situation.

The weather had continued to be at its finest; the sky was bluer, the colors move vivid and deeper, as the sea was when Neptune and I came to it. A ship stood on the horizon as if painted on canvas, and my thoughts were channeled in the direction of the *Petroc,* wondering if it was still hidden in that creek? Would its Captain know of the dinner party at the house tonight?

For some reason, I thought of Miss Phoebe, and how vague she had been last evening at dinner, with just Trevor and me. She had stared at me all through the meal, and afterwards she had asked me when would I visit her gallery again, as she had something to show me.

"Any time you like," I assured her, and although she didn't offer a definite time, I now thought about it and felt it would be appropriate for me to visit her this afternoon when I returned to the house, perhaps after lunch.

With this in mind, I led Neptune back through the trees, reluctant to hurry, for I was almost at peace with myself, and I wanted the feeling to stay with me as long as possible.

From a distance, I thought I saw Hadrian Wilkes's carriage, and I guessed he was visiting his patient, Arnie Polden, at Barton Farms. Then I lost sight if it as I crossed a meadow and went deep into the forest of copper beeches, and did not think about Hadrian or Lu as I might have done. I made up my mind I would go look in on Arnie Polden, perhaps tomorrow.

With this thought, I came into the stableyard, and after a polite conversation with Jeffers, I left Neptune with him and entered the house, going up the back way. As I stood on the landing between the old gallery and Miss Phoebe's part of the house, I decided I would go along to see her now. I was still in my riding habit, but I hurried along with determination to learn what it was she wanted to show me.

I was suddenly conscious of the shadows around me in the corridor, and I shivered in spite of myself, and chided myself for being so fanciful. But if ghosts could ever haunt an old house, surely Mullins would have its share, and

Miss Phoebe's gallery would indeed make them come to light. . . .

I shuddered, then tapped on the door. Old Norie answered, staring at me suspiciously.

"I came to call on Miss Phoebe," I said, defying the woman with my bold gaze. But she did not budge, her own defiance challenging mine. I recalled Taryn's warning that she guarded her old mistress like a watch dog.

"An her do be arestin', Miss, her do," she said, distrusting me all the way. "I canna' disturb me mistress, no." She shook her head, crossing her arms over her ample bosom. "Can't it wait, Miss?" She was adamant, and my resolve to see the old woman dissolved. Miss Phoebe probably did need all the rest she could get for the festivities of the coming evening.

"Yes. It can wait, of course," I said, giving in. But I met this old servant's cold, accusing eyes, which were not as unseeing as many would have thought, in spite of her great age. I was certain that she had been the informer that night I was abducted. And for the same reason, I believed she knew far more than any other servant about what was happening at Mullins. Yes, old Norie knew, and I was tempted to confront her with it, here and now.

I seethed with anger at the thought that she could have been the instrument that had caused my abduction that night. It took all the will power I could muster to face this old servant and not try to make her confess, but I knew that if I did confront Norie, she would be placed on her guard, and perhaps she would even make things wose, by revealing the truth to Roc St. Coryn.

My thoughts went rampant in those brief seconds I was in front of her. I knew things could become terribly difficult if Roc did learn the real truth and, in his anger, swooped down on my timid little cousin. He would hurt her far more than he could ever hurt me.

The old woman was eyeing me with obvious suspicion. She had seen Trevor and me together; I could even guess that she disliked Trevor intensely, for how else could she have turned informer for Roc St. Coryn and Robin? She might be capable of anything, but above all, she would protect her mistress from Trevor, who had made it clear he did not have much patience with her.

Thus, I averted my own eyes from the old servant, and

stepped back while she looked me over, and I said, "Do give Miss Phoebe my regards, Norie, and tell her I called to pay her a visit. But I shall see her tonight at the dinner party." I smiled, but even then she did not budge from the doorway, and she nodded and waited until I moved out of sight before she closed the door.

As I made my way back to my rooms, I thought that I sensed something truly evil, but could not explain why even if I tried. There was nothing more for me to do but to change my riding habit, and look over the costume I had taken from one of the deep old chests. I had to see what could be done about letting out the waist seams of the lovely Venetian velvet, and guide Pansy through the fitting and pressing.

We worked for several hours. I went down to a solitary luncheon, for Lu did not emerge from her rooms, nor did Miss Phoebe. The house was unusually silent, but there were smells from the kitchen that told me Cook was busy baking, and I was certain the servants were all there, for I hadn't seen a one except my own maid since midday.

I wandered around through the house after my luncheon of cold meat pie and a glass of cider, admiring the decorative flowers. Trevor had arranged for musicians to play for us tonight, so there would be some dancing and a great deal of merrymaking for our twenty-two guests.

I stood for a long moment in the Great Hall, looking at the beauty of the room, its Elizabethan window and the marvelously worked tapestry of the Civil War, and I marveled at Miss Phoebe's great talent for depicting the scene.

I heard a slight noise behind me. I jerked around, my heart thudding in an uncommon manner.

It was Taryn. She was smiling when she saw me. "There you are, Roma. None of the servants knew where you were, but I thought I'd seek you out before I had to go back to the Reach." She walked over to where I stood, and as I felt relief washing over me, I wondered if, lately, I hadn't been letting my imagination run away with me.

CHAPTER SEVEN

"I came over to see if I could be of some help," Taryn said, as her gaze traveled over my pale lime green muslin. I somehow felt she approved of it, and that she was appraising not only its simple cut, but its color, which did suit me very well. I could see no covetousness in her manner, and I believe this was why I liked her as she went on. "But I needn't have worried. Mrs. Pascal has assured me that all is going smoothly." She glanced around the Great Hall, admiring it.

I agreed with her. "Mrs. Pascal would be hard to outdo with her knack for handling the servants," I laughed. "She is a marvel of a housekeeper. I am sure Lucretia is a very lucky mistress to have her."

She inclined her head to one side and laughed. "I should think so. Any great house would do well to have someone like her. But," she sighed, "I can't stay long. I've left Jon with our cook, for Hadrian has gone off and had not returned when I decided to come over. I took the short cut, using the old trap and Bluebell, so I must get back to the Reach in time to get us ready for tonight's party. Trust Hadrian to be kept late on these occasions."

I remembered I thought I'd seen Hadrian in his carriage earlier, and was about to remark on this, but I thought better of it and said instead, "You should have brought your things over here, Taryn, and stayed. I'm sure Mrs. Pascal would have been only too pleased to have readied a room for your use."

The smile lit up her eyes. "It's just as well I didn't. I don't want to leave Jon too long. Mannie's hearing is not too sharp and as Jon is asleep, she might not hear when he wakes up. I must get back." She met my inquiring look.

Surely this woman had borne shame and humiliation at Roc St. Coryn's hands, I thought, bearing this child she seemed so detached from. I had firmly accepted in my own mind that Roc was fully capable of committing such a misdeed and I resented it more than I cared to admit.

"You are wondering about the father of my son, Roma. I will tell you, although you are indeed the only one I will ever say this to. I have kept the identity of Jon's father a secret, even from my brother. Somehow, I feel you will be my friend."

Her eyes arrested mine, and I felt my skin burn with embarrassment that she should have guessed my thoughts. My lips went dry and I ran my tongue over them as I said, "I . . . Taryn. You must not feel you have to explain . . . anything to me. I'm sure Roc St. Coryn is a complete *blackguard* where all women are concerned." I could have bitten off my tongue as soon as I said it.

Her expression confirmed this. "Roc St. Coryn had nothing to do with Jon, Roma," she said quietly, a cold light in her eyes. "No, it was not Roc, but Trevor. Trevor is Jon's father."

For one long moment she watched my face, and then she repeated her statement. "Yes. I can see that would stun you. Trevor is Jon's father. It happened during that tragic time seven years ago, when Trevor came home, and Philip and Kate were planning their wild elopement." She seemed her usual calm self, and smiled across at me. "What ever made you think of Roc St. Coryn?" She lifted her brows, amused, her voice now husky and warm.

Why did I feel such an acute sensation of relief? I could only stammer, "I . . . that is, everyone tells me . . . Roc St. Coryn is such a . . ." I stopped, blushing hotly, and could not continue.

"Roc did have a way with women, Roma. It's true. And, it's most likely he does have a trail of illegitimate children left behind him. But Jon is Trevor's. I'm surprised that more people have not seen the resemblance, and I'm sure Hadrian suspects it, but he has not interfered, not by one word or look. He would not betray me, either."

"Then you are fortunate," I said softly.

"Yes. In that respect, I am fortunate. I hoped you would understand how I felt when I learned he was to marry an heiress. He promised he would marry me, back then, but then that awful tragedy happened, and Trevor left afterwards. Of course, when I learned I was to have a child, it was too late, and I wouldn't reveal it to him. Not then. Trevor didn't know about Jon until recently. That I had a son, I mean." She never flinched.

I didn't know what to say for a long moment, then I managed, "He doesn't know then, that Jon is his son?"

She shook her head. "No. I believe he too thinks the

child is Roc's. But, for all purposes, it is best that he thinks so, for Lucretia's sake, and for his own, I suppose." She sighed, but her eyes never left my face.

But I was astounded. She was swallowing her pride to confide in me, and I could not help but admire her.

"I do understand, Taryn, and I commend you for being so brave. You are fortunate to have such a good brother to help with your son, under the circumstances."

She made a small grimace, the first detectable sign of discomfort. "I . . . I went away to have Jon, to a distant relation who lives on the moor. She helped me, and fabricated an excuse for needing my care and help during those months. It was only when she died suddenly that I knew I would have to face my own fate, and take Jon home with me. Father had died by that time, and Hadrian could do no less than to accept the situation, such as it was."

Again, I was at a loss for words and feeling mixed emotions. Then, I said, "Will you not let Trevor know he has a son? He might have changed his plans," I lied, for I knew he would never do such a thing. It disturbed me that Taryn was telling me all this, and I wondered what her reasons were. Perhaps she only needed a friend to confide in.

"Naturally, I should like to have Jon know about his father. And Mullins is his right, too, even if he was born on the wrong side of the blanket. So were Roc and Kate. Perhaps Lucretia won't have a child—a son, that is. Then Jon would be here," Taryn answered.

I saw her point. "But if you keep all this from Trevor now, bringing it forward in the future would surely do far more harm than allowing it to be known now. Trevor might not accept the truth, if you allow him to believe Roc was responsible." I remembered with a touch of bitterness and fear what Trevor would do to any woman he considered his possession, should he learn some other man found her attractive.

Her smile was sardonic. "Yes. I've thought of that too, but I have not yet found the courage to speak up. To tell him the truth—seven years late—" she sighed heavily. "Jon could easily have been Roc's, you see," she told me, her eyes on my face, and I was thankful she could not know how my heart quivered. "He was always . . . after me. And Trevor, in those days, was quite jealous of Roc's attentions." She looked sadly alone, remembering, I suppose, the wayward feelings of the heart when love was promising, and I averted my eyes, for I didn't want to see her hurt or allow her to see how much her words were affecting me.

I could envision this beautiful woman and those handsome men. That Trevor had seduced Taryn, and then refused to marry her, seemed unjust. I couldn't help but wonder if, when he looked at Jon, he had ever guessed just who the father was. He must have been curious, knowing by his age that Jon could be his son. Would he not have shown some emotion, even if he assumed the child might be Roc's?

It occurred to me then and there that something far more deeply disturbing and passionate lay hidden under this woman's countenance than she was revealing to me.

"I wanted to talk with you, Roma, to explain. I think we are friends, and I thought perhaps you even might help me to decide whether or not to tell Trevor about Jon. Sometimes, a friend can be worthy to know *all* in one's life. Will you be that friend?" She appealed to me, and I was moved by her voice and the need I heard there. Yet she seemed uneasy, and I rushed to assure her of my willingness to be her friend.

"Of course," I said. "I'm glad you felt you could trust me as a friend."

"I did so want you to understand. I was certain I could confide in you," she said slowly. "You are not disturbed by what I have told you?" She seemed uncertain, her eyes wide and searching.

"Of course I am not disturbed. You must not worry." I thought of Lucretia, and apparently, this was on her mind too, for she said, "Your cousin may resent me—Jon. She is quite frail, I can tell, and she does seem to depend on you for strength. I hope we can be friends, for all our sakes."

I laughed as lightly as I could. "You must not ever worry about Lucretia. She would never harbor resentment, no matter what anyone did."

"Then, Trevor is very fortunate—lucky in both aspects, wouldn't you say?"

"What aspects?" I asked.

"That he is to marry a woman of means, as well as one of such virtues. She will make him the perfect wife."

I thought of Lu's predicament, but I didn't feel I could tell Taryn. So I said instead, "Have you been told about the changes in the wedding plans and the ball, Taryn? Trevor wants them hurried up a bit."

For a moment, she looked as if she hadn't heard me, but then she said, "Oh, but yes. Mrs. Pascal was telling me about it when I came in. Well, what is the rush? Does Trevor think the bride may change her mind?" she asked, amused, and I smiled too, but said nothing.

She made a move toward the door, and I fell in step with her. "I must be getting back. Mannie will worry. I understand that Trevor has gone to Plymouth to fetch one of the guests?" she asked, and I told her it was true, but that he should be back early enough. She said goodbye and left me at the foot of the grand staircase, promising to see me in the evening. "I know I can trust you to say nothing of this to anyone, Roma. We shall discuss it again, if I may be free to do so. Until then, let it be our secret."

"Of course," I said. As I ascended the stairs, I thought that if Trevor were indeed told of the child's parentage, he just might not claim Jon as his son. He could easily deny it.

I thought now of the resemblance between Jon and Trevor, although I hadn't even suspected it before. Surely as time went on, Trevor would notice it?

My own feelings now toward Trevor were at ragged ends. How I, too, needed a friend to confide in, to tell of the ordeal I had been through, but knew I could never dare to do so.

I was in this frame of mind when I reached my rooms, and found Pansy had laid out the gown I was to wear this evening. She was not there, so I took this time to try to sort out my thoughts.

It was of no use, however, and I decided I would go along to Lu's rooms to see if she would see me. But neither Lu nor her maid was there, and this puzzled me. Still, I thought, if Lu had felt strong enough to leave her rooms with her maid, she must be feeling much better and by evening she should be fine.

I returned to my own rooms, and rang for Pansy.

It was quite late when I finally dressed for the evening. I came out of my warm scented bath, feeling somewhat relaxed in spite of my heavy spirits.

Pansy's face was flushed as she said, "Mister Trevor he do be back, Miss, and 'im do be askin' that 'ee come straight down to the Bower, he do." She seemed overly nervous, and several times I caught her glancing around furtively, jumping at the least little sound.

"Very well, Pansy," I said, uneasily. "Mister Trevor and his guest have only just arrived, have they? I thought I heard a carriage some time ago." I slipped into the dressing room and sat down at the small table to have my hair brushed and arranged into a crown of curls, before I dressed in the gown laid out over the small settee. Certainly, I was not going to rush.

"Oh yes, Miss, they'm have. But I reckun' that 'ee heard the musicians come in earlier, that would be they 'ee heard. Them be down in the servants' wing havin' refreshment and the like."

She began to brush my hair, but she still seemed nervous.

"I suppose Miss Lucretia is getting dressed too," I said glibly. "She and Tulip were not in her rooms earlier. Do you know if they had gone out for a walk, Pansy? I have not seen my cousin all day, and I suppose Tulip has been with her." I smiled in the mirror, inwardly envisioning Lu with her maid. It was no secret in the house just how Tulip adored her mistress by now.

But Pansy's hands fumbled, dropping the brush on the floor, and after she'd picked it up, her face seemed blotchy and strained. Poor Pansy! I said, "Pansy, you are upset over something. You are as nervous as a cat. What is it, pray tell?"

She swallowed hard, and stared at me in the mirror, her hands trembling violently.

"Oh Miss. Them two went out quite early, they did, and none of us know just where they did get off to. But . . ." she stopped, biting her trembling lip.

"But what, Pansy?" I frowned at her. "Surely it doesn't matter if they went somewhere," I said, thinking of the secret rendezvous my cousin and her lover would now make and keep, "just as long as they are back in time for the dinner party. They are back, aren't they, Pansy?"

She shook, groping for support on the back of the chair I sat in, and I turned around to stare at her.

"No, Miss. Them did not come back, not as yet, 'ee see, and that do worry me, for 'tisn't like them, now, is it?"

I was silent, staring at this frightened maid; yes, she was frightened, but why should she be? "Do you know in which direction they went, or if they took a conveyence—a carriage?" I asked softly.

She shook her head. "I didn't see them go, Miss, no. It

do seem strange, it do, for none of us did, that be for sure."

I waited for this to sink in. Well, it wasn't all that late, I told myself, and Lucretia did have Tulip with her, wherever they went. I was certain it was to meet Hadrian Wilkes somewhere, and that he would make certain Lu was here on time. No harm could come to her, not with Hadrian or Tulip looking after her. Of this I was positive.

So I said, "Well, Pansy, I can't see why we are worrying, can you? They will come back, for my cousin would never miss her preparations for this dinner party." I tried to be cheerful, positive, and turned back toward the mirror. "Finish my hair, Pansy, and help me into my gown. It does look beautiful, don't you think?" I made a gesture to the sheer finery, pleased myself, and knew its simplicity and long flowing lines would do much to restore my confidence.

I had given Pansy a couple of gowns I'd discarded, and had told her she could make them into a costume for the night of the masquerade ball, and if she wanted Tulip to have one, I shouldn't mind. The servants were to have their ball too that same night, as was the custom, for all the guests brought their maids and grooms, and this would add extra gaiety to a great manor such as Mullins.

Pansy and her sister were terribly excited over this ball, as it would be their first since coming to the manor to work. And now I began to talk of the party because I thought it might take her mind off Lucretia and Tulip for the moment, and I said, "I'm sure you won't want to miss seeing all the guests arrive tonight, Pansy. It will look almost as grand as the ball next week. Smaller occasions sometimes are better than the big affairs, for then one can get a good look at all the fancy clothes. You will watch, won't you?"

She began to help me into my gown. "Oh yes, Miss, I wouldn't want to miss that, no I wouldn't!" She shook her head, and I saw the old spark return to her eyes. "I told Tulip, and her did agree, Miss, that we'un have not seen dinner guests at the house, not as yet, and Tulip and me were waitin' fer this event, we were, 'tis so."

The gown was of the finest Venetian velvet, amber to match my eyes, with a high waist that accentuated my full breast and slender body, with the folds flowing out around my ankles in a gentle swirl. The short puffed sleeves left my arms bare, creamy against the velvet, and I felt satisfaction when I looked in the long oval looking glass in the corner and noticed the swell of my breasts curving up from the low decolletage, my crown of curls lending me a regal look.

My eyes, too, were unusually bright, matching the amber earrings I chose to wear with the amber pendant. These gems were what my mother had left me, and I felt I did them justice with this lovely gown. My color was heightened in spite of my deepening fears. I wanted to rush to Lu's room and find her there, as ready as I was for this dinner party.

It was when I turned to Pansy to thank her, that I remembered to ask if Trevor know that Lucretia had not yet returned home.

She shook her head. "That I wouldn't know, Miss, no. Mister Trevor only asked for 'ee to come down as quickly as 'ee could."

This would upset Trevor, I knew. He would be angry. I had to give Lu time, I thought, and I would have to keep him unaware until she did show up.

"Pansy, I want you to let me know immediately when my cousin arrives, will you? I shall go down to the Bower now and see Mister Trevor, but there is no point in upsetting him. You will inform me, won't you, when they've arrived?"

She agreed. "Oh I do hope them will get here, Miss, I do. No need to tell 'ee my fears, what with all them smuggler ships and old slavers we do be ahearin' are in these parts. . . ."

"Pansy! Stop that at once!" I cried. "You must not think such things. I tell you, they will be here soon. We can count on it, and don't you start worrying until there is something to worry over. Now," I smiled, "you must hurry if you want to watch the guests arrive. And remember what I told you. Let me know when my cousin has come in."

I turned and left her then, and made my way down the spiral staircase, aware that Combes was just lighting all the candles and placing them in their sconces. The old steward's face seemed more flushed than usual, as if he were dismayed by something. But when he saw me, he smiled curiously, as if we shared some amusing secret.

"Good evenin', Miss," he said.

"Good evening, Combes. Is Mister Trevor with his guest in the Bower?"

"Aye, Miss, Mister Trevor do be in the Bower awaitin' 'ee. Said to tell 'ee to go right in, that he did. The gentleman, he be taken to 'im rooms. The journey were quite tirin', I 'spect it were."

"Oh. I see," I said, and wondered how I should face Trevor alone. "Thank you, Combes. I shall go right in now."

He moved over to open the doors for me, and bowed slightly as I entered the Bower, then closed the doors behind me. Trevor was standing beside the window, his hands in his pockets as he stared out into the garden. I saw that he had changed into his dinner clothes, and when he turned to face me, his eyes were light and smiling. He hurried over to me, took both my hands in his and let his eyes rove over me slowly and possessively. My color heightened beneath his look.

"You are beautiful, my darling," he said.

I met his eyes, and saw the possessiveness there. "Roma, my sweetest. I have much to tell you. Come. You must sit down and prepare yourself for the news I have." He led me to a chair near the fireside, but I did not sit down. I watched as he went over to the table where a small tray with a crystal flask and goblets was placed, and he poured brandy in both goblets, then raised his eyes to me.

He seemed like a man possessed. An uneasy feeling began to take hold of me as I studied him; the dark blue velvet coat he wore looked well on him, with the cravat neatly tied, but something in his expression frightened me.

He came over to me slowly, deliberately, and when he stood close to me, he handed me the goblet. He had a strange, almost devilish look about him, and my heart dipped in fear.

"Roma, our course in life has a new direction, and all because of your pretty little cousin," he announced, smiling. I had to hold onto the goblet tightly to keep from shaking.

"What . . . what are you saying, Trevor?"

"Just this, my sweet. Your little cousin has run off with Hadrian Wilkes, and has left her fortune to you, my darling Roma. Now there is no one to stand in the way of our happiness."

My heart was pounding, but before I could say anything, he said, "I know this is stunning. I know just how you feel, my love, but thank God it has happened, and I will tell you without further delay just how it came about." He lifted his glass to his lips, his eyes on my face.

"But, how can you know this?" I managed to ask.

"My dear Roma, it came as an astonishment to me also. Lucretia left me a note, as well as a note for Sir George, leaving the entire estate to you. Her instructions were quite clear. She, this day, has eloped with Hadrian and—" He stopped, smiled and pulled a letter from the pocket of his coat. "It should be a shock that she would choose a penni-less doctor, but for her to be so generous to me, and to you, my sweet, by giving us the fortune, stunned both Sir George and myself. Read it for yourself. I see the disbelief in your face." He laughed loudly then. I sat down on the chair, trembling.

I took the letter with a sense of detachment. It was brief, but it was her handwriting and I had to believe it. I looked up from it and said, my voice almost a croak, "But why . . . why should she do this? Leave me her wealth?"

And what of tonight, and the guests who would be arriv-ing? I thought numbly. How would Trevor explain all this?

He took the letter from me and replaced it in his pocket, then took my hands and pulled me to my feet, so that I faced him. He kissed my hands, both of them.

"Sweetheart, I shall tell you what you are thinking. To-night we shall tell our guests that you and I are to be mar-ried. And, to answer your question of why your little cousin was so generous—why, my darling, she knew that you could not be my bride without her money, and timid little Lucretia wanted a soft way out for herself. Can any-thing be more to our benefit, my love?" He pulled me to him, bringing his arms about me, and kissed me on the mouth, then stepped back, and laughed.

"You are truly shocked, aren't you? But Sir George is here to make all this legal and right for us, which we shall do in the morning. I must admit, it shocked Sir George, but he can have nothing else to say, since she did write him full instructions as to her wishes. It's like a rich plum fall-ing into our laps, wouldn't you agree, my sweet?"

I was shocked. "But why didn't she leave *me* a note— some word of this?" I moved away from him, annoyed and still in the fog of confusion. "It's not like Lu to do such a thing, without letting me know—"

"Roma. She didn't want you to guess her secret feelings. That's my surmise why she didn't. Perhaps there's a letter on the way for you somewhere, but what is more important now is the fact that you will be my wife, and she made it all possible. We must make the most of it, you and I." His eyes reflected his feelings, and his touch was too possessive on my hands. I pulled them free, and was silent as he went back to the table and refilled his goblet with brandy. I hadn't touched my glass.

All this was what I had longed for, I realized in that moment; I now could be free to marry Trevor, to be the mistress of this lovely old manor, and to have my stolen inheritance restored to me. It was beyond all expectations. Lucretia had been more considerate than was necessary, I thought, and I realized I was reluctant to accept it all, simply because I couldn't believe it.

"I find it too incredible that Lucretia would simply write off her fortune like this, without first a word to me, or even a note. I . . . knew she and Hadrian. . . ." I began, but stopped, when I saw the look pass over Trevor's face.

He lifted his glass of brandy and took a long swallow, then came back to where I stood. "Well, whatever you knew about those two, you can be sure of one thing now, my dear, and that is they won't stand in the way of our plans for the wedding and our future. Sir George confirms this by saying everything is legal enough and that you will receive the full inheritance. And they can't claim anything afterwards. Let's not waste our thoughts on a generous but foolish child. Let's you and I think of our own good fortune. Come here, Roma." He held his arms wide open, but I backed away, angry, puzzled.

"But I can't let her do that, Trevor! I won't. When everything seemed to turn against me, it was Lu who gave me a home, and an allowance. I will not let her give it all back to me. She will need some support—"

He placed his goblet down and took my arm. "Of course. I know how you must feel, Roma. You're simply stunned to find you have inherited your own fortune again. But don't do anything so foolish, not right now. I'm here to see that you use good, clear thinking. Give Lucretia time, and she will no doubt get in touch with you, but I wouldn't count on that for some time. Do you know, I am so relieved that now I feel Lucretia was just a burden I was forced to carry. Does that make you feel better, my love?"

I was not relieved; my conscience would not allow me

relief. "I simply cannot understand why she would go without telling me. And, where would they go to?"

"At this moment, I'm not the least interested in Hadrian Wilkes or his new-found love. Only us. Come here, my sweet."

I didn't move, but he gathered me into his arms, pulled me to him and held me tightly. "I love you, and I can't and won't live without you." He drew back his head in order to see my face. "Well, darling? Don't you have an answer?"

I couldn't trust myself to answer, and when I didn't, he stepped back and, staring at me, he took a ring from his pocket and placed it on my finger. It was a large garnet, in a circlet of diamonds.

"There. This makes you mine, Roma. For all the world to see. Oh, Roma. You are my great need. I will be a possessive husband, jealous of your every moment." His hands stroked my throat, and at his touch, I cringed inside and moved out of his embrace, forgetting the ring in the frustration I felt.

"I must find Lucretia, Trevor," I said uneasily. I didn't like his possessiveness. "I must discuss . . . all this," I gestured with my right hand, feeling the weight of the unfamiliar garnet I had not acknowledged, "with Lu. And before I see Sir George. I am certainly surprised that Sir George consented to help restore my inheritance. He is so unbending in his attitude towards me, I know!" I couldn't hide the bitterness I felt, and I turned my back on Trevor and walked over to the window, my eyes on the dark red sunset but my mind a thousand miles away.

I felt Trevor's hands on my shoulders, and he turned me around and tilted my chin. "The devil with all else, except us, Roma. Face it. Sir George did come around, and I'm afraid you'll just have to accept the fact that Lucretia and Hadrian Wilkes are gone, for a while anyway. We can't wait for them. We have our dinner guests arriving within a few hours, and we shall indeed announce to them our intention to be wed. You will make a most lovely bride, the loveliest bride Mullins has ever had. What can be better than this, Roma? Of course you will see Sir George, and we shall get all the snares and entanglements cleared in time for the wedding. I shall see to it personally."

The door opened, and it was Combes who came in with Taryn after him.

"I thought you might be in here, so I asked Combes and

he confirmed it himself, and let me in. I trust I'm not intruding on anything?" Her voice, as well as her eyes, was full of that rich amusement she always showed. Her gown was a deep plum shade of rich heavy silk, adorned simply with a small turquoise brooch pinned at the firm swell of her breasts.

Trevor took a deep breath, then as Taryn's eyes moved from me to him, he spoke. "No. You're not intruding, Taryn. But we've some news to share with you, haven't we, Roma? Do come and join us in a glass of brandy."

She lifted her eyebrows, and gave a soft husky laugh. "And just what great news do you have to share with me? And," she glanced around the room, then at my gown, and at the old steward who kept busily stoking the fire, "where is the bride-to-be at this hour? I would have thought she would be here. But, in fact, I am quite put out with my own brother for abandoning me. I finally bribed Mannie to keep Jon tonight, and hurried over in the trap, simply because Hadrian is tardy. Have you any knowledge of where my errant brother might be? I thought of stopping in at Barton Farms to see if he could still be with Arnie, but I thought better of it, and decided I might be needed here."

Trevor went to the table and filled another glass, brought it to Taryn, and then he said, "I can assure you that Hadrian is not at Barton Farms with his so-called patient Arnie Polden, Taryn. And what I do have to tell you may come as a complete shock, but one we'll all have to accept."

Her eyes sparkled with unfeigned delight. "You make it sound sinister," she laughed. "But I am all ears and can't wait. What is this shocking news?"

Uneasily, I waited too; I had believed from the beginning that Taryn had somehow suspected I, not Lucretia, was the woman Trevor loved, and that he was only using Lu for the wealth she would bring him. Even as she'd confided in me earlier her secret of Jon's paternity, I was certain she had suspected I was closer to Trevor than Lu was. But I could see she had not suspected the situation between her own brother and my cousin.

"Your brother and my former bride-to-be ran away together sometime today, Taryn," Trevor said bluntly. "They have eloped."

Surprise, not shock, registered on her face. "You've got

to be joking, Trevor. Surely, you wouldn't be here drinking to the occasion if Hadrian had carried off your bride?"

Trevor shook his head. "I'm not joking. They eloped, it's true."

She glanced at me anxiously. "Hadrian and Lucretia? How on earth did they have the nerve?"

Trevor laughed darkly. "It's beyond all of us, but the important thing is we have a dinner party on hand with guests arriving, and we can't disappoint them. I shall introduce my new bride-to-be, the woman I love, Taryn. Roma has just consented to be mine, so it does work out for the best, after all. Let us drink to this moment."

Taryn's face blanched with the shock she was now experiencing; her eyes darkened as though they had dilated and couldn't see properly, and for one dreadful moment, I thought she was going to faint.

She looked at me, and under her gaze I felt as if I had betrayed her. She had confided in me all her shame of having a child out of wedlock by this man, how she'd hoped to marry him, and had not been courageous enough to confront him with his son. And now this.

Words seemed to fail her. She put her hand to her throat and swallowed deliberately. Tense and distressed, she stood, watching me as if I were a complete stranger. That her brother had gone off with Lucretia without a word had not bothered her, and she had taken it in stride; but this news seemed to shake her deeply.

Trevor said, "We must rejoice in this elopement of your brother and Lucretia, Taryn. Roma will marry me, as I truly always wanted her to." He smiled at me, but I averted my gaze, knowing a certain resentment at the mockery of his manner toward Hadrian and Lu.

Taryn stared at Trevor. "But I . . . believed you. . . ." She stopped, ran her tongue lightly over her lips as if they had gone dry, then she seemed to compose herself and her thoughts, her voice taking on the old amused tone.

"And now that the . . . heiress has run off with my brother, what are your plans for that lost fortune, or am I being too ridiculous in asking such a question? I can't imagine Hadrian doing anything so rash, but you, Trevor?" She lifted her silky brows, and I saw beneath that mask of amusement. How that must have cost her, I thought. "Have you decided your shipping business will pay well enough?"

His laugh was hard, mirthless. "The inheritance belonged to Roma in the first place. It was all hers by rights, you see, Taryn, but Lucretia's father stripped Roma of it when she was a child, and then gave it to his own daughter not more than a year ago. She could do no less than to give it back to her, since she so desired your brother."

"I see." Taryn looked at both of us, and her eyes found the ring on my finger. "Then, you two must have known each other before—" She didn't finish, as she saw Trevor move closer to me, placing his arm around my waist. I saw what could only be suspicion in her expression.

Trevor nodded. "Of course we knew each other before I knew Lucretia. And thank God for that! But, come. Let us drink to this occasion." And he lifted his goblet.

As Taryn sipped her drink, she eyed us both speculatively. "How on earth did you learn of Hadrian and Lucretia? And how could she have wanted to part with a fortune left to her? I don't understand. Hadrian didn't leave me a note. It's not like him." I thought there was a bitter note in her voice, almost as if she were accusing Trevor. "Did you receive a message from him, by any chance?"

He took a long swallow of his drink. "No. Hadrian didn't leave a message. Sir George Thorpe, her solicitor, and I received word from Lucretia at Liskard, on our way back from Plymouth." He shrugged. "I suppose she felt somehow obligated to both Roma and myself. Who knows? But whatever she did it for, I know one thing for certain, and that is she gave me the right to marry the woman I love, and who loves me. I could have asked for no better arrangement than this."

Taryn, her face pale, watched me with wide-open, startled eyes. Never had I felt so guilty. I knew of her secret, and I couldn't help but think that she must have been harboring some hope that she herself might yet become Trevor's wife.

It all seemed wrong somehow, like a dream out of control, and in my heart there was a throbbing of fear. I could not rid myself of this uncanny sense of disaster lurking around me as I considered the evening I had to face.

"Roma," Taryn said huskily. "Did you know of this clandestine romance between my brother and your cousin? I certainly didn't know Hadrian was infatuated, not in the least. It seems unlike him in every way to go off like that, leaving his life of caring for the sick, especially with no one else to look after his patients properly." A slight frown creased her forehead.

I hesitated; I felt at once I was under some smothering scrutiny, as if I would be made to take the blame if I admitted that I had known of the situation between Hadrian and Lucretia. I resented this. According to both Taryn and Trevor, this knowledge would seem treason to them.

She was giving me a strange look, but I met her gaze steadily, and said, "I could have no idea, especially since Lu did not leave me a note either. I believe it is out of character for Lu, as well as you say it is for your brother, Taryn."

Trevor's voice was rough with impatience. "Then, I suggest that both of you did not know those two as well as you thought. The facts are in front of us," he barked, bringing out the note in Lu's own hand, and shoving it into Taryn's hands. "This is the proof, and by God, I accept it as Sir George does. It frees me to marry Roma now."

Taryn studied the note, then lifted her eyes to meet Trevor's as she handed him the note. A smouldering emotion, long buried, seemed to come to the surface for one split second, and I thought she was going to break down and burst into tears. However, she did not do so, but lifted her chin with what I believed was a cross between defiance and acceptance, and this puzzled me, even though I was relieved.

"Well. You are now the heiress, and the next mistress of Mullins, Roma. I congratulate you both." She lifted her goblet to her mouth, her eyes wide and light with speculation. "Have you informed the servants of this slight change of . . . brides? I gather from the look of things," she gestured with her hand around us, "that you've just been told about it yourself, Roma?"

It was only then that I became aware of Combes. He hadn't left the room, but was standing near enough to us to have overheard everything we had said. It didn't seem to bother Trevor.

"Not yet, no, for as you guessed, there's been little time, but of course they will have to be told. I'm sure they will have no objection." He looked down into her face, with mockery in his manner.

She smiled, defying him. "No. I dare say the servants here will have no objections. They are loyal. By the way, Trevor, as I was driving the trap over, I caught a glimpse of a strange ship in the estuary, heading toward Mullins. Is it one of your vessels?"

Trevor gave me a swift look, obviously irritated that she had dared confront him with it. "Well, it could be one of my vessels. One was in Fowey three days ago." He frowned down into his goblet. "Which does remind me that I must tell Mrs. Pascal to lay four new places, as new guests will be here." He looked at me. "Shall we make our announcement together, Roma? Let's go to the kitchens and see just how loyal they are. Come with us, Taryn. Combes will lead the way."

I was reluctant to tell these servants I was to be Trevor's wife instead of my cousin Lu; I felt they had already accepted her, and that I would certainly be under suspicion, as well as scrutiny. But most of all in this moment, I felt an unreasonable apprehension tear through me, and I could do nothing about it. I seemed to be carried away along this quicksilver tide of happenings, unable to do anything to change its course, as we made our way into the servants' quarters.

Trevor proudly announced our arrival. Mrs. Pascal hurried up to us, to see if all the preparations were satisfactory; Cook was pink, and I thought jolly on first glance, but it took only a few minutes to realize everyone was as tense and restless as I'd felt them to be earlier in the day, and it added to my apprehensions.

Trevor told them of the change of plans. It came as a shock, and for one silent moment, no one dared breathe. It was only when Trevor told Mrs. Pascal that there would be four additional guests at the dinner table that the housekeeper seemed to throw off her shock and become herself. She eyed me with keen, all-knowing eyes.

"It do come as a . . . shock, Miss, it do, if 'ee'll pardon me fer sayin' so." She bent her head in a most discreet manner to both Trevor and myself. "Fancy little Miss Lucretia going off like that, and with Doctor Hadrian! Why, Miss Taryn, 'ee too, must be shocked, that 'ee brother runs off with the prospective bride? I do say, what a shock 'tis!"

Taryn laughed, her old self again. "Well, it is true, isn't it, Mrs. Pascal? The Wilkes are infamous for eloping with the women-folk of Mullins."

There was a shocked silence after this reminder, and the housekeeper blinked, surprise in her face. "Why, so 'ee do be right, Miss Taryn. That were true, weren't it?" She glanced back at Cook and the maids lined up, their expressions revealing the superstitious fear that was running among them.

Pansy stared at me. She was taking this very hard, so I went over to her and took her aside. "Did you have any inkling from Tulip, Pansy?" I questioned her in a low voice.

"No, Miss, I didn't!" She seemed to choke over her emotions. "It do be all so strange, Miss, it do. Nary a word did me sister say, she did not." And I guessed then that Pansy would somehow tie this to that past tragedy of Kate St. Coryn and Phillip Wilkes. "It do be queer, it do, for it weren't like Tulip, no it were not! What will our mother and father say to this?" Her eyes were round as saucers, fear shining in them.

But Trevor laughed out, trying to dispel any reason for superstition. "I say that there's no reason to link that past elopement to what's happened here today. Apparently these two people are very good at escaping and carrying out what they wish. Pansy," he said he walked over to stand beside me, "your sister must have gone along with them, for Miss Lucretia would not have gone without her, I judge. But in any case, they will have to come back one day, as Doctor Wilkes does have a practice, as well as a house and land. Let's leave it at that, and get on with the celebrations. Combes?" He turned around to where the old steward stood fidgeting with the wine goblets he'd brought in, and now Combes looked up, his face rather pale. There was something of strain in his eyes.

"Combes, will you fill up these glasses? We shall have a toast, but first have Jeffers and his wife in, will you? We shall be in the Bower. Mrs. Pascal, do gather all the housemaids and servants, including Miss Phoebe and old Norie, in the Bower, in five mintues' time?" He was generous with his smiles. "We shall toast the future mistress of Mullins."

"Very well, Mister Trevor," she said, but I felt she was very perplexed at Trevor's apparent joy, which was something she couldn't quite make out. "Did 'ee say there were to be four new guests? Will them be all gentlemen, or—" Her question seemed to take Trevor by surprise.

"They will be gentlemen, Mrs. Pascal. They aren't the regular sort of dinner guests, but I could not see any alternative but to invite them to this affair. And do send a word up to Sir George. I'm sure he may want to rest before the evening begins, but he may want to join us for this small celebration drink."

Sir George. I did not care to see him. No. To see Sir George, and his unmoving, cold eyes, would serve only to stir up all the venomous thoughts I'd stored up inside for him and my Uncle Doyle. I would delay seeing him as long as I could.

I said, "Please don't bother Sir George, Mrs. Pascal. Knowing him as I do, I should think he would refuse anyway. I would prefer to allow him all the rest he can get, after such a long and tiring day of travel."

There was a restless silence but, after a moment, Trevor agreed, and we left the kitchen and went to the Bower, where Miss Phoebe and her maid Norie had already arrived. Miss Phoebe, dressed in her finest silk of pale lavender, looked as if she had just stepped out of one of her own tapestry scenes from her gallery. Her eyes were far more alert than they had been previously, and I noticed she was watching Trevor and myself with that keen look she sometimes had, as if she were scheming a plan to place us both in one of her scenes. If she missed my cousin, she didn't say so, although I caught her gazing around the room as if she were searching for Lucretia.

It was Taryn who told Miss Phoebe that I was to be Trevor's bride; and it was she who took upon herself the task of explaining that her brother had run off with Miss Lucretia. As she did so, I found myself thinking, "Why, she is enjoying this! She is making it sound like what happened to her brother Phillip and Kate St. Coryn. And the old lady is devouring it with the fascination of one delighting in gossip!" Old Norie stood back, her face in shadow, but I saw how ashen it became as Taryn related all the events which had taken place this day.

Norie had crept out, I noticed later when all the servants had come into the Bower, with a whispered word to Combes as she went, and his face seemed to pale to that same ashen shade, and he became nervously impatient.

Trevor had listened as Taryn explained the situation to Miss Phoebe, and he was amused, saying to me in a low voice, "This will put the old woman into a more confused world, Roma. I sometimes think that after we are married, I shall lock her up somewhere, although so far she has not been harmful in any way. It's just that she—" He stopped, seeing my expression.

"I cannot think you would do such a horrible thing to Miss Phoebe, Trevor! She is keen, and far more so than you give her credit for! To lock her up would be a sure death sentence, and cruel beyond imagination. How can you even suggest such an awful thing?" My eyes were blazing at him, and I could barely keep from making a scene.

Carefully changing the subject, I asked Trevor, "Who did you say the four extra guests you invited are? They seemed to upset Mrs. Pascal's careful dinner arrangements, although I'm certain there is plenty of food. Who are they?"

He took my hand in his, turning it over and then kissing the palm, taking advantage of this opportunity to make amends. "They are from the ship, *The Black Tusk*. Two men are but passengers, to be sure, but very important ones, as they are going out to the Americas to start a trade enterprise. I should like it very much, sweetheart, if you would be your very nicest to them, and to the Captain and his man tonight. It will mean much to them if they can know that in the future, they will have an open invitation from the mistress of Mullins. Indeed, I am very proud of you, and I want you to be exceptionally beautiful and welcoming. Can you do this for me, my sweet?"

Fear froze my whole being. I recalled what Hadrian had told me that day in Fowey when he'd pointed out that ship in the harbor, and also the taunting words of Roc St. Coryn that same day. Dear God in heaven, I thought, as I stared at Trevor. What ghastly nerve he had to bring those men here to Mullins.

"You can't be serious!" I was hardly aware that I spoke, but the words seemed to echo in my ears and I knew it was I who had uttered them. Then, no matter how chilled I was by fear, I knew I had to learn the truth. "What are you planning?" I vaguely remembered how he'd evaded Taryn's inquiry earlier about the ship in the river, but now he'd actually admitted it was present, and that the Captain was coming to dine with us and our guests.

"Oh, but I am very serious!" he laughed, pressing my now moist hand tightly. His head was close to mine as he pulled me aside to speak confidentially. "It's all working out so much better than I'd hoped. My plan is to have you introduced to these men, for it is best to start our married life with the understanding that you will be my helpmate in my business, my darling Roma. We shall rid the manor of traitors, weed them out, and build an empire that will stretch clear to the Americas, and we shall be rich beyond our imagination!"

Thus in a span of scarcely five minutes, I learned the truth I had been deliberately refusing to face ever since I'd come to Cornwall. So much had happened to me since the hour I'd set foot in Mullins. I now understood that all along, Trevor had been following a devious plan to build an empire with his wife's fortune, and that he cared about little else aside from money.

I felt myself go pale with horror, as if my blood had turned to ice. I could not answer him. I looked around at the servants by the door and, somehow, I sensed their nervous glances and I was conscious of how Miss Phoebe kept nodding her head, her eyes brighter, her mouth smiling, her gold-filled teeth showing as she watched Taryn and Trevor and me throughout this most impromptu celebration.

If anyone else was aware of old Norie's hasty exit they gave no sign, but I was aware of it, and it occurred to me she had set out to warn someone. Who would she warn, I thought, biting my lips until they hurt, but Roc St. Coryn. How on earth would he figure in this night? Had he not warned me of what he would do to prevent that slave ship from coming up the river to Mullins? Hadn't he been furiously outraged by Trevor's plan to enslave good Cornishmen like Arnie Polden and Cal Pascal? And suddenly, I could not stop myself from thinking of Hadrian.

Hadrian Wilkes. A doctor, and one who'd aided and befriended Arnie Polden. Had he not suspected Trevor's motives for having that ship in Fowey Harbor? Hadn't he, too, feared for all the good Cornishmen who'd needed badly to earn some extra money in these hard times?

Fear flashed through me like a flaming dagger. No, I reasoned, as I turned to stare up at Trevor's profile, his face flushed with proud achievement. To the astonishment of all, he began handing out gold sovereigns to each and every one of the servants.

"For your loyalty in serving me at Mullins," he said, smiling down into the startled faces of the maids as well as Jeffers and Combes and old Soady, who had come in with the men.

In the distance, the muffled sound of approaching car-
riages and horses came to me, and it was the cue for us to
prepare for the first jangle of the bell that would signal the
arrival of the guests.

CHAPTER EIGHT

For the first time in years, Mullins was having a banquet in
the Great Hall. The candles shone down upon the guests—
Cornishmen and their ladies, dressed in their finest silks
and velvets and sitting at the long table. The table itself
looked splendid, set with silver, rose-bordered china, and
large bowls piled high with fruit.

At one end sat Trevor, a little overconfident, I thought,
laughing a shade too loud and too long at every jest that
was made. I sat facing him at the other end, trying hard to
act as unperturbed as Trevor, but toying with the dishes set
before me, conscious of all the eyes upon me. I knew that
each guest here was viewing me rather suspiciously, because each had learned of the highly unusual change in
Trevor's wedding plans.

They were long-standing friends and neighbors of the St.
Coryn family, except for the four new arrivals Trevor had
invited at the last minute. I suspected many of these people
had been at Mullins on that memorable and tragic night
when another ball was given, and had witnessed the drama
that resulted in the death of Edward, his daughter Kate,
and her lover Phillip. Possibly they had known, too, of the
hatred that stood between Roc St. Coryn and Trevor, but if
they did remember, not one of them saw reason to ac-
knowledge it.

Taryn sat on Trevor's left, and she chatted happily with
the man next to her and with other ladies she seemed to
know quite well. On my left and right were the two men
from London, Mister Rockingham and Mister Jenkins. To
look at them both, no one would suspect that they were
involved in the slave trade, but I knew they were and
abhorred their presence more than anything.

The servants hovered anxiously about the table, a mixture of fear and awe on their faces as they served the elaborate dinner. I could see how their eyes often rested on Cap-

tain Whitney, the man who sat across from Taryn; they were frightened, there was no doubt, and I shared their feelings.

Captain Whitney was a pale, slender man dressed in a fawn-colored coat and matching breeches. His eyes were a curious pale brown, without sparkle, and his face was unlined and free of all emotion. His long, sensitive fingers held the knife and fork, then touched the wine goblet stem as they might explore a man's throat, and I was shocked at my own thoughts as he looked up and met my eyes. I felt cold all over.

I signaled to the maids to fill the goblets once more, and the musicians played their instruments softly from their place on the dais at the far end of the room. The hum and chatter of voices rang in my ears; I glanced at the man on my left, and noticed that he was looking around the room as if to memorize it all.

Through course after course, the men helped themselves liberally, and occasionally wiped their mouths with lace-edged handkerchiefs, coughing awkwardly. Jenkins, on my left, said, "Is it true that St. Coryn's father, old Edward St. Coryn, had a bastard son who stole his ship and sailed it out to the Spanish Main?" He said it so that everyone down at this end of the table could hear.

"Aye, and the most impudent, bloodthirsty youth I'd ever clapped my eyes upon, that was Roc St. Coryn. Just like his father, I can vouch. We've heard since that time that his ship carries a full complement of women on every voyage, and most of them, poor souls, were kidnapped along this coast. Needless to say, if he was a scoundrel as a youth, he would be one today," replied the man nearest Jenkins.

Rockingham laughed. "He must be the curse of the family. I take it he's not been seen around here for quite some time then?" He frowned and sipped his wine.

The man who spoke, one of the genteel farmers whose name escaped me, said stiffly, "Oh, he's been back here. We all know that for sure, but he hides in the creeks. Naturally, one cannot get direct answers from servants," he chuckled, "but they know where he is, and by God if they were my servants, I'd horsewhip them until I got the truth out of them, or see to it they were transported! We have enough of that smuggling around here, and I wouldn't put it past Roc St. Coryn to be the biggest devil in on it. Just like his father, he is, I'm told." He drank down his wine, still shaking his head.

How I detest these people, I thought, and I suspected that most of these men were capable of any of the evil deeds they credited to Roc St. Coryn.

"But tell me, if you can," Rockingham queried, and his glance included me, "is it true that he killed his own father, over some nasty quarrel? Bastard sons are unusually touchy, I know, but I've heard rumors that this one made it look like a suicide, and afterwards took the ship to the Spanish Main."

At that moment, silence fell over the room as a strange man was ushered in and hurried to the side of Captain Whitney. The man whispered in the captain's ear, and Whitney jumped to his feet, speaking to Trevor from the side of his mouth so that I could not hear. Trevor, too, stood up, just as the bell in the front hall jangled loudly and sounded through the Great Hall.

Everyone seemed to freeze until Trevor gave the signal to Combes to open the door. "Now who the devil's that?" Trevor roared in sudden anger. I could see that he was upset by what Captain Whitney had said to him, and as Combes disappeared into the outer hall, I knew that Trevor was completely alert, and as wary as Captain Whitney was next to him. I wondered how the unknown man had come into the house, unless he'd been admitted by one of the servants from the kitchen, but I didn't dwell on this.

Taryn's face paled, and I wondered if she had heard what the Captain had said to Trevor. But everyone at the table seemed restless, and kept their eyes on Trevor as he stood waiting for Combes to return.

"Well, Combes?" His voice was like an explosion in the room. "Who comes to Mullins during this banquet?"

There was no immediate answer, but in the door directly behind the old steward, was the man I feared most. He said, "Roc St. Coryn, at the service of all you gentlemen." He walked into the hall, a pistol in each hand and a smile on his lips. "Don't move, Whitney," he said, "and the rest of you, stay where you are. I have you covered, all of you, and the first one who moves will have a bullet through his head."

Looking up toward the gallery above, I saw Robin with a pistol in his hand, and another man I recognized beside him, while at the door leading toward the servants' wing stood Tamblyn, with Jake Polden pointing a pistol straight at Captain Whitney's throat.

Our eyes met across that long space, Roc's and mine, and it set my heart pounding so fiercely that for one moment I had to turn my face away, knowing it would surely betray me. The fact that he was behind Trevor did little to stem the panic rising within me, for Trevor's eyes were now on my face too.

"I pray you be seated, gentlemen," Roc said, and I saw Combes close the door behind Roc and stand aside as if he were at attention.

"I will not keep you long. As for the ladies present, I would suggest they be escorted into the Bower, except Miss Roma Kendal. I wish her to remain seated."

There were long gasps, and outraged exclamations of protest, but the arrogant Roc threw back his head and laughed, and it rang through the hall and in my ears.

"Do not be frightened, ladies. My men will not harm you. You all know me well enough to know I shall not rob you of your jewels. It's your men I want, and Miss Roma." There was hatred and fear in the faces of all the men.

Then he came towards me. My heart felt near to bursting as I thought that I was now the woman he'd thought me to be when he'd abducted me: the true heiress Trevor was going to marry!

I shut my eyes, the light of the candles beating against them in swirls of red and gold and violet, and I opened them quickly to find that all the ladies were now standing uncertainly, and that Roc St. Coryn stood in front of me, his strong white teeth flashing in that bronzed face, his eyes dark and dangerous.

His presence in this room created a completely different atmosphere. I was astonished that in so short a time a strange feeling of intimacy had sprung up between us. It was alarming, yet somehow not wholly unpleasant. How could that be? I calmed my nerves and saw things clearly for the first time.

It no longer mattered what this man had done or what he was. The simple truth was that I had fallen in love with Roc St. Coryn.

This was the man I wanted, not Trevor. And the probability that I could not have him made not the slightest difference to the way I felt. I could pretend no longer, not even to myself.

I knew that this man had the power to stir my body and mind to depths I could not yet comprehend, and although I knew he would never feel the same way about me, I knew I could never be the person I was before that night on his ship. That shallow, selfish, embittered socialite Roma Kendal no longer existed. No man was capable, I knew in that moment, of stirring me so deeply or so permanently as Roc St. Coryn. A sense of desolation I could not quite understand came over me as he stood looking down into my guarded eyes.

But he did not speak immediately to me. "Ladies, please leave the hall and go into the Bower. My dear Auntie," he purred as he leaned over and touched Miss Phoebe's withered cheek, "you will forgive a truant nephew, won't you? I shan't be long, and then we shall have a nice long chat."

"Roc! You naughty boy! How like you to come like this, and to a party! You always did do the outrageous, just like Edward." Miss Phoebe's eyes were almost sparkling with pleasure. "You've come home, haven't you? I knew you would."

"Now, Auntie, don't be sentimental. I've business to see to, and we shall talk afterwards. Do try to convince all the ladies that they shan't be robbed."

All of the women left the room but Taryn and myself, and it seemed she felt she should remain. The men sat frozen in their seats at the table. No one spoke a word, but every man watched as Roc stood there smiling down at me.

There were five men against eleven, but the five were armed, and the eleven men had supped and drunk too well, and none were armed, except for Captain Whitney.

When Combes closed the door after him, Robin and his companion came down the staircase from the gallery and took positions at either end of the long hall, watchful, ever alert, so that if a man dared move, he would meet the fate that Roc had promised.

Captain Whitney looked right into the barrel of Jake Polden's pistol, and he passed his tongue over his lips but did not speak. The two men nearest me sat and surveyed the scene with bland bewilderment, as if all this had nothing to do with either of them. Trevor alone was seething with pent-up fury, his face darkened with the tell-tale flush of hatred.

But Roc simply passed his gaze over the company of men and then looked down at me. "I have made this special call on you, my lady, to return a most valuable article belonging to you. I would not allow another night to pass without these being in your possession. You left them that night you came to my ship's cabin."

My face drained of all color. So he meant to humiliate me further, as he had threatened he would do in front of Trevor. But I met his eyes steadily and said, "Then it is a most generous gesture on your part, Captain." He sheathed one pistol and placed his hand inside the red velvet coat he wore so casually, and pulled out the articles I well remembered.

He cocked one eyebrow, and bowed gallantly, then placed my chemise and the pink peignoir into my hands, and my cheeks flamed scarlet, knowing all eyes were accusingly upon me.

"It was my pleasure, of course," he said gravely. "Robin laundered them, and because they were . . . slightly torn, Robin mended them with expert stitches, so that no trace of the torn places can be seen. He placed them in my own personal chest, for my lady to wear when she made another visit. I discovered them but by chance this very day, and have returned them."

There was nothing I could say but what was on my tongue. "Then it was very generous of Robin, Captain, but remiss of him, too."

"I was sure you would see it that way, my lady, but now that they are returned, can we not call a truce? Perhaps you would be generous and pour some wine into a goblet for me while I rob these gentlemen of their wealth."

My delight was the inexplicable delight of a woman in love, in that brief, delirious moment, and I did as he wished, handing him the goblet of wine. I did not care now what Trevor would think. That he was glaring down the table at me in a most savage manner was obvious to one and all, and I marveled that he could restrain himself from attacking this half-brother he hated.

"Thank you, my lady Roma," Roc said, accepting the goblet, and turned from me. "You are aware, aren't you Trevor, that we keep a good cellar here at Mullins? And, of course, my men and I are responsible for this, and Combes keeps a good watch over it. This wine does improve over the years and should not be drunk too soon."

"The Devil take you!" Trevor exploded. "Of all the confounded, brash—"

"Be careful what you say," Roc said, smiling. "Now. I shall relieve these gentlemen of some of their belongings." He bowed, and his eyes turned upon Rockingham to my right.

"Your ring, sir, and I'll have that watch fob," he said, "and empty your pockets into my pouch here, if you please."

The man obeyed, his florid face now purple with indignation. But he did not challenge Roc, and Roc slowly made the circuit of the table, each guest in turn losing the money from his pockets, the rings from his fingers, and any other jewelry he wore.

As he came to Captain Whitney, Roc bowed again. "Good evening, Captain. I salute you on your bold venture up this estuary, but I must warn you of the plight of that black vessel. It will be going up in flames and sunk in the river before daybreak. Your sword, sir, if you please. And what have you in your pockets?"

Even from where I sat, I could see a thick vein standing out in Captain Whitney's forehead, and although he did not show emotion on his face, I could well guess the fury raging within him as his sword clattered to the floor.

But it was Trevor who spoke. "You'll pay for this, God damn you, Roc!"

"Hardly. It is you and your guests who are paying. And so are the crew aboard *The Black Tusk*." He watched Trevor's scowling face, and he smiled in satisfaction. "Those helpless captives will be set free."

"You're a black devil!" Trevor said savagely, and Roc laughed in his face.

"You'll find out just how black I am, as I expose you for what you are. I am here to reclaim the inheritance that you cheated me out of, under all your pretenses of being the 'legal son' of Edward St. Coryn." His eyes were like flames, and I knew he was enjoying this moment he had dreamed of for so long.

There was something evil and frightening about the pure hatred between these two men. I trembled inside, yet I was fascinated at the same time, as was Taryn. She just sat there with a knowing smile curved on her mouth, and I knew a sense of anxiety, my heart in turmoil.

Naturally, I told myself, she had known Roc, and perhaps better than most, and even though I knew Trevor was the father of her child, I wondered in this moment if Roc had loved her in that past.

But this was only a fleeting thought, as Trevor blazed back at Roc in fanatical fury. "You bastard, you! How like you to twist something into what you want and wish were true! But I am the legal son of Edward St. Coryn, and what is more important, the whole of Cornwall knows it, too! There's no way you are going to make any court believe otherwise." As these words tore out of him, I noticed how Roc's eyes moved over Taryn's lovely smiling face, as if he weren't even listening to Trevor.

"Ah, good evening, Taryn. Taryn Wilkes. But, it is not just 'Taryn Wilkes,' is it?" His voice was cool and smooth, but his face betrayed the venom he meant, and her face went white. For a split second she seemed not to know what he was saying, and he continued, "But it's Taryn Wilkes *St. Coryn,* isn't it? Married in civil court seven years ago in Falmouth to this man who calls himself the son of my father, who in reality is the bastard son of his mother and my father's worst enemy, Maximilian Bronson. And now, this man is about to commit bigamy, by marrying Miss Roma Kendal. That makes you an accomplice, does it not, Taryn?"

In the long silence that seemed to stretch into eternity, tension, sudden and sinister, crackled in the room. Taryn shot Roc a venomous glance.

Trevor's face went livid. "You . . . *dare* insult me with these trumped-up lies! I'll kill you for this, Roc, so help me God! You! A no-good bastard of my father, coming into this hall and pouring out these lies—" He stopped, unable to go on, for words failed him. I saw Taryn's face turn toward Trevor, as Roc's laughter rang hard in the hall, his voice cutting through Trevor's protests.

"Then you deny this marriage to Taryn seven years ago, Trevor?" he goaded, and he glanced at Taryn's ashen face. She seemed to hold her breath, staring at Trevor.

"By God, yes! I deny it and more!" Trevor said, half standing now, his hands gripping the edge of the table. But Robin behind him pressed his pistol to the back of his head, and he sat back down reluctantly.

Taryn caught her breath in a gasp audible even where I sat. "Trevor! How can you—"

He turned on her savagely. "Be quiet, Taryn, you fool.

This bastard has made a death warrant for himself, I'll see to that. What's more, there won't be any more threats after this night, by heaven and hell. Who do you think you are, coming to Mullins like this? A wicked pirate, robbing the neighbors as if it were sport. By God, you ought to be horsewhipped!"

Suddenly, I felt a peculiar calm. It was as if I were watching something outside myself. Shock was gone, and in its place I felt only a curiously objective puzzlement that I could look down this table at Trevor and see the face of a stranger. There was suddenly a steel barrier between us.

"Not this night, Trevor," Roc said. "And now, gentlemen, men of Cornwall, I have a bold request of those who did not come off *The Black Tusk*. I need you men to witness the burning of that ship, thus ridding our coast of this pestilence, before they fill her hold once again with unsuspecting prisoners."

One and all stared at him in utter distrust. "It is perhaps a little crude, but under the circumstances very necessary, that I ask that the men who came off that ship remove their breeches and hand them over to my men here. Likewise their stockings and shoes, for I fear if I leave them without taking precautionary measures, they may thwart my plans."

"But you don't understand! This will end in disaster!" Trevor shouted, only to be silenced by two of Roc's men.

"By heaven! This is just too much! Have you not made sport of us enough tonight? Trevor, for God's sake, do something to this fool of a half-brother before all hell turns loose!" Mister Jenkins exploded, looking at the helpless Trevor in disgust.

"He is no half-brother of mine, I am glad to say," Roc said calmly, unperturbed. "But no. I'm afraid I must insist you do as I say. The others," he said, and gestured to the Cornishmen as he did so, "may rise from their seats and leave the room. You must remember my men are posted throughout this house. Make no mistake about what I say. And now, you will please leave. He bowed, confident, and held the door open for the men to file out, anger still on their faces.

When they were gone, Roc turned to me and said, "My lady, perhaps you will be good enough to come with me while these men disrobe? They might not care to undress themselves before you in public."

"No!" Trevor thundered. "Roma, you are staying with me!"

Roc held my chair for me as I stood up. His eyes met those down the table. "The lady is going with me, for she has no choice," he said challengingly. "And Taryn. You may do as you please, but I suggest that you, too, leave the hall."

He turned then, and opened the door for me to pass through. Taryn, after a moment's decision, swept from her place beside Trevor and passed Roc as he looked back over his shoulder and called, "I shall give you five minutes, but no more. Robin, Luke, Jake, Tamblyn—keep a close watch upon these gentlemen. I shall not be long."

He followed me into the entry hall and shut the door. I turned to Taryn.

"Is it true you are married to Trevor?" I felt no qualms asking her this candid question.

For a split second she seemed startled, then she glanced at Roc and lowered her eyes, still very pale. "Yes." She looked up again at Roc, wetting her lips with her tongue. "But how on earth did you learn this, Roc?" Her tone was full of bitterness, I thought. "And . . . when?"

Roc's voice was cold. "Just this past month, Taryn, when I paid my final visit to the magistrate in Falmouth. You were in on Trevor's devious scheme, weren't you?" He grabbed her by the arm, as if he would shake the truth from her, and her eyes widened in fear. Seeing this, he let go of her and stood back, his nostrils flaring with the fury he was now trying to hold in check.

"I'm sorry, Taryn," he said. "I can't forget what he did to Kate."

She stared at him. "What are you talking about? What did Trevor do to her?" Her mouth trembled as her face contorted with jealousy. "She was a flirt, and any man would have succumbed to all of that! Besides, she was eloping with my brother, if you remember." She threw back her head, proud, defying him to recall that tragic night.

"So you were willing to accept blindly what Trevor set up as the truth, Taryn? But, of course, you would have done anything for Trevor, wouldn't you? He married you, and you didn't even realize that you were never really to be his wife, living here as mistress of Mullins as you desired. No. You didn't even guess that he committed bigamy more than once during these seven years, marrying rich little

French girls for their family fortunes and then sending them off into that cavity of human bondage the Spanish Americas are built upon, now did you?" His voice was rough, cold, and deadly.

"But what you did know, Taryn, was that he was using Roma Kendal in this manner, for he fed you his great plan and said it would mean a fortune for you both; her money would go into Mullins, but she would somehow disappear like all the rest, and you would then be mistress here at last. And your son," he said coldly, "would be Trevor's heir. He promised you this, and you went along."

It was terrifying, and it sent my memory reeling back to that night I met Trevor for the first time in Lady Cecilia's house in London. How he'd schemed to get me until he learned which woman was the heiress, and then he'd changed his plans to wed poor little Lu. Oh, dear God in heaven! I nearly swooned as I realized that he'd intended to have Lu placed on that ship, *The Black Tusk*.

The reality of this evil scheme was staggering, but it served to steady my racing pulse and brought me down to earth, as Taryn said sulkily, "Very well, Roc. Yes. What you say is true. But I didn't know, as you yourself said, about those other women. And I was very upset when I learned he was going to marry now. He'd written me all this, you see, and when I met his bride-to-be, Roma's cousin Lucretia, I fell in with the scheme. I knew he didn't love her, for she was so timid! I marvel that she had the courage to run off with my brother. But," she said as she looked up at me with accusing eyes, "what did matter was that Lucretia gave her fortune to Roma, and I understood clearly then that the picture had changed." She looked at me with hatred in her eyes, but I saw sorrow there too.

"You were the woman he loved and wanted all along, and I never guessed it. Oh, yes, I see it all now." She laughed incredulously, as if some insight had opened a closed door for her. "Do you know, I can now actually believe that he was planning to have me abducted and placed in the hold of that slaver?" She shuddered, a long quivering breath escaping her. "He's capable of it."

But Roc was frowning, and I saw at once that he was somehow grasping the truth. It was time to have my pleasure in seeing his face as he learned he'd abducted the wrong woman that night.

I smiled at him, the silence in the entry hall around us

broken by the strokes of midnight echoing from the tower clock in the stables. He was dumbfounded for a fraction of a moment as I said, "It's true. You kidnapped the right women at the wrong time," I challenged. "My cousin, Lucretia Kendal, was too frightened to stay in the Blue Boudoir, so I was moved there. But evidently, when Norie informed Robin, she did not know that the wrong Miss Kendal would be taken."

He laughed in his familiar mocking manner. "Ah, but I did have the right woman. You were his possession, or so he believed, and still does apparently."

My face flamed. "I am no man's possession. No one is going to turn me into a piece of mindless property!"

"But you were a willing, giving, warm woman in my possession," he mocked, "and my revenge struck home. For I can wager that he got the message I intended he know."

That stung as it was meant to, and I was conscious of Taryn's expression.

"So it is true." She looked at us both, the truth hitting her. "You know Roc, and quite well. Of course, you have been hiding in a creek somewhere, and that is why Arnie Polden came to Mullins that night. Of course it's true! He is a member of your crew, and they're all working for you—Cal Pascal, Jake, Tamblyn, all of them. Hadrian was sure of it." She looked at me. "But you knew he was here, didn't you, and you didn't breathe a word of it." She smiled, mockery touching her eyes. "I can guess why. I know the power Roc has over certain women, and Trevor wouldn't stand for that. He is a jealous, possessive man. Possessive especially where it concerns the woman he wants. He could kill you for this, Roc. I know Trevor."

"Just as he killed my sister Kate, Taryn. And my father. Yes, and Phillip too, and he made it all seem like a blunder on my father's part, and then suicide. Yes. For do you know why? It was Kate who had wrung the secret of Trevor's birth out of my father, and she taunted Trevor with it, because he had raped her and said he would make her marry him."

"How can you know all this, Roc? It was you who left here, immediately after the deaths, and you couldn't know that you were Edward's heir?"

"Kate left a letter. Miss Phoebe kept that letter, and in her confusion, she waited for me to come back. It was

through old Norie that she learned where I was, and she
sent the letter to me. Kate was frightened. She wrote that
letter before she was lured out the window of the Blue Boudoir by a note from Phillip saying he'd meet her; he, in
turn, was lured by a note from Kate to meet her there. In
her letter to me she told all. It was I who guessed at Trevor's
cunning, but even now I still am uncertain of just how he
carried it all out that night, murdering all three of them.
But I intend to drag the truth from him, after I attend to
this most pressing matter of that slaver in the estuary."

Stunned, Taryn could barely get the words from her
throat. "It is . . . true then that Trevor is . . . not Edward St. Coryn's son?" Her hand went to her throat, and
then nervously touched the brooch she wore pinned on her
gown.

He nodded. "It is true, Taryn. He is not a St. Coryn,
legitimate or illegitimate. He is the bastard son of Maximilian Bronson, my father's enemy."

Her face was like a death mask. "Then . . . you think
Trevor knew this seven years ago?" Her breath was coming
fast, and I felt sorry for her then.

"I'm sure of it. Kate left it all in the frantic letter she
wrote that night, after the party. You see, Miss Phoebe
found the envelope, and the small note from Phillip was
enclosed. It was not a note of two people planning to elope,
but wanting to discuss something, as I knew Kate liked to
do. And I shall learn the whole truth before this night is
out."

Suddenly, he frowned. "What is this about Hadrian running off with Roma's cousin, Taryn? When did this happen?"

She shrugged. "Today, it seems. Hadrian didn't so much
as leave me a note, and it was Lucretia who left notes for
Trevor and for Sir George Thorpe, her solicitor, and
Roma's, I believe." She studied me questioningly. "Isn't this
so, Roma? It seems she left instructions that gave Roma her
full fortune, making her the heiress Trevor so needed."

She would be bitter, I thought in a rush of compassion,
in spite of the lie she had told me earlier that Trevor did
not know Jon was his own son. I felt I could understand
what she must be suffering now, knowing that her son was
not a St. Coryn, and would never inherit Mullins.

"Taryn," I said, holding out my hand to her, with a
pleading look, "I . . . I don't know what to say—"

"You were in on his schemes too, were you not, from the beginning? You would be his mistress, while your cousin was his wife, and the two of you would have used her fortune to get what you both wanted. I was to be—" She stopped, turning from me, and from Roc, as her humiliation was complete. Her shoulders began to shake, and I would have gone to her had Roc allowed me to, but he took my arm, holding me back.

"He used you, Taryn, as he has always used women, and he would have used Roma, too," he said, "but I stopped it, didn't I, Roma?" His voice was soft, low, and I measured that look as he was measuring mine. How right he was, oh dear God, I thought, how right he was.

Before I could answer, however, the door to the great hall opened and Robin stuck his head out. "Yes?" Roc called over my shoulder. "Have the gentlemen done as I have commanded them?"

"Them has, Cap'n, them has," he answered.

"Very well then. Tell Jake and Tamblyn to tie their hands behind their backs and escort them to a bedroom above. Close the door upon them and turn the key. They will not trouble us, while we attend to our business."

"Aye, Cap'n."

"And Robin?"

"Eh, Cap'n?"

"When you've finished there, come with Tamblyn and Jake and Luke to join us in the Bower." He pointed toward the closed doors. "The musicians are safe in the kitchens?" I remembered seeing those men almost slinking out of the Great Hall earlier, although I had forgotten about them until now.

The little man grinned broadly. "Aye, Cap'n. Safe-and-sound-like, as 'ee would wish," and he gave a form of salute and closed the door.

I stared at Roc, puzzled, as Taryn sobbed with her back to us still. My voice was low as I asked, "What are you going to do?"

He waited a moment before he answered, and he was not smiling any longer. I noticed that his eyes were dark with thought. But he shrugged it off and said, "Let us join my men in the Bower, shall we? There is much to do before this night runs out, and much wrongdoing to be brought to light, I dare say."

As Combes let us into the Bower, the loud jangle of the

bell shattered the room, with shouts from outside. Roc turned to Combes "See who it is, man. Simms," he called to a man standing on guard beside the windows, his gun cocked, "go with him and be careful."

The two men left the room, and I was conscious of the tension as everyone seemed to listen to the impatient ringing of the bell. Then suddenly, a loud voice shouted out. "That ship's on fire! It's blazing like hell and there's people aboard her, screaming like banshees, they are! Hurry, before it's too late!"

"What do you mean, there are people aboard? No prisoners were to have been taken yet—" Roc bellowed, rage and not a little fear in his voice.

It seemed then that reality was forcing this strange nightmarish drama into the open, but even so, there was a terrible fear in my heart that I could not totally explain. It was as if everything was moving too quickly, carrying all of us to some dreadful climax. I felt a hand on my arm and I looked up into the face of Roc St. Coryn.

"Come with me, hurry! Those people must be saved and we've no time to lose." He opened the French doors and we stepped out into the garden. The night was heavy with the pungent scents of autumnal flowers, like Mother Earth herself, and I glanced up into the sky and saw the pale gold crescent of the new moon high above the dark trees, with traces of autumnal mists beginning to trail across it. But there was a shout behind us before we could cross the garden, and Roc turned to see Jake Polden coming after us.

"We got to get out there afore it goes! Cal Pascal and Arnie do be aboard her, they do, and maybe more local folk, so Mister Trevor let me and Tam know!" Even in the dark, I could see the man's face was white with anger and fear, and all the old forebodings I'd experienced now took possession of me.

There was no time to talk, and Roc pulled me forward with him through the garden gate and along the lawn towards the river, where even now the flames were like orange tongues licking up through the shadows between the trees.

Men swarmed behind us, around us, in front of us, and I could not guess where they all came from, their figures and faces all shadowed in the blackness of night.

As we neared the ship, however, we could see that, being anchored in the middle of the river, it would be difficult to get to, but there were already some men in rowboats trying to reach it, silhouetted against the orange light on the water. But the sounds from the ship brought a freezing chill to the very marrow of my bones, and I listened in horror, as those around me did too, to the moaning and screaming of those people trapped within the bowels of that evil prison.

"God Almighty! Listen to that! It sounds like a human pyre, burning alive?" Someone cried beside me as we reached the old stone quay.

"And so it is!" Roc shouted. "There must be hundreds of them trapped inside! Come along, we have no time to waste. We'll need all the boats available, but some of them might be able to swim for it. Stay here, Roma. Don't leave!" And before I could protest, he had flung himself into one of the boats waiting there, filled with men. I suddenly became aware of Combes standing beside me.

"Did 'ee ever see such a sight, Miss? An' that ship, her do be burning like it were wildfire. We 'uns can only pray them mightn't be too late, it do look like, wouldn't 'ee say?"

"It's tragic," I said, agreeing with him, feeling helpless because I could do nothing but watch as the flames leaped up the tall masts.

" 'Tis bad enough, that them be foreigners like, m'lady," Combes said, and I knew he too felt helpless, "but with our own on it, why that do make it our own special-like hell, now, don't it? And Tam, he do believe his girl Tulip be down in that pit, along with our good Doctor and Miss Lucretia. But that don't sound reasonable, do it, Miss? No man alive could be that wicked, even if it be Mister Trevor himself." He shook his head in disbelief.

Shocked, I watched the murky light of the fire and water and shadows, hearing the sounds of pain and suffering as if from afar, my own soul gripped with terror now for my cousin and her maid and Hadrian. For now I knew Trevor could indeed be what I'd not thought possible earlier. In him was some quality of deliberate and cruel depravity which, because of the age we lived in, had been well concealed. I shuddered violently as I watched the men climb the ladders to the deck of that burning ship.

It seemed an eternity; it would be forever imprinted on my mind, that flaming ship in the indigo night, strangely vivid scenes of men and women with fiery halos running back and forth, screaming, perhaps dying as they jumped from the burning deck to the swirling river below, or scrambled over the deck rail down the ladder, into a waiting boat.

Boatload after boatload of the escapees were rowed back to the quay; the swollen river was now crawling with frantic arms splashing through the treacherous eddying current, and I watched spellbound as the first of the rescued were lifted out and placed safely on the quay, their sobs frantic, crying out in foreign tongues their terror and their gratitude. The only language I could distinguish was rapid French.

Hamilton came to me. "Oh, Miss," he said in a hurried voice, "Master say 'ee are to take 'em to the house, 'ee do, without delay. 'Ee'll know how to do it, he say."

"Hamilton," I cried, reaching for his arm before he could return to one of the rowboats. "Have they found my cousin, Miss Lucretia?"

He looked down at me, startled, I thought, as if I'd lost my senses. "Do 'ee know fer sure that she be on the ship, Miss?"

"Combes believes she is, and with Doctor Hadrian and Tulip." I found myself almost screaming now, in my own panic.

"Then I best be gettin' back, Miss. That ship, she be doomed, and 'twon't take nothin' to sink her! He tore away from me, and I somehow knew there was no purpose in my staying to watch.

I turned to Combes, who by now was helping some of these frightened, sobbing people. Together, we managed to convey to them that they were to follow us, and we led them through the darkness up toward the house, where the welcome light from the opened doors streamed out like beacons. When we reached the house, I saw the bedraggled, wretched state these people were in, huddled together, fear in their emaciated faces.

There seemed to be scores of them, and they stared in dumb horror at the elegantly gowned ladies who, as they stood behind Mrs. Pascal and the cowering servants girls, were staring in equal fascination at the scene before them.

"Mrs. Pascal," I said, suddenly resolute, calm, and in command. "Pray bring these poor, wretched souls into the Bower. Bring warm blankets and hot food. There will be others, and we shall have to organize ourselves properly. Get these ladies to help, for we're in need of every pair of hands. Their husbands are fighting for their own lives out there on a burning, sinking ship, so bring in bandages, salve and hot water. There are some badly burned people here, I believe. We must make them as comfortable as possible, for they have suffered much." I turned to Combes.

"Please do go back to the quay, Combes, and please, when you've word, let me know immediately, will you?" I searched the old man's face, and I knew he was as anxious as I was to learn the outcome.

"Aye, Miss, that I'll do," and he turned swiftly and disappeared into the darkness.

It was well into the night when I stepped from the Bower into the entry hall, every nerve of my body tense and waiting for the news I needed to hear: that Lu and Hadrian and Tulip, along with Cal Pascal and Arnie Polden were safe. But Combes had kept returning to the house with dozens of people who we all now knew had been destined for slavery in the New World, most of them having been chained in the hold of *The Black Tusk*. Their tales shocked everyone that night, as the story came out in bits and pieces, especially from fifty-odd French *émigrés* who had practically sold their souls to *Monsieur* St. Coryn to help relocate them in England.

As I left the Bower, however, I was dimly aware that I had not seen Taryn for some time, and had I thought with a clearer mind, I might have remembered I hadn't seen her since she'd stood in this entry hall hours ago with Roc and me, her back to us, silently sobbing in her defeat, knowing how Trevor had used her.

But I didn't want to think about that now. Instead, my heart was yearning for knowledge of my little cousin's safety. How could I have been so blind, I thought, not to have guessed the truth? My guilty conscience would ride me for a long time, for Taryn had been right: I would have gone along with Trevor, had not Roc St. Coryn abducted me that night.

I stood in the silent entry hall now, facing this moment of truth. The candles in the old chandelier were dripping over, the wax spilling down on the stone floor, and the light they gave seemed to me almost sinister. I walked slowly over to the door leading into the Great Hall, and opened it wide.

It looked like a still-life painting drawn by a professional artist, the table, the plates and dishes still there, the silver bowls still piled with fruit, the wine goblets half empty. The chairs were pushed back, as if the guests had just risen from their supper and withdrawn to the Bower, where I heard the rise and fall of murmuring voices. It was a strange and forlorn moment, for the candles here too were sputtering and dripping, many of them guttering out, and I realized that no one had remembered to extinguish them. Their light flickered and danced upon the walls, eerily reminding me of that burning ship in the dark river. I wondered who had misinformed Roc by telling him no prisoners were on board.

The clock in the stable tower struck two; thin high notes, an echo of bells, I thought wearily. I turned to go back into the entry hall, when a sound from above made me look towards the gallery. And there, staring down at me with narrowed, unsmiling light eyes, stood Trevor with an ugly gash slashed across his face, and a pistol in his hand.

He stood there staring down at me for what seemed an eternity, and then he slowly descended, never taking his eyes from my face. I backed away from him, trembling violently, and found the table to support me.

He was clad only in his shirt and breeches tucked hastily, I saw, into his boots, and I was conscious now of blood upon his shirt, and guessed what must have happened. In a room somewhere above, he must have fought with one of the crew from *The Petroc,* a savage and brutal struggle for life, and Trevor had come away the victor.

But now he stood at the bottom of the stairs, watching me, saying nothing for one long and dreadful moment. Then he moved across the table from me, and sat down in one of the chairs, still holding the gun.

When he spoke at last, it was in the same familiar manner, possessive, sure of himself and of me. "I managed to get free. I'm taking you with me, Roma. Sir George is waiting for us with a carriage. Sit down for a minute. I must get my strength, and we must have a talk. Sit down." He waved to the chair opposite.

I did as he bade, simply because my knees shook so that I was afraid he might see them. He smiled at me. "That was a pretty piece of conversation you two had," he said. "And if I didn't know you as I do, I would say that you had visited that bastard on *The Petroc* and that he seduced you, my love." There was no mirth in the laugh he gave, and I shrugged my shoulders without answering him, for however much he had guessed it now seemed of little consequence. The only thing that mattered now was to know what plans he had. I would never be able to trust him again.

"You know, my darling, that I will never be merely on the edge of your life, nor you mine. It must be total—all. Do you understand that, Roma?" His voice had an edge I feared. He watched my face.

"I know that you are too possessive, Trevor, and I do not want to be possessed. I want and need to be myself, not a shadow of a man who places a ring on my finger."

"But that is what love is all about, my darling Roma. Complete possession. Love itself is an imprisonment, and that is what I have to teach you."

"You never will!" I blurted out.

He stood up slowly, his eyes on my face as he moved, catlike, around the table to my side. He took my hand and pulled me to my feet, and with his free hand he tilted my chin, then began to trace the outline of my face. He must have felt my every muscle tense and resistant, but it didn't worry him.

"Do you really think I trust you, my darling? Oh no, not until you're married to me and I have a claim on you. I know Roc, and I know too the power he has over women. So you had a little fling with him. I don't mind. But get this straight, my sweet. You are my love and nobody is going to take you from me. I intend to keep you by my side for always, from this second. Roc St. Coryn be damned!"

Losing my temper with Trevor now was the last thing I should have done, but all the fury rose inside me, and I shut my eyes against his closeness, hating him with all my being.

He was mad with jealousy and greed. I knew that now as I stared up into that face, the gash bleeding so that it dripped down onto my gown.

He twisted my wrist and pain shot up through my arm. "That was just a little reminder that you are not to make a sound as we go. Don't underestimate that warning, Roma. I will kill you if I must." And he led me toward the stairs which he'd come down a while ago from the old gallery.

We were halfway up those stairs when a voice shouted down at us from the gallery. Stunned, we both looked up to see Taryn.

"Don't come any closer, Trevor!" Her voice was hoarse, as though her throat were raw. "You aren't going to take . . . her . . . anywhere." She stood with difficulty, I saw, a pistol in her hands, and it was pointed at us, cocked.

Caught off guard, Trevor was momentarily surprised, but still he laughed. "Get out of my way, Taryn. You know what this means to me. We must get away before that bastard Roc gets his hands on her."

"You left me for dead, using your treacherous tongue, as you're using it now, as if I'd be welcome to go along with you and her!" She laughed, near hysteria. "I was the one foolish enough to race back to your side, to cut you free, and you turned on me, you tried to kill me, as you did my brother. You murdered them, all of them, and perhaps Hadrian, too, has died because of you!" She was breathing hard. I could hear the gasps even as Trevor tightened his grip on my wrist.

"You're mad, Taryn. Mad with envy," he laughed, "and you're greedy, for you wanted to be mistress, the lady of the manor—"

"Stop! Greedy? Jealous? You make me sick! No, Trevor. You've done your last treacherous act. You've committed bigamy many times over in your greed, murdering your heiresses whenever you had their wealth, and you promised me—*me*—all the glories of having our son as the heir to Mullins. But you're not even a St. Coryn, and Roc is! Oh yes, and you still dream that this beautiful Roma Kendal will be yours, all yours!" She laughed. "Couldn't you see that she loves him? Couldn't you guess that Roc has already won her?"

"He'll never have her, no! She is mine! Now you get out of our way, Taryn. I warn you, I'll kill you or anybody who tries to stop me."

CHAPTER NINE

Another voice cut in from the hall below us, causing Trevor to jerk around. "I am stopping you, Trevor!" It was Roc. My heart wrenched in pain, with a mixture of joy and fear. "She is already my woman, do you hear? You have lost out, Trevor. The woman you want most is now my woman. She knows you and hates you for what you are!" he shouted. "Ask her, and she will tell you." Stunned, I was barely conscious of the dripping candles as, one by one, they sputtered out and cast only a dim, flickering light on the walls and on Trevor's face as he looked down at me, spinning me around to face him.

"You lie!" And his free hand struck me across my face. In that split second, two blinding charges exploded around us, roaring and echoing in my ears, and I felt such excruciating pain tear through me that I lost my breath, and I was aware of falling.

I put my hands out in a futile gesture to grab the bannister. Trevor, too, seemed to spin around, as a grey fog swirled up and engulfed me. From a long way off I heard shouts, but I lost them in the overwhelming mist.

There was pain behind my eyes, the explosion still echoing in my ears. I wanted to lie down and sleep; I wanted to forget that Taryn stood above me, her face a mask of pain and guilt; I wanted to remember no more the candles in the Great Hall, and Trevor's murderous hand rising to strike me; I wanted to forget that Trevor had betrayed my cousin, and the fog I sank into was the merciful haven of sleep I longed for.

I wanted to dream. In this dream, I wanted to believe that Roc St. Coryn loved me as I wanted to be loved by him, and as I surely loved him. But my dream was a tortured nightmare of that burning ship and the hellish cries and moans of the doomed in her bowels, of Lucretia and Hadrian. I tried to get up, but I could not and remained in this fog. . . .

Long afterwards, or so it seemed, voices hovered over me like wings whirring in and out of darkness and light. Faces bent over me, and hands lifted me and carried me. Someone bathed my face and my throat, and I felt a scorching pain sear my whole body, and then at last, my head was upon a pillow.

I must have slept after this, the dull heavy sleep of exhaustion, for when I opened my eyes it was daylight, and the curtains had been pulled back, and there was Roc sitting by my side, holding my hand in his own strong one, and fondling my curls, which spilled over the pillow and the chemise I was wearing. Behind him, the muted light from the window, warm, soft yellow light of the autumnal sun, poured into the room, touching a vase of yellow and bronze crysanthemums.

"It's all right, my darling," he said in a most tender voice. "I am with you, and I shall never leave you again. I promise." His concerned eyes were upon my face, and for me it was an incredible moment of unexpected joy.

But the horror of that night flooded back as I came more fully awake. I stared at him. "Roc. . . ." The voice, unlike my own, croaked. The pain in my heart must have showed in my eyes, for he leaned over me and touched my cheek with his lips.

"You mustn't distress yourself, my love. Trust me. Everything is all right. You must believe that."

But I persisted, remembering. "Lucretia—"

He placed a finger over my lips. "She is safe. I promise. She and Hadrian are alive, thank God. Your pretty cousin is in her rooms, being looked after by all her adoring servants, and anyone else who happens to be in this house. They are spoiling her. But you have me to look after you, my darling. None of us can be more thankful than myself that you are safe and with me again."

I could hardly believe it, so incredible it seemed. "The ship?"

"It burned and sank, as it was destined to. All those people were set free, so you must not worry over their fate, Roma. It was nearly a tragedy, because in my haste to put a stop to Trevor's slave trade, I failed to examine the ship myself, taking the word of a near stranger who claimed to know the vessel was empty. If we had not been able to save those poor people, I could never have forgiven myself."

I could only stare at him, knowing joy and pain, and in this joy I was certain I should awaken and find his presence and voice all a dream. But I remembered too much of that night. I moved my tongue over my dry lips, and asked in a faint voice, "Taryn—" I stopped, for I could not go on, seeing his eyes darken.

He hesitated, choosing his words carefully before he said, "I suppose you will have to know sometime, Roma, and so I will tell you now." He pressed my hand tightly.

"Taryn . . . died that night."

I digested that slowly. "*That* night? It wasn't last night?"

He smiled. "Four nights have come and gone since that night, my darling."

"That long?" I found myself frowning. And as I moved

my arm, a pain shot through my left side and I saw that I was bandaged over my shoulder and left arm.

"You were shot, my darling, by Taryn's gun as it went off when she began to fall. You see, when she slipped up to the room to free Trevor during all the commotion of the burning ship, Trevor betrayed her; he took the knife from her and they fought, and she gashed his face open before he plunged it into her. He left her there to die, but she dragged herself along the gallery, where she turned a gun on him." He brought my hand to his lips, almost bowing over it as if in deep meditation.

I had no words then, my throat raw, my mouth hot and dry as I imagined that horrendous scene.

"It was her gun that went off as she was fainting, and her bullet struck you, just below the shoulder. Oh, my dearest, dearest love! I thought I'd lost you, and I near died in that second!" His voice was full of love and tenderness, and I could have wept then as I realized my dreams had come true.

I swallowed hard. "And Trevor . . . ?" I couldn't finish.

"My shot came nearer to killing him," he said darkly, "and by heaven I wanted him to die! But he is saved for the gallows, along with his henchmen, that captain and those two 'businessmen.' They will be dealt with by the law in Bodmin."

Again, I wet my lips. "But what of Taryn?" My throat was hurting, and I knew there were tears close to the surface. I thought of her son, Jon.

"She died, just after I got to her, Roma. I told her Hadrian was safe, and she died knowing that." He was quiet as I was, as we both reflected on all she had told us of her own ordeal. I glanced at Roc, and found his eyes warm and loving on my face.

"Today you will marry me, my darling. Today I want to make you my wife."

He spoke so seriously that I didn't know what to say, so stunned was I. I must have looked like an ecstatic schoolgirl.

"The vicar from Pelyn is here to perform this marriage; I have had him at call these four days, for this very hour. We shall not put it off any longer than it will take for me to send for him, as he sups now in the kitchen with Cook and Combes. I say, my darling. You will make a most beautiful bride. And I shall spend my hours making you well again."

I felt myself blush under his eyes. "Can this be true?" I asked, disbelieving. "You care for me? I would have thought—" He cut me off.

"Of course it's true, my darling. You are the woman I love, and I am going to make you my wife. I love you, Roma. Can I dare hope that you feel the same about me?"

"I love you, Roc," I said simply.

"That is all I need to hear," he answered, and he leaned over and kissed me hungrily, and as passionately as I remembered.

The door opened and it was Pansy who stuck her beaming face in, but when she saw us, her face went scarlet with embarrassed delight.

She curtseyed to Roc, who insisted she come in. "Will you stay with your mistress while I go down to fetch the Vicar, Pansy?"

She blushed deeper, but she said, "Aye, Master. That I will." And I saw that she was only too happy to do so.

Roc turned to go, then looked at her and said, "Help freshen Miss Roma up, for in about an hour, she will be receiving some guests." Then he winked and gave a laugh, while Pansy bubbled over with excitement, and he left the room.

Because my throat seemed far too sore to try to talk, I allowed the maid to tell me in her own words just what had happened to Tulip and my cousin that day. And this suited Pansy, for as she went about bringing me my newest dressing gown, a pure white muslin trimmed in amber ribbons, she chattered almost feverishly, with comical gestures and expressions that made me laugh.

"Oh, 'ee had us frightened to death, 'ee did, Miss, but it were me sister what near went mad with shock, her did! 'Ee see, Miss, Tulip went with Miss Lucretia to meet Doctor Hadrian. Her had a note, it do seem, from the good Doctor to meet near the North Lodge, and o' course, Tulip went with her. 'Twas at the old mill, to be exact," Pansy said, as she helped me into the gown. I winced as I moved my arm, but she was careful and very gentle with me.

"But he weren't there, so Tulip says, her did, Miss. And the way Mister Trevor jumped out at them both, why it near frightened poor little Miss to death as it did Tulip! He twisted a rope around Tulip's wrists and tied her up inside that old mill, and gagged her with cotton, he did, so's she couldn't scream out for help."

Pansy brought a basin of warm water and began dabbing my face and hands, then said, "Her had to watch in horror what he did to poor Miss Lucretia, Miss. That were the worst part, so Tulip says. Her was like a piece o' limp rag, just fainted dead away, and he laid her out on the stone floor, mind you, and brought her to her senses by passin' a strong smellin' salt under her nose."

I could imagine it. Poor Lu, what a shock she must have had! But I looked at Pansy and said, "I thought Mister Trevor had gone to Plymouth. How on earth did he manage this, with Sir George Thorpe . . ." I had forgotten about Sir George, and in my mind's eye, I saw Trevor as he'd been that night, saying, 'Sir George is waiting with a carriage.' I frowned. Had he been in on all this murderous business?

"Oh, him were coming by hisself, him were, Miss. Why, Hamilton fetched him from Bodmin, where they 'twere met by Mister Trevor, so Hamilton he say. And Hamilton, he didn't know about Mister Trevor's dark deeds, no he didn't!"

It must have been because I was still a bit light-headed that things seemed so fuzzy, and I was glad for the tray one of the other maids brought in and set down beside the bed, which Pansy then placed across my lap.

"It's Mister Roc's orders that 'ee eat this, Miss, afore he comes back." She removed the cover, and the aroma of the chicken leg and thick soup made me realize I was famished.

While I was eating, Pansy talked on. "Mister Trevor forced poor little Miss Lucretia to write that letter to Sir George, Miss, he did, for Tulip watched him and listened. And he beat her, hittin' her across the face with his hand. An them didn't know poor Doctor Hadrian were in the next room, unconscious, he were, an' tied up and gettin' ready to be thrown into that black hole in that old ship, right along with poor Tulip and her mistress! I say now, Miss, bain't that a scary thing to happen to any body? Why, I do wonder how poor Tulip stood, I do, poor thing!" Her eyes were wide with fear at the picture her sister had painted, and I knew it would be remembered as vividly as she imagined it.

I only nodded, saying nothing, and eating the hot soup

Cook had sent up for me while Pansy talked away. "It were hours, so me sister said, afore they knew what were agoin' to happen to 'em, and her mistress were mostly in a dead faint, but some of us believe her were knocked out just like Doctor Hadrian were, Miss. Ooo-oo, but he were a wicked man at heart, were he not, Miss? An him killin' poor Miss Taryn like he did and all, I say. 'Ee could have knocked us over with a feather, so Mrs. Pascal do say, all o' us, and we'd not be more surprised at his black heart. One would allus of thought that of Mister Roc, 'im being so hot-tempered an' all." She looked at me sheepishly, but I averted my gaze.

I looked at her and said for her benefit, "Life is full of surprises, Pansy. I find this true." I stopped and ate a bit of chicken; it tasted heavenly. "Tell me, did Arnie Polden and Cal Psacal come out all right?"

She nodded her head. "Aye, and they'm two'll have a long time in forgettin' what Mister Trevor put 'em through! Why, when me father, Tam, and Jake got to 'em, they were taken out fer dead, Miss. Arnie," she shook her head, and truly looked mournful, " 'im'll lose his leg, so the Doctor say. An' 'im only a young lad an' all."

It was a sad moment. Reflecting upon the fates Trevor had planned for all those people was not pleasant, but that we came out alive and had righted some of Trevor's wrong-doing made me thankful.

Then Lucretia came to me and the pieces fell into place. She sat beside my bed, her eyes widely innocent and starry, and told me how much Roc loved me. She told me that from the moment he lifted me in his arms and carried me here, he kept constant vigil over me, making the most impatient demands on all the servants to see that I recovered.

"He loves you, Roma dear," she said, "and you are most fortunate. I find Roc St. Coryn all that a woman like you could ever need. And he is so good-looking, so marvelously good-looking, while underneath his outspoken manner he is as gentle as a lamb."

Her smile was radiant and my heart nearly burst with happiness, for two reasons: that she was right about Roc, and that she herself was safe and as happily in love with her own choice as I was with mine.

"You must tell me all," I said, trying to be strong, yet knowing I was not yet well enough to move about, for fear of reopening the wound. "Hadrian? Is he all right?"

"I'm happy to say yes to that question, Roma. Do you know that we were both drugged, before we were actually placed on that ship?" she told me, her face paling a little as she spoke, "And that was why we could not be found so easily when Tamblyn and Roc came searching for us. I suppose I should be thankful I didn't get to see the . . . tortures that must have'been going on." She shuddered.

"Thank God you were found in time."

She nodded, and inclined her head to one side. "Trevor, as you know, tried to persuade me that we should marry before the set date, and although I didn't want to, I was actually going to do it. But I believe he was suspicious of Hadrian and me, and even had us watched all along. What he didn't know was that I would never have had the courage to run away with Hadrian, and Hadrian would never have left Wilkes Reach or his medical life. He is much too involved with all his patients." She paused and looked at me. "He loved you rather possessively, didn't he? All along, even before Papa died, he loved you, and had you been the heiress you should have been, he would have married you. Oh," she made a face, wrinkling her nose and shaking her curls, saying, "I know all that, and I too am guilty of wanting a protector. Please say you forgive me for taking the man you wanted to marry."

I tried to laugh but it was hard, and I took her hand in my own. "I . . . oh, Lu! You truly saved me, you little goose! It is I who should ask forgiveness—"

She placed a finger over my lips. "Don't talk so, Roma dear. We both have much now, and we must never lose this preciousness."

We were both moved to tears, saying no more of it, but knowing we'd covered a span of time together that would bind us forever.

Then she continued. "Trevor forced me to write that letter to Sir George. You must know that he and Trevor had plotted all this together, thinking that if I could be persuaded to give you my wealth, which was what Trevor needed, then it would be easy for them to persuade you to be a party to all the wicked plans he had in mind. But as I wrote it, Roma, I *knew*, and I prayed, that you would see through that letter and know me; that I could never do such a thing without telling you, that is, to go off with Hadrian as that note said."

"And you were right, Lu," I cried. "I simply couldn't believe it!"

"And Hadrian?" I searched her face. "What are your plans?"

Her pretty face blushed pink, her eyes starry. "We shall be happy together, Roma. I am going to marry him, of course. And we shall live at the Reach. I am very interested in his work. I want so very much to be near him."

It was a long moment before I could ask, "And what of Jon? Hadrian's nephew? He was Trevor's son—"

"He was Taryn's son, and he is indeed Hadrian's nephew, and like a son to him, as well you may recall, Roma. He shall live with us, and naturally be one of us. I want it so, and Hadrian is pleased."

The door opened and Pansy brought in Miss Phoebe, the old woman's face alive with secretive pleasure. She looked as if she could hardly contain herself, and I wondered if all of the excitement around her had given her inspiration for one of the fantastic picture dramas she worked in silken threads.

"So, Roma Kendal," she said gleefully, and I saw Lu go pale and silent beside me and guessed that she still was extremely sensitive to this old lady and her playful ghost tales. It occurred to me then that Lu would be most happily settled in Wilkes Reach, away from Mullins and its ghosts haunting the rooms, and I too had to smile, as the old woman said, "You and I have indeed come up with all those answers we needed to finish my story, don't you think?"

She looked down at me from the foot of the bed.

"What can you mean, Miss Phoebe?" I asked, feigning innocence.

"I knew you would be the one person I could rely upon, the first day I saw you in my gallery, Roma Kendal. You took such an interest. You are an artist on the piano, and you would understand all the sensitive questions and mystery that must go into telling one of my story works." Her old face was like a child's, beaming with delight.

"So what answers did you arrive at?" I asked her as she sat down across from Lu and beside me.

"Why, the answer to why Edward was killed that night. I could never believe that Edward could commit such a crime. And it was that evil mind of Sarah's son that planned it, carried it out in his diabolical way. And so, it is all solved. It shall go down on my tapestry, thanks to you, my dear." Her eyes were bright, alert, and one would never suspect that she sometimes lived in the past.

"Why me, Miss Phoebe?" I was mystified.

"Because you brought Trevor down here, my dear. You are the woman he wanted, and Roc knew this." Her old eyes sparkled with mischief, and I knew then she was a wise old woman. My face went crimson as I remembered that she must have known then about the night aboard *The Petroc,* or suspected anyway what went on there.

"But it was. . . ." I stopped, for I saw Lu's expression. I had wanted to remind her it had been my cousin who'd been Trevor's chosen bride, but all that this quaint and dear old woman had said was true.

"He confessed, you know," Miss Phoebe said after a moment's pause. "Trevor confessed to murdering Kate and Phillip Wilkes, and then making Edward's death seem like a suicide. Oh, yes. He was bad all the way through, Sarah's son was." And then she was reflective, as both Lu and I were in that moment before the door opened, and Roc with Hadrian and the Vicar from Pelyn church entered, and my future as the wife of Roc St. Coryn began.

We were married that day. For me, it was the most romantic way to begin my life with Roc. He wanted to waste no time, for his longing for me was as great as mine for him—ever since that night aboard his ship. When my shoulder healed, as it did rapidly for I was a healthy young woman, I could meet the demands of being Roc's wife as well as the mistress of Mullins. Nothing blighted my happiness, nor Roc's. I was still stunned that I was his bride. A very lucky me, I thought then, and still think so, in the year that has passed since that day.

Much has happened since then: Trevor was tried for the murder of four people, along with the captain of the ship and even Sir George Thorpe, for their crimes in kidnapping the French emigrants to exploit them in the New World, and they went to the gallows, along with Mister Rockingham and Mister Jenkins, on a cold late October day, just before Hadrian and Lucretia were married.

When I wrote to my old friend Lady Cecilia about the fate of these Frenchmen, she rushed down to Cornwall, stunned at the sordid story, and took them in her charge, finding places for them in Cornwall.

Lucretia and Hadrian were married not long after my wedding. It was a beautiful, gay wedding in the village church, with all the household staff and Mullins' farmers there to celebrate. They were destined for a sweet life together, dedicated to each other in their compassion for the sick and distressed. They took Jon with them on their honeymoon to Scotland, before returning to Wilkes Reach six weeks later.

Lucretia kept the inheritance; I insisted, for I had my own happiness, although it was sometimes a turbulent one, for I discovered that I could be a jealous woman, and a passionate one. But I did not want Lu's money; there was no place for such greed in my life with Roc. He gave freely, and took freely. Sometimes I think Roc liked to tease me, in repayment, he said, for the jealousy he had felt of Trevor.

So Lu kept her money; Roc wanted it that way. He loves Mullins as much as I do, but he also wants to show me some of the faraway places he's seen, so we've decided to take a voyage to the West Indies, sailing on *The Petroc*. We shall come back, of course. Mullins is a place to come back to, and our children shall be born here.

Miss Phoebe set to work on her tapestry story, and she completed it just before she died quietly in her sleep one night.

But I shall always remember what she said to Roc and me when she presented her tapestry to us: "Kate's ghost is at peace now, my dears. She will no more haunt the Blue Boudoir, and I shall feel easy that her murderer was caught, so that she could rest in peace."

It was with great sadness that we buried that dear old woman next to her Edward at Plyn churchyard. We are born, we love, and we die, but Mullins has its story in those beautiful works one patient St. Coryn woman thought to give her time and effort and love to, to be cherished into the future.

THE END